MW00932351

The Raven's Ring Pin

JOHN ANACKER is fascinated by Norse/ Viking culture and mythology, drawing from his research in these topics to write this book. He is a former academic administrator, now focusing on writing and art.

The Raven's Ring Pin

John W. Anacker

2004
Llewellyn Worldwide, Ltd.
St. Paul, Minnesota 55164-0383

FIRST EDITION
First Printing, 2004

Cover art © 2004 by Matthew Archambault
Cover design by Gavin Dayton Duffy
Editing and interior design by Connie Hill
Map, pp. vi-vii © 2004 by John W. Anacker

Library of Congress Cataloging-in-Publication Data
Anacker, John W.
  The Raven's Ring Pin / John W. Anacker — 1st ed.
     p.   cm.
  Includes glossary.
  ISBN 0-7387-0433-4
   I. Title.
data pending

Llewellyn Worldwide does not participate in, endorse, or have any authority or responsibility concerning private business transactions between our authors and the public.

All mail addressed to the author is forwarded, but the publisher cannot, unless specifically instructed by the author, give out an address or phone number.

Any Internet references contained in this work are current at publication time, but the publisher cannot guarantee that a specific location will continue to be maintained. Please refer to the publisher's website for links to authors' websites and other sources.

Llewellyn Publications
A Division of Llewellyn Worldwide, Ltd.
P.O. Box 64383, Dept. 0-7387-0433-4
St. Paul, MN 55164-0383, U.S.A.
www.llewellyn.com

Printed in the United States of America

To my father and mother,
Ed and Stella

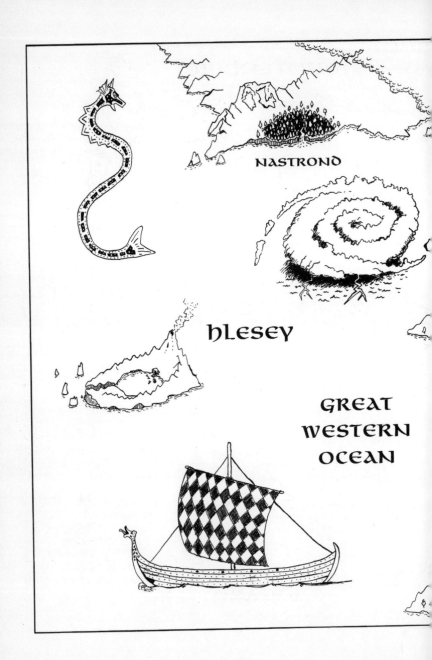

NASTROND

hLESEY

GREAT
WESTERN
OCEAN

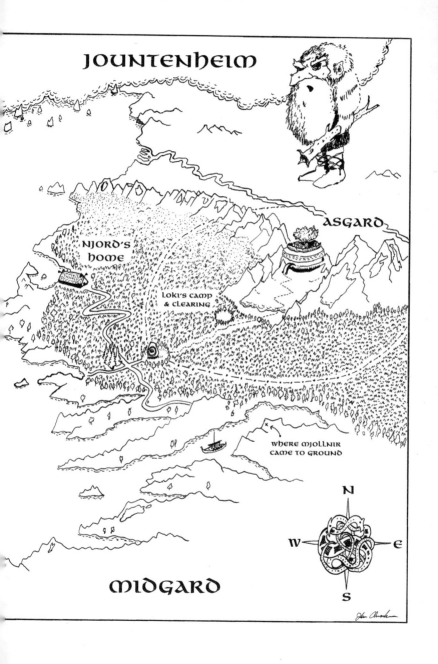

JOUNTENHEIM

ASGARD

NJORD'S
HOME

LOKI'S CAMP
& CLEARING

WHERE MJOLLNIR
CAME TO GROUND

N
W E
S

MIDGARD

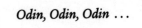

Odin, Odin, Odin ...

Chapter 1

The pine cone whizzed past Thokk's head, careened off his frantically flapping wings and bounced off a nearby tree trunk. Weaving desperately, the raven dodged among the pines and firs, hoping that another missile wouldn't dislodge the meager scrap of bread clamped in his beak. Finally, with a sense of overwhelming frustration, he swooped to a stop on a high branch well out of reach of his human attackers. With a quick snap, he gulped down the hard-won crust.

After awhile he was joined by the source of his anger and irritation, a much larger and weather-beaten raven named Rag. Spitting with fury, Thokk said, "Once again you have ruined a perfectly good opportunity to pinch food from a clutch of tourists. The dolts were ripe for the picking. Didn't you see that feast they were setting out on their picnic table? All you had to do was distract them while I glided in to snatch that wonderful, soft loaf of white bread." Here a dreamy expression filled Thokk's tar-black eyes, only to quickly harden again into anger. "But noooo . . . You had to be all friendly with that little girl, sitting quietly as she came closer and closer. How could they not help but hear me trying to undo that plastic bag? I wish it had been you who had to dodge those pine cones. Just look at my wing." Thokk held up the injured appendage, flapped it in Rag's face and then went on. "To think I daily risk my glossy feathers to feed your mangy hide. Just look at you! You're a mess. Don't you ever preen your coat or trim your claws? Look at how carefully I keep my legs and claws. Not a nick or scratch. I say, if you weren't so God-awful big, I'd never have taken you in. You had better thank your ancestors that Grackle and his gang of crows run at the very sight of you."

To all this, Rag said nothing. He never did. Some terrible childhood catastrophe had left him both an orphan and completely mute. He just looked at Thokk's clever and cocky face with a calm, steady glance, betraying neither anger nor dislike.

With a groan, Thokk rolled his eyes and said: "Well, come on then, let's go home."

Like two black leaves caught in a puff of wind, the ravens launched off their high perch and flapped off through the trees. It was late July in Yellowstone National Park. The air was full of shimmering waves of evergreen pollen and the smell of pine. The sun was warm, but not hot. The sky was a clear azure blue. A small herd of buffalo, grazing in a golden meadow of ripening grass, ignored the two black shadows that flew low over their backs.

As the two ravens glided along, Thokk glanced over at Rag and wondered for the thousandth time about his friend. Even though Rag was unkempt and dusty, there was a dignity about him that went beyond mere appearance. Something very good and profound was hidden behind his sad eyes. Unfortunately, this concealed dignity seemed to make him incapable of many practical things, like stealing food. Thokk only shook his head and marveled at his own folly for sticking with such a strange and, at times, completely useless partner.

Suddenly something caught Thokk's ever inquisitive eye. With a deep throated "quork," he signaled for Rag to stop while he himself veered onto the branch of a slender old lodgepole pine. Down below, several people were engaged in a beehive of activity. A beat-up orange pickup truck had been backed up to a slight depression in a small meadow. Crates of equipment, shovels, tents, and other camping gear were being unloaded from the truck bed and spread out over the ground. A car, bouncing as it drove across the uneven ground, pulled up beside the truck and disgorged several more people, including a tall elderly gentleman with white hair and skin like leather. He at once began giving orders and pointing out where tents should be positioned and equipment stowed.

All this was of immense interest to Thokk. Long-term visitors were always more welcome in his territory than day tourists. More permanent guests could be flattered and courted until they were trained to provide a regular supply of treats. All that was needed was time, and these people appeared to be planning to stay for months.

After making a mental note of the location of this potential gold mine of food, Thokk nodded to Rag and the two resumed their journey. Their destination was not very far away—just over a clump of Douglas firs and across a broad asphalt parking lot full of cars. With a graceful glide, both ravens alighted on the roof crest of their home, the Geyser Inn.

Thokk was extremely proud of his home, even though it was an exceedingly awkward and gloomy structure. A gigantic log cabin several stories tall, it sat brooding on the shore of Yellowstone Lake. From its moss and lichen-encrusted roof, Thokk and Rag could survey the lakeshore for dead fish and the surrounding picnic tables for scraps of food. Or, at least, Thokk could. Rag was usually looking for something else.

Rag had an obsession. He loved shiny objects—anything that sparkled. He was forever peering at the ground and rustling under leaves in search of some new piece of junk. Over time he had amassed a collection of bottle caps, coins, nuts and bolts, and even a wedding ring. Rag stored his treasures in the attic of the Geyser Inn. Every evening he would squeeze through the slats of a broken air vent and deposit his latest find beside a rafter. He would then roost on a nearby ceiling beam. It was here that Rag now retreated, not only because the day was getting on, but also to evade Thokk's bitter jibes.

"Yeah, just leave me to fend for myself, you incompetent crow. Go mope in your dusty cave," Thokk shot after Rag as the latter disappeared.

The next day Thokk awoke hungry. After the pine cone incident and Rag's escape, he had not been able to find anything to eat—not even a dead squirrel along the road. His empty stomach made Thokk's mood black. When Rag emerged from the attic into the early morning light, Thokk eyed him angrily and growled: "Did you get your beauty sleep, my friend, or did the rumblings of my stomach keep you awake all night? I'm sure a few thin shingles couldn't have possibly blocked out the sound. I suppose you satisfied your hunger by gnawing on one of your precious treasures. You do eat them, don't you—a bolt-and-bottle-cap soufflé perhaps? Maybe you saved a slice for me since it was your fault we lost that loaf of bread yesterday. No? . . . Well, I tell you what! Today you're going to learn to beg, since larceny seems to be below you. Perhaps a good dose of humiliation will rekindle your interest in thievery. Who knows, it might even unstick that stubborn tongue of yours."

In reply, Thokk's partner bobbed his head twice and looked out over Yellowstone Lake. The sun had just risen and the water, tinged with salmon and pale yellow, sparkled with a thousand fallen stars. Rag seemed enraptured by the sight and was unable to remove his eyes from it.

In disgust, Thokk scoffed, "Come on, you empty-headed bag of feathers. Gawking at sunrises will not fill our bellies. We have dark deeds to do. Our first stop is that new campsite. You know, the one with the orange truck and the whole gaggle of people. Perhaps we'll make their breakfast."

Unfortunately they did not. The people at the camp-site must have risen before dawn, for when Thokk and Rag arrived, they were already hard at work. Not a scrap of food was in sight. With a weary sigh, Thokk alighted on the crown of a nearby pine tree. Rag perched on a limb a few feet lower. Bending down, Thokk said: "Even though we've missed their feeding time, we might as well stay and spy them out. Maybe they'll have a snack midmorning or drop a candy bar in the dust."

All through the long morning Thokk and Rag stayed perched high in their tree. There they tried, without success, to understand the meaning and purpose of the human activity that went on below them. At first the people paced around the shallow depression in the ground with a long silver tape and now and then pounded a stake into the ground. After numerous stakes were positioned, bright orange strings were stretched between them to form a large grid. Shovels and wheelbarrows appeared. Soon the humans were busy digging up the top layer of grass and dirt and carting it off.

Once a large area had been cleared and a smooth under layer exposed, the elderly man and two assistants began to excavate a deeper hole with small spades. Every once in a while, the men would put down their trowels and begin to gently dust away dirt with a brush. At these times, an air of excitement would come over the site. Everyone would gather around. On one such occasion, the searchers lifted out a black obsidian arrowhead, next a needle made out of bone, and then a broken shard of pottery—all Native American artifacts.

"Fools," Thokk muttered with a sneer. "If they want to dig for real treasures, they should check out the dumpsters behind the inn's kitchen." But then suddenly, Thokk's mood brightened. "What's this?! I think they're quitting for lunch." And indeed, as he spoke, shovels were leaned against trees, brushes set aside, and two large red coolers placed atop a folding metal picnic table. The people began to talk and laugh. The hiss and pop of opening soda cans floated through the air.

An eager gleam filled Thokk's eyes as he whispered to Rag, "This is it! This is our chance. I'll go first. You just stay back and watch. Follow my every move. Remember. You'll be doing it next."

Rag dutifully nodded his head, and, together, the two ravens left their perch and glided down to the edge of the excavation. Once on the ground, Thokk hissed, "Wait here."

Confidently, Thokk turned his attention away from Rag and hopped over toward the picnic table surrounded by humans. With a loud croak, he turned all their heads in his direction. For a second, everything was quiet and then Thokk did an amazing thing. With a frenzied flap of feathers, he did a somersault—an awkward, ungraceful flip. The crowd of people gasped in amazement and then laughed. Here was something completely unexpected, strange, and hilarious. All of them would tell the tale of "that crazy raven in Yellowstone" for the rest of their lives. The gift of a story like that was worth a reward. The tag end of a ham sandwich sailed through the air and was deftly caught in Thokk's beak. Glowing with pride, Thokk glanced backwards, fully expecting to see Rag admiring his expertise. Of course, Rag was nowhere to be seen.

Rag was on the bottom of the excavation pit, pecking at a silver object peeping through the dust. His keen eyes, much sharper than any human's, had caught the faint glitter of metal as his ever-wandering eyes had turned away from Thokk's performance. He had immediately fluttered down to investigate. He grew more and more excited as he scraped dirt away from the buried object with his beak and claws. What appeared was a strange piece of silver jewelry.

It was a large brooch, or more accurately, a ring pin, as Rag was to later learn. It was about the size of an apple and shaped like a crescent moon, with a big bulge in the middle and two smaller ones on each horn. The middle protrusion contained a large carved eye, while the other two were filled with extremely tiny symbols. Surrounding the eye and symbols were intricate borders of interlaced ribbons.

As Rag looked closer at these ribbons, he began to see that they were really violently contorted animals, their limbs extended to fantastic lengths and positions. Around one side, right along the central bulge, a rather deadly looking stickpin was attached. It extended between and beyond the encircling horns of the brooch. The whole thing looked vaguely like a tadpole with the stick pin as the tail.

As he scraped the last bit of dirt away, Rag had the queer feeling that this was not a mere bauble, but a special talisman of great worth. A sense of awe and foreboding overcame him as he lifted the brooch in his beak and flapped out of the hole and onto the branch of a nearby pine tree.

Thokk sputtered angrily as he dropped down on the branch next to Rag. "What are you doing?! I told you to watch me and instead you wandered off. Good God almighty, you have the attention span of a starling." And then, in a voice full of sarcasm, he cackled, "What piece of junk have you unearthed now?"

As Rag set the ring pin down, Thokk fell silent. Even he felt the mysterious power of the brooch. It glittered in the strong afternoon sunlight, painful to look at, its polish strangely undiminished by burial, its silver surface untarnished.

Thokk gasped, "Ugh, if that isn't the weirdest thing you've ever found. It's creepier than a cabin full of cats. Go get rid of it! Why not drop it in the lake or, better yet, down a geyser?"

Rag, unmoved by these suggestions, picked up the pin and looked his friend straight in the eye with a piercing glare. Thokk, for once abashed, looked away. Rag then launched himself into the air, flew to his secret hideout in the inn and deposited the brooch among his other treasures.

Thokk shook his head in dismay as his friend disappeared. An unpleasant premonition filtered through his mind and settled in the pit of his stomach. Under his breath he cursed. "This is a bear's toe! The beginning of something big, bad, and very, very ugly."

Chapter 2

Splashing through the cold rain and slush, the car carrying Samuel Johnson finally came to a halt in front of the Geyser Inn. He shivered when he looked up at the brooding castle of burled logs, darkened dormers, and leaking gutters. As he stepped out into the downpour, his breath came in puffs of steam and the rain on his shoulders felt like someone was poking him with icicles. Even now, in late October, the sodden sky was flecked with snow. Under his breath Samuel cursed. Yet again, his father had dragged him away from home to a new, unfamiliar, invariably worse, place to live. Samuel did not like to remember how many times before this had happened to him in his short, fifteen-year-old life.

"Come on, Sam," growled Jim, Samuel's father. "Stop gawking and give me a hand with these bags."

Sullenly, Samuel trudged to the back of the car, grabbed a tattered duffle bag, and followed his father up the inn's steps. Glancing backwards, he saw his short, slightly chubby mother, Carol, sitting rigidly in the car's front seat, her large eyes staring straight ahead and her mouth tightly pursed.

The inside of the Geyser Inn was little warmer than the outside. Samuel shuddered as a trickle of water ran off his light brown hair and seeped down his neck. Goose bumps appeared on his fair skin and he had to rub rain out of his hazel eyes. His father motioned for him to wait while he went in search of somebody. The inn appeared to be abandoned. Miserably, Samuel peered around and saw that he was in the middle of a huge lobby. The ceiling soared more than four stories from a worn hardwood floor to a gloomy ceiling criss-crossed by dark wooden beams. At the room's center, sitting like a huge, squatting troll, was a gargantuan fieldstone fireplace. Several wagon wheel chandeliers hung down from the beams—their meager light barely illuminating the far corners of the room. Countless layers of varnish and shellac coated the log walls and railings like coats of maple syrup.

Samuel heard a cough. He turned around and saw that his mother had finally followed them into the inn. With shaking hands, she was lighting a cigarette. The sudden flare of a match illuminated her freckled complexion, red hair, and green eyes. In a sad voice she said: "This is really not what I expected. I thought this place would be . . . well, more modern and not so far from the nearest town. We must be fifty miles at least from West Yellowstone. To think we'll be here, by ourselves, all winter."

Just then Jim reappeared, walking behind a nervous young man at least ten years his junior. Jim's worn plaid shirt, carpenter's pants, and pot belly contrasted sharply with the man's slender build, cheap polyester suit and somber tie. The man said: "As I told you several times, I've left a detailed list of the projects the director and I thought you should concentrate on. But you know, the most important thing is to just keep the furnace running. We really, REALLY, don't want the pipes to freeze up. If you can keep the boiler's pilot light lit, we wouldn't care if you watched TV all winter. Now, if you would please excuse me, I must be on my way."

"Sir," Carol said with a hesitant wave of her hand. "Is it always so cold?"

The young man stared at Carol and then chuckled nervously as he glanced sideways at Jim. "Lady, this is as warm as it gets."

"Oh," said Carol and then, feeling a need to explain her question, she went on. "This weather is just such a change from where we've been living. Do you know that it was still ninety degrees in Big Bend National Park when we left three days ago?"

"Don't worry so much, Carol," growled Jim. "Everything will be just fine."

"Well, I must be off then, before it really starts to snow," said the young man as he quickly backed away toward the door, nearly tripping over himself. "My car's just outside and I'm all packed." And then with one last quick backward glance and a frozen smile he mumbled: "Good luck."

For a moment, Samuel and his parents were left staring at the empty doorway of the Geyser Inn. Jim was absent-mindedly twisting a strand of his big black beard. Carol blinked and said nervously, "Honey, do you really think this is such a good idea?"

"Now don't start in on me again!" snapped Jim, his eyes narrowing. "You were all for this when I first got the letter. If you hadn't listened to Doris and Betty, you'd still be as happy as a clam."

"Yes, but I didn't know we'd be so far away from everyone. I'll never have anyone to play cards with or even talk to."

"I think my job, our livelihood, is a lot more important than your social life."

"Really? Well, maybe . . ." Carol stammered, but then said more heatedly: "But I think this is all unfair to Samuel. He's not going to get a proper education way out here in the woods. You know how bright he is. He deserves better."

"Look, Carol!" shouted Jim. "We've been through all this before. The school in Gardner, Montana, will give Samuel his assignments and grades over the Internet. We've got it all worked out. You know that."

"I'm sorry, Jim. It's just that now that we're here, things don't look so good," Carol said, with a catch in her voice.

"Well, too bad!" yelled Jim. "You should have married a lawyer instead of a maintenance man. I'm doing the best I can and you never, ever, give me credit for it.

Well I'm tired of it!" With an oath, Jim spun around and stamped out of the lobby.

For a few seconds Carol stood stock still, tears welling up in her eyes. She sat down on a suitcase and sobbed quietly. Samuel was left staring at his mother and feeling a mixture of resentment and anxiety.

A short time later Jim reappeared and led Samuel and Carol to a large restaurant kitchen. It was a brightly lit room with stainless steel counters, a huge gas range and monstrous industrial appliances. Off the kitchen was a hallway that led first to a small break room and then to an office. At the end of the hallway was a set of stairs leading to a series of small bedrooms and a lone bathroom with a shower.

"Here's how it's going to be," Jim said. "You get the first bedroom, Samuel. Your mother and I will take the second one. We'll use the break room as a dining room and the hotel reading lounge as a living room."

Dejectedly, Samuel pushed the door open to his room. Several steel-framed bunk beds with sagging wire springs filled the space. One narrow window, splattered with wet snow, let in a pale shaft of light. On the dusty floor several dead flies lay like the victims of some insect catastrophe. A rickety dresser with several missing knobs occupied a corner. With a groan of dismay, Samuel sank down on a bed and put his head in his hands. One of the flies rose from the dead and began to feebly buzz, on its back, across the floor.

Over the next few days, the Johnson family managed to create a home out of the Geyser Inn. Jim and Samuel moved all but one set of the bunk beds out of Samuel's room, repaired the dresser, and put down a thin wool rug over the bare wooden floor. Samuel put up a few posters, where he could find wall space, and scattered his models, books, and one sports trophy around the room. He and his dad also converted the office downstairs into a place for Samuel to do his schoolwork and the break room into a dining room.

As Jim and Samuel finished moving things around, Carol appeared and said: "I guess we have a home of sorts now." And then with a tentative laugh she said, "I certainly can't complain about having a kitchen that's too small."

"It'll be the first thing you haven't whined about!" snapped Jim, and, without another word, he turned around and marched out of the room. Carol, a little stunned, began patting her pockets in search of a cigarette.

Samuel muttered, "I think I'll go outside."

Carol looked up and seemed about to say something. Instead, she looked away and waved weakly for Samuel to go. Samuel could see that her lower lip was quivering.

Once outside Samuel's mood improved. The weather was glorious. The air was sharp and clear. The sky was full of hurrying white clouds. A stiff wind hissed through the firs and turned Samuel's cheeks bright red. All afternoon he walked along the shores of Yellowstone Lake, skipping stones into the water and jumping over boulders. In his travels, he saw a herd of buffalo, a huge bull elk, and, in the distance, a coyote. A pair of ravens even seemed to follow him around.

For about a week Samuel lived outside. Then one morning he awoke to what he thought was the moaning of a ghost. For a few dazed moments he lay in bed paralyzed with fear. As his groggy mind became clearer, he realized that what he was hearing was the wind howling through the power lines outside his window. The air in his room had turned so cold that he could see his breath. That afternoon it began to snow and it continued snowing for what seemed a week. Next came days of incredible cold and then more snow. The drifts outside of the Geyser Inn grew higher and higher until it seemed like the entire world was mummified in snow. And so it went day after day, week after week, on past Thanksgiving, past Christmas, and past New Year's Day.

"I hate this place," Samuel said one day to his mother.

"Humph," was all his mother said as she stared at a small portable TV positioned at the end of the kitchen counter. The sound of a game show filled the room with a dull roar.

"I really hate this place," Samuel repeated. "I have nothing to do. Those assignments I get over the Internet from that cheesy school in Gardner are way too easy. I'm always done by lunch."

Carol shrugged her shoulders and blew a cloud of smoke out of the corner of her mouth. A little more forcefully, Samuel went on: "That dopey computer in the office is too weak for any good games and we only get one channel on the TV. I don't have any friends. I have no one to talk to. I can't even go outside. The snow is too deep, the air too cold, and Dad saw a wolf by the dumpsters two days ago. I feel like I'm on a rock-et ship crawling to a distant star. It might as well be outer space outside."

With a savage edge to her voice, Carol turned on Samuel. "I'm sorry life's the pits for you. But you know, there's nothing I can do about it. So stop bugging me and let me alone. In fact, get the heck out here. Go somewhere else."

Samuel spun out of his chair so fast that it tipped over and went clattering over the tile floor. He stomped out of the kitchen and into the main lobby of the Geyser Inn. For a few seconds he seethed with anger, his breath coming in hoarse gasps. But then he felt like crying.

Dejectedly, he began to wander about. First he went to the inn's reading lounge, which doubled as their living room. Of all the rooms the Johnson family inhabit-ed, this was the most pleasant. It was full of overstuffed chairs and bookcases crammed with old books. The floor was carpeted and the walls were crowded with old photographs and the heads of stuffed animals. Yet Samuel did not stop here; he felt too restless to sit and read a book.

Absentmindedly, he re-crossed the main lobby and began to ascend a flight of stairs. These led to the inn's three maze-like upper stories. On each floor, hallways crisscrossed each other or led to dead ends. Doors opened up to huge suites, tiny electrical closets, or to stairs that seemed to go nowhere. Only a few small light fixtures hung from the walls. These provided scanty patches of cold, watery light. Everything was gloomy, cold, and, except for the boards under Samuel's feet, deadly quiet. He didn't like to wander around up here, but at times like this, it was the only thing left to do.

After roaming around for a while, Samuel found himself on the fourth floor, looking down a hall filled with closed doors. Half-heartedly he began to try door-knobs, in case one was unlocked. One after another he twisted the brass handles, only to find them latched, until he tried the last one. To his surprise it turned eas-ily in his hand. Cautiously, Samuel cracked open the door.

Inside was a maintenance room full of shelves, brooms, and boxes. A lone light bulb dangled from the ceiling. It barely blinked to life when Samuel pulled its chain. Nothing particularly attracted his attention. The shelves were full of cleaning supplies and the boxes full of toilet paper. But then, when he was about to turn around and leave, something caught his eye. Just peek-ing out from behind a stack of paper towel cartons was the corner of another door. As he stared at it, Samuel noticed something strange. A loose label on one of the cartons was gently flapping, drawn toward the door by a slight breeze. Something was eerie about that draft. It was if something big was breathing behind the door. Suddenly, the light bulb fizzled and flickered. Shadows leapt across the walls. An electric chill ran down Samuel's back. Walking backwards, he stumbled out of the room and into the hallway. He quickly shut the outer door. Maybe another time he would return to investigate the hidden door, but not today.

Chapter 3

Samuel stared out the window of the inn's reading lounge at the tremendous blizzard that howled outside. Curtains of snow, like mad giants, raged through the trees in the dim dawn light. The room was filled with eddies of frigid air and a continuous symphony of creaks and groans as the wind sought out every crack and gap in the old log walls. The lounge windows, many opaque with frost, rattled like chattering teeth with each fresh gust. Samuel shivered as his mother called him to breakfast.

After breakfast, Samuel spent all morning plowing through his school assignments, stopping every once in a while to listen to the storm. As he worked, Carol sat in the kitchen playing solitaire, her inert body slumped against a counter. She and Jim had quarreled over breakfast, a change from what had been weeks of frigid silence.

When Samuel had finished his homework and eaten lunch, he asked if he could be excused. Carol dully nodded assent, her eyes never meeting Samuel's. With a sigh, Samuel walked out of the muggy warmth of the kitchen and into the chill of the lobby, pausing by the fireplace. Glumly, he listened to the wind moan and whistle down the flue, rustling the pages of a magazine left on the hearth. It was then that he remembered the fourth-floor maintenance room.

Actually, Samuel had thought about the hidden door for more than a week. It seemed to prey on his imagination. He kept wondering what inner sanctum of the Geyser Inn might be behind the door's wooden face. He had even dreamed about it—a nightmare in which he opened the door and found it led to a hallway full of windows. At each window he saw something different: a cold cruel man laughing at something unseen, a giant tree rustling in the wind, a small boat battered by a storm, a huge white creature half hidden by shadows, and finally, a window full of laughing, mocking faces from which waves of sound seemed to pour out like water, drowning him in noise. Samuel had awakened shaking and sweating, unsure of where he was. Now, as he stood in the lobby listening to the Geyser Inn creak and moan, he made a decision. He would swallow his fears and open the door. At least, he told himself grimly, his efforts would fill up a few empty hours.

With a quickness in his step and a thumping heart, Samuel ran upstairs to the fourth floor and located the maintenance room. He pushed open the door, turned on the light, and began moving boxes. He worked fast so that his imagination would not have time to play upon his jitters. What appeared was an unusually narrow door, shorter than Samuel was tall by a couple of inches—the top of it on a level with Samuel's eyes. A faint draft eddied across his cheek. He nervously reached out and grabbed the door knob. It was locked.

Frustrated, Samuel stepped back. He then remembered seeing his father open a locked door once, using only a plastic card. Hurriedly, he began to search the shelves and soon found an old red laundry tag. Gritting his teeth with determination, he slipped the tag into the crack between the door and its frame. Shimming the tag upward he caught the door bolt and wedged it back. Carefully, he pried the door ajar. As the tag dropped to the floor, he pulled the door open and found a very small closet lined with wooden slats. Bits of chicken wire, tarpaper, and newsprint showed through the gaps like the lining of a torn coat. Light barely penetrated past the closet's threshold. Nailed to one wall was a wooden ladder leading to a trap door set into a high ceiling. Samuel shivered. He felt like he had entered a coffin.

For a long time Samuel stared up at the trap door. It beckoned with a mysterious allure. What hidden world was behind its surface? Samuel hesitated a second longer and then began to climb the ladder. About three quarters of the way up, he suddenly realized that he had left the laundry tag outside. If the closet door were to close for some reason, he would be locked in. The walls of the closet seemed to close in and the shadows grew darker. Samuel trembled with indecision. But then he thought, "How could the door possibly shut by itself?" With a shrug, he began to climb again.

At the top of the ladder, Samuel placed his hand on the trap door and gently pushed. It moved slightly. He shoved a little harder but was unable to open it more than a crack. The hatch was very heavy and his perch, with one arm extended over his head, exceedingly awkward. Samuel bit his lip in frustration. Desperately he placed both his hands on the door and held onto the ladder with his legs. Shaking with fear and strain, he gave the door a mighty heave. For a fraction of a second the door resisted and then sprang back on its hinges. At that moment Samuel heard three things: first, the trap door landing with a thud on the floor above; next a whoosh, as the warm air of the maintenance room was sucked up into the unheated space above; and then finally, and most disturbingly, the unmistakable slam of the door below as it was drawn shut by the rush of air. He was plunged into what seemed like complete darkness.

Totally unnerved, Samuel lost his balance and began to waver back and forth. He frantically reached up and barely got his grip on the floor above. Sweating and swearing, he froze in horror. Only after his eyes had adjusted to the darkness could he see that a little light was filtering in from above. Carefully he climbed down the ladder, his hands and legs shaking. Feebly at first, but then with growing urgency, he tried the closet door. It was indeed locked. He wanted to pound on the door, to yell and scream, but he knew that with his father in the basement working on the furnace and his mother watching TV several floors below, no one could possibly hear him. Samuel glanced up, gathered his breath, and then reclimbed the ladder; it was his only choice.

He emerged from the trapdoor onto a rough wooden floor. At first, all he could see were faint jumbles of boxes and piles of roof shingles. Slowly though, as his eyes got used to the dim light, he saw that he was in a long attic with a soaring ceiling.

Samuel began to shiver. The temperature in the attic was very low—well below zero. He had a sweater and shoes on, but they weren't nearly enough to keep him warm. Anxiously, he looked around the room for something to provide additional warmth. As he stumbled about, he tripped over an old cardboard box. It split open and spilled out what appeared to be bolts of cloth. He discovered, upon closer examination, that they were really large bed spreads, cached away in the attic long ago. Although they were musty, and mice-chewn, Samuel gratefully wrapped one around his shoulders.

Feeling a little more secure and brave, Samuel began to further investigate the attic.

Around the trap door the floor was strewn with stacks and piles of discarded and forgotten junk, but as he walked through the clutter it thinned and ended. Soon he was walking in an empty, cavernous space. As he progressed, the light grew stronger. Up above, he could see row upon row of rafters supporting a roof made out of planking. At regular intervals a wide log beam stretched over his head and across the width of the room. Everything was coated with dust and seemed gray and ancient. A fine mist of ice crystals danced faintly in the murky light. Through this twinkling haze, Samuel saw a large round airway piercing the attic's end wall. This vent had a number of louvers missing. The resulting gap let into the room an occasional gust of snowflakes and a shaft of faint, dreary light. Where this watery illumination met the floor, Samuel spied something small and shiny.

His curiosity aroused, Samuel walked over to the object, peered at it for a few seconds and then carefully picked it up. It appeared to be a piece of costume jewelry. He turned it over in his hands and was struck by its weight and the large carved eye that stared back at him. He was about to put it in his pocket when, suddenly, there was a ruffle of feathers, and a harsh, angry voice squawked, "Go away."

Chapter 4

On the very day that Samuel was trapped in the attic of the Geyser Inn, Thokk awoke amidst the storm that raged outside. He was jolted to consciousness by a harsh blast of arctic air that furiously shook the tree in which he was roosting. Annoyed, he fluffed his feathers and buried himself deep under some snow-laden branches, hoping their shelter would keep him snug. Unfortunately, the wind sought out his nook, stripped away the warmth gathering under his feathers and pelted him spitefully with shards of hard-packed snow.

In his discomfort, Thokk attempted to think of some other way of escaping the storm. Rag's attic hide-out immediately came to mind. He imagined his friend perched snug and secure on a rafter, safe from the wind and snow. The longer he thought about the attic, the more it seemed a perfect refuge. With a shake of his feathers, he launched himself into the swirling air.

Immediately Thokk was blown helter-skelter, like a newspaper grabbed by a gale. A downdraft caught and smashed him upside down into a snow drift. Painfully, he rose to his feet, stunned and bewildered. With great difficulty he began hopping toward the inn, which emerged and disappeared in clouds of blowing snow. Suddenly the inn vanished in one tremendous billow of flakes and Thokk was sent skittering and tumbling across the ground. For a moment, he lost all sense of direction as everything went white. Mercifully, the inn reappeared, and he was able to struggle the last few yards to the shelter of its walls. For a long time he stood half buried in a drift, gasping for breath and summoning the strength to fly the remaining distance to Rag's home. As he waited, streamers of snow hissed around him like angry little ghosts. Finally, bruised and unhappy, he fluttered up to the vent that marked the entrance to Rag's hideaway.

As he squeezed through the broken louvers, Thokk uttered a harsh croak, which echoed off the walls. Adjusting to the dim light he spied Rag about fifteen feet away, perched on a beam. With several awkward flaps, he alighted next to his friend, who sat stone still, head bowed and mind comatose from cold and hunger. At Rag's feet was his treasure trove of shiny objects. Conspicuous on top was the silver ring pin he had found last summer. It shone faintly in the dim light, curiously free of dust and dirt.

His friend's silence grated on Thokk. "A little pity would be welcome," he grumbled. "You don't know what it's like out there! It's colder than a dead moose. But of course you don't know what it's like outside because you haven't been outside for, what, about a month. Ever since you found that big ugly silver pin, all you do is sit up here and expect me to wait on you."

This awakened Rag from his somnolent state, but instead of being angry or hurt, he only smiled with a bemused glimmer in his eyes. This irritated Thokk even more and his voice went up an octave. "Yeah, you just roost up here all day like a smelly old owl while I have to go out and find us dinner. I guess you're too good now for even scavenging, let alone begging and thievery, but you're more than happy to accept my charity. I feel like I'm having to feed some enormous mutant chick that won't grow up! It is completely beyond me why I put up with you. Any other sane raven would have ditched you in a minute." Then with an even stronger edge of sarcasm, Thokk added, "What do you do all day while you're up here guarding that ugly old brooch? Polish it? Admire it? Calculate its value in pine nuts? Not that anyone would give you a fish fin for it. I know, perhaps you're bewitched by it. Maybe the hee-bee-jeebee mojo god gave you a case of twinkle fever! Seriously, what is the good of that piece of junk? Here, why don't you let me get rid of it for you!" With that, Thokk darted his head past Rag and clamped the ring pin in his beak.

The indulgent look in Rag's eyes vanished, replaced by a much more ominous glint. With a lunge of his head, he also clasped onto the brooch. A fierce tug of war ensued, with the ring pin finally spinning out of both their grasps and landing with a clink on the wood floor below. Both ravens stared at the brooch for a moment. Just as Rag raised his wings to swoop down and retrieve it, a loud boom reverberated through the attic.

Thokk and Rag froze, directing their eyes toward the source of the commotion. Minutes passed without any discernable noise. Then intermittent shuffling sounds came from out of the gloom that encased the far end of the attic. Slowly, a small human, wrapped in an over-sized blanket, emerged into the dim light, paused for a moment, and then quietly walked toward them.

Rag and Thokk watched nervously as the young man approached. The closer he came, the more un-nerved the birds became. Finally, when Samuel stopped directly below them and picked up the brooch, his closeness became too much for Thokk. With an in-voluntary shudder, the raven flapped his wings and sounded a warning call.

Now Samuel—for, of course, it was Samuel—heard not a harsh caw, but "Go away," plainly and clearly.

In utter shock, Samuel jerked around, the hair on the back of his neck standing on end. When he spied the two coal-black ravens perched just a few feet above his head, he nearly jumped out of his skin. He froze, and without removing his eyes from the birds, said in a hoarse whisper: "Who's there?! Wh-where are you?"

Thokk and Rag nearly fell off their perch. Instead of the usual ugly stream of guttural grunts and chirps of human speech, they heard what Samuel said flawlessly in their own language. "What trick is this?" gasped Thokk.

Samuel saw Thokk's beak move and fully understood what the bird had said. His eyes nearly popped out of their sockets.

"You said that!" shouted Samuel.

"Said what?" sputtered Thokk.

"'What trick is this?'" answered Samuel.

A moment of silence passed as Thokk, Rag, and Samuel stared at each other in amazement. Finally Samuel stammered: "What is happening? Am I really talking to a bird? How can that be?"

"How would I know?" spat Thokk. But then his eyes opened wide and he gasped, "Wait, I do know what's happening! It's that God-awful brooch. It's casting a spell on us or something!"

"What are you talking about?" croaked Samuel.

"That piece of junk you're holding in your hands. We found it last summer, and ever since then I knew there was something evil about it. Just looking at it gives you the creeps. It's awful."

Samuel looked down at the brooch and then, after a second of hesitation, softly said, "I don't think it's so terrible."

Suddenly, neither did Thokk. As the full potential of being able to communicate with a human sunk in, Thokk's mind began to race. A clever glint entered his eyes. "You like our brooch then?"

"It's kind of weird looking, but it seems to let us understand each other."

"That it does, that it does. I, for one, have never been able to talk with a person before—not that I have really cared to. Perhaps we should test it. Put it down and walk away and see if we can still speak to each other."

Samuel set the ring pin on the floor, walked a few feet away and said, "Hello, hello, can you hear me."

Thokk shook his head and cawed. Samuel walked back and retrieved the pin. Thokk then said, "While we're at it, let's do one more experiment. Give me the brooch and see if we can still understand each other." This they did and found that it worked, no matter who was holding it.

"Well, well, isn't this amazing. We have a real magic brooch here," chuckled Thokk as he dropped it back into Samuel's hand.

Samuel nodded and rubbed his fingers over the surface of the brooch. Suddenly he asked, in a hesitant voice, "Can I have it?"

"No! Of course not!" snapped Thokk. "It's ours and we want to keep it. But," Thokk paused, looked slyly at Samuel, and said, "we could be your pals, though. Then you could see the brooch anytime you liked."

Samuel considered for a second and then said, "I could use a friend or two. I sure don't have any right now. It's just my parents and me here at the inn." Samuel then lowered his eyes and said: "Yeah sure, I'll be your friend."

Thokk clicked his tongue and said. "Good, good . . . But of course it's not quite that easy."

Samuel quickly looked up and said suspiciously, "What do you mean? You're the one who suggested being friends."

"Indeed," cooed Thokk. "But you have to understand, Rag and I are not used to having people as friends. We rather think ourselves better than that. You're such messy, ugly creatures. But you seem like a nice enough chap, and perhaps we'll make an exception for you. What's your name?"

"Samuel."

"I'm Thokk and he's Rag, but don't bother talking to him, he's mute as a fish." Here Thokk paused and looked craftily at Samuel. "Now if you're going to be our friend, you have to promise us a couple of things."

"What things?" answered Samuel, mistrust in his voice.

Thokk clicked his beak and said, "Well, first of all, you can't tell anyone about us or our hideout. We don't want some fussy adult coming along and kicking us out because you've tipped over the nest. Second, you have to always give us back the brooch. It's ours and we want to keep it. And, finally," here Thokk paused for dramatic effect while Samuel frowned, "you have to bring us food every day, without fail."

Samuel grimaced at this last request and Rag gave Thokk a sharp look. Thokk swallowed hard and quickly sputtered, "Well, it's winter you know. Times are tough and we have to spend most of our day hunting for food. But, if you were to bring us something to eat every day, then we could take time out of our busy schedule for a visit."

Samuel eyed Thokk with anger. The last condition had seemed too much, especially the "without fail" bit.

He wanted to just pocket the brooch and run. But then, with a shudder, he remembered that he was locked in the attic. All at once he felt chilled to the bone and he noticed that his toes and fingers were numb. He looked away from the ravens and toward the shadows that hid the trapdoor from the fourth-floor closet. Rag noted Samuel's abrupt change of mood and nudged Thokk.

Not very sympathetically, Thokk asked, "What's the matter? Are you changing your mind?"

Samuel answered, anxiety edging his voice. "No, it's not that. It's just that I'm trapped up here and I'm getting really cold."

"What do you mean, 'trapped'?"

"In order to get up here, I had to go through a door. Once I was through, it slammed behind me and locked. I don't have the key."

Thokk thought for a moment and then said, "Perhaps Rag and I can help you, but first you need to agree to our conditions—all three of them."

Samuel nodded reluctantly.

"Good, that's settled. So let's think of a way to get you out of here. How did you open the door in the first place without a key?" asked Thokk.

"I used a plastic tag to pick the door lock, but I dropped the tag on the other side of the door. I'd look for something else to use, but I can barely see in this light."

"What did the piece of plastic look like?"

"It was flat and about as big as my palm."

"Does it need to be plastic?"

"No, just stiff. A piece of cardboard is too flimsy."

"Well, let's search the attic and perhaps there's something here that will work just as well."

Samuel, with Thokk and Rag flapping behind, walked back to the piles of boxes surrounding the attic entrance. Fortunately for Samuel, ravens can see much better than humans in the dark. Soon Rag discovered a shingle fragment that matched what Samuel had described.

With the shingle in his mouth, Rag hopped over to Samuel and dropped it at his feet.

"This will work great," Samuel said with enormous relief. "Thank you."

"Oh, it's the least we can do for a new friend," answered Thokk in a voice bordering on insincerity. "In any case, you had better be on your way; you do look a little blue. Just don't forget what you promised—NO TELLING. And, oh yes, just a little something else to keep in mind: meat is better than bread, and whatever you bring doesn't have to be overly fresh. In fact, I have a fondness for week-old coyote."

With these words in his ears, Samuel promised to return the next day. Carefully he handed the ring pin back to Rag, who grabbed it in his beak. Thokk said goodbye, and Rag nodded his head. Samuel climbed down the ladder, found the door, and began to jiggle the shingle under the door bolt. With a click, the door gave way and swung open, revealing the musty maintenance room. Its one dim bulb seemed to Samuel, at that moment, to be as bright as the sun.

After gently closing the closet door, Samuel let out an enormous sigh. All he wanted now was to be somewhere comfortable and warm. Quickly he descended to the ground floor and across the empty lobby. Ahead, he saw the kitchen door, a big, heavy slab of stainless steel. A band of bright fluorescent light flooded underneath like a welcoming beacon. Samuel sprinted the last few steps and through the door. Carol was just starting the preparations for dinner. As Samuel rushed in, she lifted her head and gave him a sad smile.

Chapter 5

Samuel looked forward eagerly to his afternoon visits with Thokk and Rag; winter had now unalterably lost its dreariness. Every day, after finishing his schoolwork, he would fill a plastic bag with lunch scraps, slip out of the kitchen, throw on his winter clothes, rush through the inn, and straight up to the attic.

When Samuel reached the attic he inevitably plopped down on a bundle of old bedspreads and curtains he had piled up on the floor as a cushion. The ravens would then fly down from their perch, drop the brooch in his hand, and quickly gobble up their lunch. Afterward, Thokk and Samuel would talk while Rag hovered nearby, occasionally pecking at Samuel's sleeve.

After several visits, Samuel, Thokk, and Rag came to know one another quite well. Ironically, it was Samuel and Rag who became close friends, even though the latter could not utter a word. Thokk constantly colored his conversations with snide comments about people in general, and Samuel in particular. After a while Samuel would tire of this abuse and fall silent, feeling a little hurt and angry.

Unlike Thokk, Rag was good at cheering Samuel up. He would lumber over to Samuel's side, tap the floor several times with his beak and then hop onto Samuel's forearm, bobbing his head up and down in a clumsy fashion. This routine inevitably brought a smile to Samuel's face and got him to laugh.

One day, while the ravens were finishing their dinner, Samuel asked Thokk, "Why doesn't Rag ever say anything?"

Thokk looked up, glanced at Rag and said, "Something very bad happened to him when he was a fledgling. I think his whole family died in some gruesome disaster, and he was left alone and abandoned. As a result he went muddy in the head. His memory was wiped clean and he totally lost his ability to speak. He can't even remember his own name."

"I thought Rag was his name?"

"It might be; it certainly fits. But, between you and me, I don't think so."

"Why not?"

"Because if it were, he would no longer be mute," answered Thokk.

Samuel looked puzzled and said, "What do you mean?"

"Well you have to understand, what happened to Rag is not an unheard-of malady for ravens. We are, despite our reputation, very fragile and sensitive birds. It is common for us to become like Rag in the face of tragedy, devoid of memory and unable to talk. We become like lost souls, swallowed up in ourselves. Although it may sound strange to you, there is a simple cure for this condition. It is for the affected bird to first remember, and then say out loud, his real name. So you see, if 'Rag' were Rag's real name, then he would have long ago regained his voice. I've certainly yelled it at him enough times."

"Perhaps he can't speak. I mean, maybe his vocal cords have been damaged or something."

"Possibly, but I don't think so. Occasionally, in his sleep he'll chirp and coo."

"How did he get the name Rag then, if it's not his real name?"

"I think on account of his flea-bitten looks, of course."

In reaction to this insult, Rag jerked his head around and quickly jabbed at Thokk with his beak. Thokk hopped back in surprise, squawking indignantly, and fluttered off to a safe distance.

Rag stepped forward and tapped at the brooch in Samuel's hand. In response, Samuel placed the ring pin face-up on the floor. Rag delicately pecked at the small symbols that appeared on its front. Samuel picked the pin back up, rubbed the symbols with his fingers and stared at them intently. They were all straight angles, with no curved or horizontal lines. Although vaguely similar to normal letters, they were completely incomprehensible to Samuel.

"I've never seen letters like these before. I wonder what they say?" Samuel commented.

"Who cares what they say?" grumbled Thokk, who was still nursing his bruised pride. "They probably say 'Please Dispose of Properly' in Chinese, no less."

"I've seen Chinese letters and these are not anything like them," Samuel replied, ignoring Thokk's sarcasm.

"Personally, I wouldn't give them a second thought," scoffed Thokk. "But, by the looks of Rag, he certainly seems to think they're some big deal."

Indeed, Rag had stood staring at Samuel all the while he had been studying the letters.

Samuel began to feel uncomfortable under the bird's intense gaze. With a half chuckle he asked, "Whatever do you want, Rag?"

"He wants you to find out what those little symbols mean, of course," sneered Thokk. "He has a habit of asking his friends to do impossible things."

"I really have no idea what they might say. I don't even know if they're letters," answered Samuel.

Rag sagged noticeably—a gleam seemed to leave his eyes. In response Samuel said quickly, "Wait, wait! Let me think. Maybe there's something I can do. Maybe I can use the inn's set of encyclopedias to find something out. Here, I'll copy down the letters, or whatever they are, and see what turns up."

From his pocket Samuel produced a ballpoint pen and, on a chunk of old cardboard torn from a box, began to meticulously reproduce the symbols. Given the poor light, the letters' tiny size, and the cold, it took him nearly half an hour to complete the task. As he labored, he became more and more curious as to what the letters might say, where they came from, and who might have created them. His eyes were burning and his fingers numb from cold when he finally finished. Carefully he stuffed the cardboard in his coat, and with a quick goodbye left the two ravens for the day.

Samuel spent the remainder of the afternoon in the inn's reading lounge. He went straight to a set of antiquated encyclopedias stored haphazardly in a bookcase. They were not in the best of shape. Spines were broken, pages ripped out, and volumes "T" and "U" were missing. Samuel sighed, took off his coat, and carefully set the symbol-filled piece of cardboard on a coffee table. He began his quest by looking up "Jewelry" and found nothing of interest, moved on to "alphabets" with no luck, and then to "symbols." After an hour of fruitless research, he gave up in despair. By this time the coffee table in front of him was weighted down with several teetering stacks of encyclopedias. Discouraged and bored, he looked around the empty lounge and wondered what to do next.

For a while Samuel sat and watched snowflakes whirl outside the window. He then listened to a CD on his headphones until the batteries on his little player went dead. Finally, he plopped himself down on an overstuffed coach with a stack of ancient comic books he had recently discovered on a high shelf. Their pages were dog-eared and brittle and the colors faded. He read half an issue of *Batman* and glanced at an edition of *Sargent Rock*. Absentmindedly, he began flipping through the remaining pile of comics until, suddenly, his hand froze over a cover half torn from its binding. There in front of him, printed in garish green and covered over with a strip of yellowing tape, were a few of the same symbols he had so laboriously copied from the brooch.

The Mighty Thor had never much interested Samuel before, but now, to his amazing disbelief, it provided the magical key to deciphering the raven's ring pin. In bold letters across the top of the magazine was printed, "Thor and the Magic Runes!" Below was a picture of a blond-haired, beardless warrior in a winged helmet, holding what looked like a little sledge hammer and cowering away from a glowing green stone. On this stone, highlighted with yellow, were carved some of the same symbols which appeared on the ring pin. A surge of hope and excitement welled up in Samuel. He now had a clue on which to proceed—the letters on the brooch were called runes.

In a rush, Samuel looked up "runes" in the encyclopedia. A short entry described them as an alphabet used by ancient Germanic and Scandinavian people, including the Vikings. It went on to say that runes were often thought to have magical powers and were carved on important religious objects and marker stones. Samuel eagerly devoured the entry, rereading it several times and memorizing every fact.

Next he looked up "Vikings," since they were so prominently mentioned in the entry on runes. This description was a good deal longer and was of less immediate interest to Samuel, although it did contain one very valuable bit of information. There, next to the written text, were two photographs of Viking artifacts. One was of a long, sinuous sailing ship. The other was of a brooch worn by Vikings to clasp together their cloaks. It nearly matched, in size and shape, the raven's ring pin. After gazing at the illustration for a long time, he closed the encyclopedia and smiled to himself.

As he sat there in the middle of Geyser Inn's reading lounge, Samuel felt a warm sense of pride. In just a few short minutes he had discovered two very important things about the ring pin: that it might have been made by Vikings a thousand years ago, and that the tiny symbols that appeared on it were called runes. Perhaps now, with a little luck, he could even translate the runes. He leaned forward in his chair, cupping his hands around his chin and resting his elbows on a stack of encyclopedias. With eyes closed and forehead creased, he concentrated on what to do next. All was quiet while he thought, except for the windows creaking in the wind and the rattle and gurgle of the inn's hot water radiators.

With a flash of inspiration, Samuel jumped up and raced into the small manager's office where he did his homework. Quickly, he turned on the computer, impatiently tapping his fingers as it whirred and clicked to life. As the screen blinked on, he went straight to the Internet.

Samuel had used the Internet often to look up school-related subjects—anything from the moons of Jupiter to the War of 1812. Perhaps, he thought, there might be a webpage on runes. Quickly, Samuel typed "Runes" into the computer. After what seemed an interminable wait, a whole list of matching websites appeared on the screen. Near the top was a site titled "Norse Runes Translator." Samuel called it up and a black screen with crossed Norwegian and American flags appeared, followed by a brief introduction giving the history of runes. Scrolling down, Samuel encountered a box where a word could be typed and the computer would automatically transform it into runes. Next was a chart that matched letters to their corresponding runes. This was the information for which Samuel was searching.

Excitedly, Samuel pulled out the piece of crumpled cardboard from under his shirt and set it next to the computer. He then began carefully matching runes to letters, using the website chart as a guide. Above each rune he wrote in pencil its corresponding letter. After a few minutes, nervously hoping his mother would not become curious about his sudden project, Samuel sat back with a grimace. All that had resulted from his efforts was a paragraph of nonsense words. He bit his lip in bitter frustration. He had seemed so close to deciphering the runes. He continued to read down the website, hoping to find some clue as to why his translation effort had failed. Unfortunately, there was nothing more to the site, except for the name of its creator, Bjorn Lillo, Professor of Medieval Studies, Trondheim University, Norway, and his e-mail address.

Samuel was stymied. His shoulders slumped as he stared at the screen. He reached out to flick the off switch when, like a bolt from the blue, an idea struck him. Why not ask professor Lillo what had happened? Surely a university professor could figure out why the runes had translated into gibberish. All Samuel needed to do was send an e-mail to Professor Lillo.

After noting the professor's address, Samuel left the "Norse Runes Translator" site and went to where he could write an e-mail. Working quickly, he typed:

Dear Professor Lillo:

My name is Samuel Johnson and I have a problem. I found what I think is a Viking Ring Pin. On it are a bunch of Runes. I tried to translate them using your Norse Runes Translator web site, but ended up with what you see below:

SIH ARSI THOM TA SKTN

FUTH HARTBML ORKHN RST BML

OJNI RSML BTH ORUF NIARSTL OMN

FUIA RS BMS IDLT ROKH RA

ISIKLT HKRO THOU FRIK

SBML UFTH OKHN SIKLT HNI

THORK HN AR BML TO SN KI

RTHOR HNIA RSNB MLOSI FUTHO

What did I do wrong? Can you help me translate the runes so they make sense?

Thank You.

Send reply to the following address . . .

P.S. Do you have ravens in Norway?

With his fingers crossed, Samuel pushed the "Send" button. He then turned the computer off with a sigh, knowing that any reply to his letter would probably take a long time.

The next day, before he began his schoolwork, Samuel checked to see whether Professor Lillo had sent him a reply. Nothing. Again, before he went to visit the ravens that afternoon, he rechecked the computer. Again nothing.

When he reached the attic, Samuel related to the ravens all that he had done and discovered the day before. Rag, at least, was pleased. He seemed to understand how hard Samuel had worked. Thokk just rolled his eyes and groused that his food ration was perhaps a little scant: ". . . due most likely to everyone's silly preoccupation with the stupid ring pin."

After a week had passed and there was no reply from Professor Lillo, Samuel began to lose hope. He had become just as obsessed with the ring pin as Rag, and the lack of any news from Norway was a painful blow. He even started to dread his visits to the ravens. Rag would always be waiting expectantly for him each day, impatient for news concerning the brooch. It broke Samuel's heart to continuously disappoint him. As time passed, Rag became more and more dispirited and would only peck at the food that Samuel brought. Rag's despair made Samuel's own frustration all the more keen.

Of course, Thokk always had something snide to say, scolding both Samuel and Rag for their apparent foolishness.

Then, one morning there it was, like the first Christmas present of the season, a reply from Professor Lillo. Samuel could barely contain his excitement as he read:

Dear Samuel:

Wherever did you get this brooch of yours? It was incredibly difficult to translate. It took me hours and hours of hard labor to make any sense of it at all.

First of all, the language that appears on the brooch is Old Norse. I am guessing that you assumed it was English. Herein lies the failure of your translation attempt. When you used the chart from my website, all that you did was switch the brooch's runes for letters. You didn't translate Old Norse to English. To better understand what you did do, you might image the French word for "friend," which is, of course, "Amie." Now imagine that I write "Amie" out in runes, ᚠ ᛟ ᚱ ᚠ, and give it to you to translate. You could use my website chart to switch the runes back to the letters "A," "M," "E" and "I" (which is exactly what you did with the brooch) but unless you know French, "Amie" would be meaningless to you. My chart cannot translate languages, it can only transpose Runes to Roman letters.

Even if you knew Old Norse, I am sure that you could not have deciphered the brooch anyway. It uses a very obscure dialect, one that even I have never seen before (and I have spent my whole life studying this language).

As I stated earlier, I spent a tremendous amount of time on this project. I hope you appreciate my efforts. In any case here is the translation:

> For the gift of poetry I gave my eye
> so into the future my sight could fly.
> From that day when my face became stark
> a single eye has become my royal mark.
> So onto this singular brooch I impart my sign
> to make it an object powerful and divine.
> Servant, say my name, Odin, thrice,
> and Asgard and your world will splice.

This is a very curious poem and I frankly can't tell you exactly what it means or from what Scandinavian country it originates. You may already know this, but Odin was the king of the Norse gods and he was blind in one eye, having given it up for the gift of poetry. Asgard, of course, is the abode of the Norse gods, much like Mt. Olympus is home for the Greek gods. I have no idea though, what is meant by "your world will splice."

My professional instincts tell me that what you have is some kind of theater prop from perhaps the late 1800s when there was a revival of interest in Viking lore in Germany and Scandinavia. The poem might be the lines from a period play. It is curious though, why anyone would go to all the bother to translate it into authentic Old Norse.

*I would very much like to learn more about where
you got this brooch and what it looks like. Please send
me an image, either by e-mail or through the post.*

Sincerely,

*Professor Bjorn Lillo, University of Trondheim,
Norway*

Samuel reread the letter, soaking up every last word
and committing it to memory, except for the poem
which he carefully copied down. As quickly as he could,
he deleted the letter, fearful his mother might see it and
his relationship with the ravens would be exposed.

It was very difficult for Samuel to do his school
work that morning. The minutes crept past, each alge-
bra problem an interminable calculation, every vocabu-
lary word an irksome chore of memorization. Lunch
was gobbled down in such a hurry that Carol repri-
manded him for his haste. "Slow down or you'll choke,
Sam. What's the big hurry?"

Without even answering his mother, Samuel raced
from the kitchen and hastily threw on his coat, hat,
boots, and gloves. It seemed a very long climb up to the
fourth floor. When Samuel finally sprinted up the attic
ladder, through the trap door and past the dim storage
boxes, it was a tremendous relief to see his friends
perched in their usual spot. As always, Rag flapped over
and gave Samuel the ring pin, and then returned to sit
next to Thokk.

"What did you bring us to eat today?" croaked Thokk.

Breathlessly Samuel replied, "I'm sorry, I forgot to bring anything but . . . "

"What!" shrieked Thokk. "Did you hit your head or something? You go back right now and get us our lunch, you twit."

"But . . . ?"

"But, nothing!" Here Thokk began to violently flap his wings and his voice rose to an indignant squawk. "I'm cold and I'm hungry and I want my food!"

Rag, who could see the excitement in Samuel's eyes, smacked Thokk with his wing. With a bitter "humph" Thokk fell silent.

"I know what the runes say!" Samuel said breathlessly.

"Ohhh, I can hardly wait," scoffed Thokk. "What do they say? 'Do Not Feed The Wildlife,' perhaps?"

Ignoring Thokk and turning to Rag, Samuel said, "The Norwegian professor figured them all out. I copied down his translation." Here Samuel pulled out the deciphered poem and read it to the ravens. By the time he was finished, Rag's eyes were shining.

Thokk, on the other hand, only rolled his eyes and sputtered, "For this I missed my lunch!"

"But don't you see? It's wonderful," Samuel said. "All our work paid off, we found out what the brooch says."

Thokk stared at his friends, his glance moving between Rag's transfixed expression and Samuel's eager, enthusiastic face. Suddenly, like the uncorking of a bottle, all the accumulated frustration of living with Rag, dealing with an especially harsh winter, and having to be nice to Samuel burst out of him. "This has gone far enough! For months Rag has been bewitched by that evil brooch and now it has infected you, Samuel, as well! It's all you dolts think about!"

"But Thokk," gasped Samuel. "It might have been made by Vikings a thousand years ago."

Thokk's eyes bulged with anger and frustration. "So what! Can you eat it? Does it keep you warm?"

"No, but . . ."

"Silence!" screamed Thokk. And then, in an only slightly calmer voice, he growled, "I must be crazy to stick around here. I'm starving and freezing in this god-forsaken cave! Instead of looking for a better place to live and for more worthy companions, I spend my time keeping company to a half-fledged car ape and playing nursemaid to a loony."

With a violent flapping of wings, Thokk swooped off his perch and toward Samuel. Samuel stumbled backward and landed on the seat of his pants. Thokk alighted on his knee, took a rasping breath and hissed. "Now you listen to me, little mammal! The brooch is great fun, it lets us have pleasant little *tête-à-têtes*. But let's leave it at that. No more talk of computers and the Internet! No more worrying about professors in Norway. Forget all about Asgard, splicing worlds, and that silly, one-eyed god, um . . . now what was his name?

Ohhh yes, Odin. Well here, let me say it three times and be done with it: Odin, Odin, Odin . . . "

Thokk got no further, for at that moment there was a blinding flash, and the attic dissolved in a hiss.

Chapter 6

Samuel, Thokk, and Rag found themselves standing outside in a broad open area covered with deep snow and surrounded by tall fir trees. It was late afternoon; blue shadows stretched across the clearing. The sky was a brilliant blue, brushed here and there with a few high, wispy clouds. It was absolutely quiet. Not a breath of wind, not a rustle of branches, not even a bird song could be heard. All three were stunned and stood rooted to the ground, staring in silence at their new surroundings. The air was cold but not bitter and their breaths came in great puffs of steam.

Thokk blinked, looked at Samuel, and then at Rag. In a voice edged with anger and fear, he squeaked, "Now look what that horrible brooch has done to us. Where in God's green earth are we now?"

Rag only nodded his head as he gaped at the trees and snow. Slowly his composure changed from fear and surprise to a look of wonderment. There was something familiar to him about the light and air of this clearing, something about the look of the trees, the quiet that encompassed them, and the deep blue, radiant sky; it was almost as if he had come home.

Samuel, on the other hand, was gripped by growing anxiety. Wherever this clearing was, it was a long way from the Geyser Inn. All he could see were shaggy evergreens and none of the prominent landmarks that normally surrounded his home—no lake off to one side, no endless ranks of lodgepole pine, no cedar-shake roof projecting above the trees, not even the distant mountains that always filled the horizon to the east of the inn. Worst of all, there were no apparent roads or trails or any other signs of human habitation. Everything was lonely and unfamiliar.

Samuel shivered in the cold air. His parents had lectured him sternly about the dangers of winter weather and on such subjects as hypothermia. Now, with his boots buried knee deep in snow, evening not far off and with no shelter in sight, he began to panic. What had happened, where was he, and how would he get back to the inn? Then, in a jolt of fear, all these concerns were erased from his mind. He saw something in the trees across the clearing that terrified him. His legs buckled and he dropped to his knees in the snow.

Standing a hundred feet away among some spindly trees was a giant. Not a large human, but a real giant, ten feet tall, thin in stature, and dressed in a gray tunic gathered at the waist by a black belt. He wore maroon pants with gray leggings held up by black, crisscrossed straps. A gray cape lined with red was clasped together at his right collarbone and, above that, a pale face rested on narrow shoulders. His nearly white hair shone in the sinking sun. As Samuel took in these general features, the giant brushed aside the trees and began to stride purposefully across the clearing toward him and the ravens.

Thokk, who had been grumbling and complaining to Rag, fell silent as he spied the oncoming giant. Samuel began to choke and cough. Rag took two steps forward, setting himself in the giant's path. Suddenly, Thokk whirled around and in a voice edged with panic squealed, "Try the ring pin, say Odin three times and get us out of here!"

In desperation, Samuel grasped the ring pin tightly in his hands, closed his eyes and shouted, "Odin, Odin, Odin." Nothing happened. Again, with his voice nearly choked with fear, Samuel gasped the magic words. Once more nothing happened. With a moan of frustration, he cried, "It's broken, it's not working."

As the giant grew close, Samuel saw that his face was clean-shaven, handsome, and narrow. A long nose and strong chin gave him an arrogant and haughty appearance. A pair of penetrating gray-blue eyes, which seemed neither kind nor welcoming, stared straight at Samuel. A large knife, set in a leather sheath, dangled at the end of a strap tied to the giant's belt. With his hands on his hips, the giant stopped in front of Rag, looked at Samuel, and then said in an icy voice, "Who are you and why are you here? You are trespassing."

"I'm sorry," stammered Samuel. "I didn't mean to trespass. I'm lost. I don't know where I am."

A look of disgust passed over the giant's face, and he turned his gaze first to Rag, who obstinately stared back at him, and then to Thokk. "Who are you, bird?"

"Ahh . . . Thokk. I'm terribly sorry about being here, we certainly didn't mean to intrude. Perhaps if you'd point the way, we'd . . . "

"What did you say your name was?" interrupted the giant brusquely, holding up a hand.

Thokk gulped. "Thokk."

"Who gave you that name?"

"My mother, I think."

"She had no right to give you that name without my permission. It is one of my special and secret names that only I may use."

"I'm very sorry," stuttered Thokk. "I'm sure she acted out of ignorance, probably from not knowing you."

"What!" shouted the giant. "How could she not know me?!"

Here Thokk was at a loss for words; he coughed and hopped nervously back and forth from one foot to the other. The giant turned to Rag and Samuel and was met by blank, fearful expressions. An amazed look crept over the giant's features. In an incredulous voice he said, "You three don't know who I am, either, do you?"

"Yes sir, that's right. We don't know who you are," whispered Samuel.

The giant stared at Samuel, Thokk, and Rag in turn with his piercing eyes. Finally he drew a deep breath and said, his voice increasing in volume and anger as he spoke, "Your ignorance astounds and amazes me! It is impossible for you not to know who I am. Everyone is taught my name from birth. Have you not heard the stories of my greatness, marveled at my adventures, thanked me every time a cooking fire is lit? Did you not listen to your village storytellers? Who were your neglectful parents?"

Here the giant paused and glared at Samuel and the ravens. When they failed to respond, he said, "I am Loki, junton of fire, lord of cleverness, god of guile, shape shifter, and blood brother to Odin. You must certainly lie when you say that I am strange to you for every golden god in Asgard, troll in Jotunheim, peasant in Midgard, and wretched soul in Hel knows of me."

As he finished speaking, Loki's features twisted into an arrogant sneer. With a toss of his head he flung a stray lock of hair back into place. Samuel and the ravens only stared back at him, frightened and confused, until Samuel, in a small voice, said, "But we're not from Midgard or from any of those other places."

"Then from where did you come? Out of what dark and savage realm did you crawl?" Loki jeered.

"We're from Earth," answered Samuel.

"Earth!?. . . I have never even heard of it. What a poor and pitiful place it must be." And then with a look of utter scorn, Loki added, "You must be what Odin refers to as a skraeling, an ugly screecher. As I remember, Odin said that skraelings have not been blessed with knowing the gods and that they live in a realm bordering on the primeval void. Yes, that must be it, you're skraelings."

Samuel and the ravens just shrugged and sat in stunned silence, speechless and pathetic, staring goggle-eyed at the giant. Loki, for his part, scowled back at them with unabashed disdain. Finally, with an irritated gesture, Loki said, "Well, I guess you had better come with me before you freeze. Perhaps I can put you to some use."

Loki turned on his heel and strode back into the forest. After hesitating for a second, Samuel followed after, afraid to go with the giant, but seeing no other alternative. Staying alone in the desolate clearing with night falling was a prospect too horrible to consider. The snow was deep—often up to Samuel's thighs—and he was unable to keep up as Loki marched quickly away. Without a backward glance, Thokk followed Loki until he also disappeared. Bewildered and afraid, Samuel stumbled along as best he could, following the giant's footsteps in the snow. Rag flapped ahead and frequently circled back to make sure Samuel was headed in the right direction.

Fortunately, Samuel did not have far to struggle. In a matter of minutes he found Loki standing in the middle of a crude campsite. A fire ring of blackened stones was filled with gray ashes and half-burned twigs, and a sooty pot sat askew on a stone, half full of ice-crusted water. Around the fire ring were several boulders and logs brushed free of snow. An enormous lean-to of spruce boughs stood nearby, under a tall tree.

Inside was a cot on which an eiderdown comforter lay in a rumpled pile. The cot's wooden frame struck Samuel's eyes, for it was intricately carved, with miniature heads topping each of its four posts, an incongruous note of luxury in otherwise primitive surroundings. Some unwashed wooden dishes and a few bones were scattered on the trampled floor of the lean-to. A large leather pack hung from a nearby tree limb. Samuel, cold and shivering, eyed the fire ring with longing.

Glancing down, Loki caught Samuel's expression and said, "Well, if you want a fire, start collecting wood."

Wearily, Samuel began trudging from tree to tree around the camp site, snapping off dead twigs and small branches. Rag helped as best he could, collecting some tufts of dried moss. Thokk gathered a few bits of bark, but mostly just sat and watched. Samuel's fingers soon became stiff and his toes numb. Finally, with a sigh of relief, he dumped a large armful of wood into the middle of the fire ring and sat down exhausted on a rock. Rag deposited what he had collected and then alighted on a nearby branch.

As Samuel and Rag rested, Loki sat on the edge of his cot, delicately plucking the needles off a small spruce twig. He then held up the stripped branch, whispered an inaudible word, and smiled as it burst into flame. Nonchalantly, he tossed the flare into Samuel's stack of wood. Slowly the fire crept from one stick to the next and soon the pile crackled and popped with a strong flame. Samuel only blinked his eyes and coughed at Loki's show of magic. He was too cold and tired for any other reaction. Even after the fire came to full life he continued to shiver.

The fire quickly burned down to embers. With a sad sigh, Samuel resigned himself to collecting another load. But before he could begin, Loki stood up and with little effort pulled the stump end of a downed tree into the fire. Samuel felt a wave of relief as the fire roared to new life. He watched as the flames greedily licked up the sides of the log.

An hour or so passed, and Loki stood without speaking, staring into the fire, lost in his own thoughts. Samuel sat dazed in the blazing warmth, mesmerized by the steam which rose from his wet boots and pants. Eventually the sun set and cold dark shadows crept out from the recesses of the forest like a gloomy tide. Only the fire's flickering flames, which seemed to grow brighter, held the darkness at bay. Thokk poked around the edge of the campfire, snapping up stray crumbs, and Rag stood on a small boulder, silently dozing in the warm air. After a while Samuel noticed he was hungry. A dull ache gnawed at his stomach.

Loki yawned and walked over to his pack. From deep inside he pulled out a leather pouch, a small silver knife, and a wooden bowl wrapped in a cloth. Out of the pouch he extracted a dried fish, black and shriveled. He uncovered the bowl, scooped out some butter and smeared it on the fish. He popped the combination into his mouth, chewed thoughtfully for a few minutes and then repeated the process.

With a whirr of feathers and a bounce, Thokk landed in front of Loki and began to hop about. The fire god smiled at this and even laughed out loud when Thokk did his usual acrobatics. He tossed Thokk a fish, which the raven caught with a snap and gulped down in one swallow. "Ha, ha, ha! You are a sly creature, aren't you! Perhaps 'Thokk' fits you after all," Loki murmured, throwing Thokk another tidbit.

When he had eaten his fill, Loki glanced over at Samuel. "Too proud to beg, are we?" he scoffed. "Oh well, I might need you."

Reaching into the pouch, Loki pulled out several bits of fish and flung them Samuel's way. Samuel quickly plucked them out of the snow and began to eat ravenously. The fish tasted awful. They were oily, salty, and their bones stuck between his teeth. Halfway though, he realized that Loki had not thrown anything Rag's way.

"Sir, I am sure Rag is also hungry."

Loki barely glanced at Samuel and retorted in a cold tone, "He is of no use to me. Let him find his own food."

Reluctantly, Samuel split his remaining fish and gave some to Rag, who, despite his usual stoic manner, gladly accepted Samuel's gift. Each quickly gobbled down his share.

After this meal, Loki pulled out a frayed woolen blanket, decorated with a faded plaid pattern of red and yellow, and threw it to Samuel. "You had better wrap up in this, it's going to be a cold night."

Loki then undid the straps around his shins, took off his shoes, which were shaped much like moccasins, and laid down on the cot. With a grunt he pulled the comforter up to his chin, rolled over and fell asleep. Samuel was left sitting on his rock in the darkness and gathering cold.

Having nowhere to lie down, Samuel passed a miserable night. He dozed sitting up, drifting in and out of consciousness. Around midnight the weather changed. The wind picked up and it started to snow. Great curtains of thick, wet flakes filtered down from the sky. Samuel was quickly blanketed with snow, which dramatically compounded his discomfort and woe. The fire sputtered and hissed as it burned down to embers.

Near dawn, Samuel awoke with a jerk from an uneasy dream and glanced at Loki with red-rimmed eyes. The giant was awake and staring at the ceiling of his lean-to, gently tapping his finger tips together. Slowly he reached out from under the protection of the lean-to and let the falling snow form a pile in his hand. Methodically, he packed the snow into a ball. It was wet and warm, and compressed easily into a tight cohesive sphere. All at once, Loki's hands froze and his eyes seemed to stare at a point far in the distance. He gave a low chuckle as a sly grin spread across his face. Suddenly, he threw the snowball at Samuel, who sprang up blinking and sputtering and wiping snow from his face. "Get up, you slothful slave," laughed Loki. "It's time you earned your keep."

After a quick breakfast of oatmeal, prepared by Loki in the sooty kettle, Loki led Samuel back to the clearing. Rag and Thokk followed and perched on a tall fir tree. It was barely dawn and the world was a uniform gray, barely visible through the falling snow. In the middle of the clearing Loki stooped and packed another snowball, examined it and with a satisfied grin said, "Now Samuel, I want you to roll as big a snowball as you can for me. Be warned, don't play weak."

Samuel unenthusiastically trudged a few yards away, formed a small sphere and rolled it along the ground. It quickly grew into an uneven mass the size of a boulder. Loki bent over, picked it up, frowned slightly, and set it in the middle of the clearing. "Keep them coming," was all he said.

Wearily, Samuel rolled ball after ball, each one requiring more effort than the last. It was miserable work. The driving snow pelted his face and made his eyes water and blink. His toes and fingers became numb with cold, yet his upper body was soon bathed in sweat. Loki grew impatient and dissatisfied with his efforts, growling, "Come on, come on! You can work faster than that!"

Gradually, two great pillars of snow rose out of the ground. When the columns reached about five feet high Loki joined them together with a bridge of willow branches covered with hard-packed snow. From there, the structure rose in one ever growing and broadening mass.

As time passed, Loki became more and more excited. He started to roll balls of snow himself, furiously lifting the spheres onto the monstrous edifice and violently packing them into place. He rushed about the clearing, gathering branches and sprinting back to his lean-to to get a needed tool. After a while, Samuel and his meager contributions were nearly forgotten.

On through the morning and into the afternoon, Samuel and Loki labored. After a while, the god's need for snowballs slacked and then ceased. Samuel was finally able to rest, sitting on the remains of an unfinished ball. He was exhausted and his breath came in painful gasps. His gloves were soaked through and when he removed one, his fingers came out white, wrinkly, and colder than a dead fish. Throbbing sparks of pain shot up from his toes as he tried to wiggle them in his boots. His undershirt was soaked with perspiration and it became chill and clammy as he rested. He began to shiver once more. Snow continued to fall, collecting on his shoulders and thighs. Through his discomfort, he watched the god of mischief labor on.

Loki was working at a frantic pace, chipping away at the rough form with both hands and a long knife. Slowly the lumpy, indistinguishable tower transformed into a massive figure at least fifteen feet tall. Arms sprouted from a barrel chest and a squat head appeared like a tremendous wart.

Once in a while Loki ordered Samuel to bring him a new snowball or fetch some willow saplings or do some other minor task. Late in the afternoon the snow stopped and ragged tears opened up in the cloud cover. It was then that Loki began to do something very curious. He would blow furiously on a small section of the snowman and then quickly rub that area with his bare hands or sleeve. This made the snow smooth and shiny, almost like marble. As the sun set and the sky turned rose and purple, Loki stepped back and admired his creation.

In front of Loki stood a brutish warrior. He was clothed from shoulders to knees with a jerkin of square armor plates, now shining brilliantly in the sinking sun. His face was covered by a shaggy beard and from under a tall helmet long tresses of unkempt hair flew in all directions.

Small, piggish eyes stared out from under heavy brows and a bulbous nose projected from his face like a knobby carrot. A great round shield, held at chest level, was strapped to his left forearm. In his other hand, he held a massive axe. This weapon rested on his right shoulder and extended above his head. The warrior's legs were bare and thick and his feet were shod in heavy boots. Around his waist was a belt made of chains and from it hung a sword. This snowman—for that is what he was—was so detailed and animated that Samuel half-expected him to spring to life.

Reluctantly, Loki turned away from his creation and began walking toward the campsite, motioning for Samuel and the ravens to follow. Samuel could barely comply. He was so stiff and cold he could only stumble along in a daze. When he reached the fire ring, he collapsed against a snowbank. His teeth chattered uncontrollably, and he felt sick to his stomach.

With an exasperated sigh, Loki stopped what he was doing and stared down at Samuel. "Here, here," he grumbled. "Don't sit in the snow."

When Samuel didn't move, Loki bent over, pulled him up, roughly wrapped a blanket around him and made him lie down on the cot. He then covered him with the down comforter and gave him a drink of water from a wooden bowl. Samuel immediately fell into a deep sleep.

Late that night, Samuel awoke briefly. Earlier Loki had built a large fire and was now staring into its embers. The pyre roared with vibrant life, casting everything into sharp contrast. All was either illuminated in a fierce orange glow or lost in blackness. Loki's features, twisted into a wily and mischievous smile, looked all the more evil and ominous in the flickering gloom. A ring of dancing shadows surrounded the campfire like a circle of vaporous witches caught in a mad frenzy. Occasionally a spark would float upward like a glowing feather or streak out like a comet and vanish with a blink. Thokk and Rag seemed frozen in stone as they slept on a branch above the lean-to, silent sentinels half lost in the night.

Suddenly, in a low, sinister whisper that made the hair on the back of Samuel's neck stand on end, Loki began muttering to himself. "Tomorrow is going to be a very sweet and pleasant day . . . a real day to remember. First I'll summon my so-called comrades. I know just how to make them come running . . . yes I do . . . Just like a hunter calls his pack of dogs . . . ha, ha, ha! Then I'll give them all a little scare, something to dent their pride and make them sweat . . . ha, ha, ha."

Here Loki paused. The popping and crackling of the fire seemed loud in the silence. Samuel was afraid that Loki had somehow sensed that he was listening. He shut his eyes tightly and tried to breath normally. But then Loki spoke again, his voice taking on a bitter and angry tone. "I'll pay them back for casting me out like an outlaw. Go live in the wilderness for a winter they said. Well they're going to regret humiliating me . . . That they will, that they will . . . ha, ha, ha."

Chapter 7

Loki's irate voice jolted Samuel abruptly to wakefulness. With a jerk, he sprang bolt upright on Loki's cot, blinking and staring in the pale gray light of dawn. Through blurry eyes, he saw Loki sitting on the edge of a rock next to the fire and gesturing fiercely for Thokk to come near. Skittishly, the raven was creeping forward with his head nervously bobbing up and down. "Come on! Come on! It's time for you to earn your crumbs," Loki snarled impatiently.

During the night the sky had cleared and the weather had turned sharply colder. Under Loki's down quilt, Samuel had kept warm. He now felt quite rested, but also very stiff and hungry. He yawned and shivered and watched as Loki finally persuaded Thokk to come within arm's reach.

"Now I want you to listen with both ears." Loki began, bending over and looking Thokk straight in the eyes. "I want you to deliver a message to some companions of mine. Just do exactly what I say and everything will turn out all right. Understand?" Thokk warily nodded his head and Loki continued. "First, I want you to fly straight east, in the direction of a long range of mountains. As soon as you are airborne, you will see them in the distance. In an hour or so you will come to the end of the forest and the mouth of a broad alpine valley. Follow this gorge as it winds upward. You will soon be over a glacier and it will lead you to a large flat-topped mountain. On this peak will be a great fortress surrounded by cliffs and deep crevasses. This citadel is called Asgard, and it is the home of the Aesir gods.

"Inside Asgard will be many palaces of different shapes and sizes. All of them will be facing a central courtyard. On the north side of the courtyard will be a hall built entirely of bright red wood. You will fly up to the door of that house, rap on it three times, and then shout, as loud as you can, 'Thor, Thor, Thor! Asgard is in peril.' You will keep shouting this until Thor opens the door."

"How will I know who Thor is? Is he a giant like you?" interrupted Thokk.

Loki gasped and then looked at Thokk, Samuel, and Rag in turn. "Don't tell me you three don't know who Thor is!"

Samuel, Thokk, and Rag all shook their heads.

Loki rolled his eyes in exasperation and declared, "You are the strangest company of orphans I have ever met. Your Earth must truly be a crude place for its inhabitants not to know of Thor. He is, alas, even more famous than I. He is the god of thunder and lightning. With his magic hammer called Mjollnir and a belt that doubles his strength, he is Asgard's most famous warrior. He is also, for some reason beyond me, the favorite of all the dull and dumb peasants of Midgard. He is as tall as I am, with red hair, a red beard, and red-rimmed eyes. Occasionally, he is even my comrade in adventure." Here Loki paused, frowned, and muttered, "Now where was I . . . ?"

"You were telling me to knock on Thor's door," Thokk said.

"That's right, well . . . when Thor opens the door, act as if the world is falling apart. Jump up and down, flap your wings, do whatever is necessary. Tell him that a huge frost giant is just outside the walls of Asgard. That this monster has captured me and will kill me quickly if he does not come to my rescue. Say that the frost giant is calling him a coward and an oaf, the son of a crow, and Odin's thrall. All this will undoubtedly make Thor furious and thirsty for blood. Volunteer to lead him, and any other god or goddess that might want to come along, back here to the clearing. And, oh yes, tell him that the frost giant's name is Jormungand." Here a particularly evil grin split Loki's face.

"Who is Jormungand?" asked Thokk.

"Let's just say that Thor and Jormungand are old acquaintances with a poisonous relationship. But you never mind, just lead Thor here and leave the rest up to me. I'll expect to see you by early afternoon."

"That soon! The journey you describe sounds much longer than a few hours' walk. Certainly Thor can't fly, can he?" asked Thokk.

"No, but Thor has a sled that can travel just as fast as you can fly," answered Loki.

"In that case, I had better be on my way," Thokk croaked. Unfortunately he said it a little too quickly.

With lightning speed Loki reached out and grabbed Thokk's leg. In a menacing voice, he said, "Just a moment my cunning friend! Make certain you act exactly as I have instructed you to act; say nothing more or nothing less than I have told you to say. Do not tell Thor or any other god that the frost giant is really just a snowman. Do not warn them in any way. If you do warn them, or if my plan misfires, I will send you and your friends straight to Hel. Do you comprehend? And don't try to run away. I can hunt you down easier than an ermine catches a lame hare." Here Loki gave Thokk a look that could crack ice.

With a nervous blink, Thokk nodded his head.

"Then be gone," snapped Loki.

With Loki watching, Thokk reluctantly flapped off, disappearing over the tops of the trees in the direction he had been instructed to go. When he had passed out of sight, Loki turned to Samuel and Rag and said with a satisfied grin, "You two, come along with me."

Loki walked straight to the clearing with Samuel and Rag plodding along behind. As they proceeded, the sun rose above the trees and the air seemed slightly warmer. It was going to be a clear and cloudless day, cold but not frigid. The brilliance of the snow hurt Samuel's eyes and he had to squint in order to see.

When Loki reached the snowman, he stopped and grinned at his creation. It was standing motionless and quiet in the morning sun, like a soldier on guard duty. Then, much to Samuel and Rag's surprise, Loki stepped up to the snowman, embraced him with both arms, gave him a kiss on his frozen lips and blew a tremendous breath of steam into his mouth. He then quickly jumped back, stumbling slightly in the snow.

A rapid and dramatic change spread across the snowman. Where there had only been shades of white, color flashed to the surface. The hues of steel and stone erupted like a discoloring disease. The snowman's face modulated to a deep blue. His nose blossomed purple, and his beard became the brilliant green of old copper. His helmet and armor plating went rust red, his arms and legs became granite gray, and his shoes went black. No flesh tones or the color of anything living or healthy appeared. When color had spread throughout, the snowman suddenly shuddered and his limbs began to twitch violently.

When the tremors shaking the snowman subsided, Loki reached under his cloak and pulled out a small ivory box, etched with a black design. A tiny puff of smoke trickled out as he gingerly opened its lid. He delicately reached into the box and pinched out two glowing sparks, which he then set in the snowman's eyes. These embers sat sparkling without dimming, like fearsome windows into the snowman's soul.

A wicked smile passed over Loki's lips, and then, as Samuel and Rag looked on in awe, he closed his eyes and began to mouth words. Immediately the snowman began to speak in a deep, rumbling voice. He bellowed, "The Aesir are worse than a pack of chattering squirrels. I will smash and mash your bones into cod cakes." Loki then lifted his right arm above his head and the snowman lifted its corresponding limb, hefting the tremendous axe high into the air.

With a shudder, Samuel realized that the snowman was no mere puppet or simple snow sculpture but something much more sinister and threatening. As it lumbered two steps forward and swung the axe about its head, it seemed as ferocious as any real flesh-and-blood monster. It occurred to Samuel that, whether he liked it or not, he was now a guilty participant in Loki's evil plans. He doubted the snowman's intended victims would see him as an innocent bystander. As the snowman let out a blood-curdling yell, Samuel knew that events were spinning completely out of control.

Finally, Loki opened his eyes and the snowman went still. He then turned to Samuel and said, "Now listen. I am going to have a little mischief with my friends. They will be here soon. When they arrive, stay next to me. Be quiet and keep out of the way. Do you understand?" Samuel, who was by now chilled to the bone, famished from lack of food, and filled with anxiety, nodded dumbly.

Loki took Samuel back to the campsite, fed him some oatmeal gruel, and wrapped a blanket about his shoulders. As Samuel scraped the last spoonful of the sticky food from his bowl, Loki scoffed, "What a nuisance you are." He then turned away and began to do some small chores around the camp.

As Loki worked, Samuel sat next to the fire, now only a few embers smoking fitfully in the chill, bright air. As the coals hissed and sputtered, he began to reflect on all that had happened to him in the past two days. Ever since his magical transportation to the clearing, he had been in the care, or perhaps captivity, of a giant who seemed only marginally concerned with his well being. He had been out in the open with only a campfire and a tattered old blanket between him and freezing to death. He had been given barely enough food to survive and forced to do hard labor. The Geyser Inn and his parents seemed to exist in another lifetime. At the thought of his family, a lump grew in his throat and he had to grit his teeth to keep from crying. Loki glanced over at him and then turned away with a look of contempt.

Rag, who had been silently watching Samuel, carefully hopped up onto his knee and pecked at his sleeve. Samuel reached out and tenderly stroked the bird's dull feathers. At the touch of another living being, a quiet sense of resolve filled Samuel's heart. He rubbed his eyes clear and took a deep breath.

Time passed and morning turned to midday, and then to early afternoon. The sun was bright, but not warm, as it filtered down through overhanging branches. A faint breeze fanned the fire and a wispy flame popped to life. Suddenly Loki, who had been disassembling his cot, paused, and an eager look of anticipation filled his face. He had heard something. For a long time he stood frozen, with his hand cupped to his ear. Samuel heard nothing but the whisper of the wind through the trees. Then all at once, Loki flung the cot aside and rushed toward the clearing, motioning with a frenzied wave of his hand for Samuel and Rag to follow. Samuel stumbled after, clutching Loki's blanket to his throat while it dragged behind in the snow.

Just when they were about to enter the clearing, Loki turned off their normal path and plunged into the forest. He began picking his way along the edge of the clearing, wading through drifts and downed timber and toward a particularly thick clump of brush. Samuel tried to follow, but was soon foundering in the unpacked snow, at one point sinking up to his waist. Loki, who had reached his destination, spun around and began to curse when he saw Samuel's plight. A look of wild panic filled his eyes. In four giant strides Loki retraced his steps, snatched Samuel up and carried him the rest of the way to the bushes.

Loki threw Samuel to the ground and began frantically scooping a shallow depression in the snow, stomping down that which he could not easily brush aside. Soon an area free of loose snow was dug. Here he crouched down and motioned to Samuel to do likewise. As Samuel knelt next to Loki, it became apparent to him why this spot had been chosen. From their vantage point, they could easily see the back of the snowman and most of the clearing while remaining hidden behind a tangle of snow-laden branches.

Soon Samuel heard what Loki had been hearing. It was the distant cry of voices and a constant clatter, like a whole kitchen of pots and pans being banged together. All at once, at the opposite end of the clearing, two massive animals appeared, drawing an enormous vehicle. This juggernaut plowed through the snow like an ocean liner in calm waters, cleaving a frosty bow wave through the drifts.

Through gaping eyes, Samuel saw that the two creatures were giant goats—huge shaggy beasts, larger than elephants. Each was covered by a brown-black coat of matted wool, now entangled with clumps of snow where it brushed against the ground. Thick straps of red leather, pierced with silver rivets, ran along their necks and backs. Each had two tremendous horns which rose in gentle twists high in the air to lethal points. Red-rimmed eyes stared straight ahead from out behind snarled tresses. Their nostrils flared with each stride, snorting forth geysers of steam.

Behind the goats rumbled a great sled, a monstrous contraption with a low floor, high sides, and an open back like a chariot. Made of bronze and gilt-covered wood, it glowed red-orange in the afternoon sun. At each corner was a wooden head, facing outward, mouth open in a silent roar. Adorning the side panels were several beasts intricately carved in low relief. All were grotesquely intertwined, their legs, necks, and tails stretched to ribbons. Each creature had another's neck in its fangs. Projecting up from the sled were several poles supporting a web of wires. Suspended from the wires were numerous rattle rings, now dancing and shimmering and sounding like a waterfall of copper cups. Standing inside the sled were several giants, all the same size as Loki. All were dressed in splendid garments or glinting mail. Their faces were grim and determined, handsome and haughty. And there in front of the sled, flapping desperately to keep ahead, was Thokk.

Up the clearing the sled sped toward the snowman, who waited for it like a statue. Then, abruptly, the goats were reined in. Their heads shook as if caught in a trap. The sled halted with a lurch and the clamor of the rattle rings ceased. For a moment silence filled the clearing. First out of the sled was a giant as big as Loki, but much broader, with arms and legs like tree trunks. He wore a tunic of steel mail that reached to his knees and was clasped around the middle by a huge leather belt. From his waist hung an enormous iron hammer with an awkwardly short handle. The head of the hammer was illuminated from within by a faint glow. The giant's legs were swathed in rough woolen stockings, clasped around with red thongs. His feet were shod in low leather boots. On one hand he wore an iron mitten burned black and gray. His beard was a brilliant red, split at the chin and braided in cords that reached down to his belt. Above the beard was a broad red face, belligerent eyes, and a torpedo-shaped, unadorned helmet with a broad band of iron projecting down over his nose. Anger surrounded this giant like bees about a broken hive. With huge strides he marched from the sled, his hammer thumping against his thigh as he came. Samuel knew that this giant must be Thor.

Following Thor, the other giants descended from the sled. Most were dressed like Thor in mail or leather jerkins, but all were smaller and thinner. One had a large empty scabbard dangling from his belt and another, with a particularly fierce face, had no right hand. The last one out was a giant dressed in blue and red, without mail or a helmet. He was far less ferocious and warlike than the rest and carried no weapons at all. His face was more noble than handsome and he was at least a head shorter than his companions. None of the giants had a beard except Thor, although a few had mustaches, plaited at their ends. There was even a lone female in the group. She was dressed in purple and had very fair skin. Her features were both beautiful and cold, and her hair, which cascaded down her sides and back, shimmered and shone like real gold.

Without waiting for the others, Thor marched within throwing distance of the snowman. The rest of the giants followed behind in a group. Thokk, who had been hovering above, perched on the candletop of a nearby spruce. In a deep, gravelly voice, Thor roared, "Who are you and why have you interrupted the repose of the gods?"

Samuel glanced over at Loki. The fire god was trembling with excitement, his teeth chattering with glee. When Thor finished speaking, Loki closed his eyes and began mouthing words and jerking his arms around in a violent pantomime. Samuel looked back to the clearing and saw that the snowman was mirroring Loki's every movement. Its voice bellowed out like a mad bull.

With an unmistakable edge of sarcasm, the snowman said, "Did I wake you from a drunken stupor, Thor? I did not know fresh air would put you in such a bad mood. I guess I should have let you be—slowly suffocating in the foul vapors of your hovel."

Thor's eyes narrowed, but he remained calm. "I am not here to trade insults. Where is Loki?"

The snow warrior laughed and jeered. "He's in my power, my prisoner, bound hand and foot nearby. Long we struggled, wit against wit, strength against strength. A truly noble contest. Of course, in the end, I won."

At this, the noble-looking giant dressed in blue and red approached Thor, put a hand on his arm and whispered something in his ear. Thor looked suspiciously at the snowman and asked again, "Who are you? What do you want?"

"Don't you know me, Thor, or has drink so completely drowned your memory?" countered the snowman. "I am Jormungand—your bane, your doom, your death. I have risen from the depths of the sea, shed my serpent skin, and taken this form. I will now settle our score, avenge the humiliation I felt at your hands, pay back the bite of your hook. I will crush you, grind your bones to dust, and scatter it for the crows to eat. I will then destroy the Aesir, cast down the walls of Asgard, and claim its riches for myself." At this the sparks in his eyes flared up and his entire form seemed illuminated by an inner glow.

Thor unbuckled the hammer on his belt and clutched it in his mitten-clad hand. It flashed red hot, casting a fierce glow on the surrounding snow. The giant who had been whispering to Thor took a step back, his face blanched white. A gasp ran through the other giants and those who had weapons drew them. Thor rasped through grinding teeth, "Well then, come on!"

"To the pit of Hel for all the Aesir," roared the snow-man as he raised his huge axe, edge glittering, high above his head and rushed at Thor. The sparks in his eyes leapt into flame, and he screamed an ear-splitting shriek. Thor stumbled a step back, raised his hammer and with a mighty throw, hurtled it straight at the snowman.

Hammer and snowman met not with the ring of steel nor the rending of stone, but with the mere whisper of parting snow. Thor's weapon hit the monster's chest dead center, passing clean through. A great gaping hole was torn, accompanied by a tremendous spray of white. The snowman froze in place, stonelike. Immediately all color vanished and the sparks in its eyes blinked out in puffs of gray smoke. Like a sand castle at high tide, it transformed before everyone's amazed eyes into a lumpy, nearly featureless figure. Meanwhile, Thor's hammer went whizzing off in an ever-increasing arc, out of the clearing and out of sight. A stunned silence fell, broken only by the muffled sound of the snow warrior's head, shield, and arms tumbling to the ground in a pile.

Chapter 8

Suddenly, from across the clearing, a hysterical laugh rang out and floated on the icy air. In fear and anger, the gods began to look one way and then another. In a furious voice Thor roared, "Who's there? Show yourself!"

With a snide snicker, Loki stepped out from his hiding place and walked toward the other gods. Samuel stayed behind, hidden in the bushes, hugging his arms and shivering with fear and cold.

"Well, well, Thor, how does it feel to kill a snowman. Are you proud of yourself or did you wet your pants again as you did when you fought the giant Hrungnir?" Loki's chuckling sounded like the braying of a donkey. "In any case, I think you certainly slew an opponent worthy of your prowess today. We all need to watch out for berserk snowmen. Perhaps Odin will even ask Bragi to compose a poem to commemorate this great victory." A tear rolled down Loki's cheek and he pointed limply at Thor, his body convulsed with laughter.

Thor's face darkened, his fists clenched, and he took a step toward the fire god. But then he halted as the

noble-looking giant, who had been scanning the northern sky, gasped, "It didn't come back, Thor. Mjollnir
didn't come back."

A look of deep concern filled Thor's face, and he too
began scanning the horizon. A murmur of alarm spread
among the other gods, some pointing skyward. A new
kind of anger, much more serious and threatening
filled Thor's face and he growled, "Loki! Where is my
hammer?"

Loki looked puzzled and stopped laughing. For the
first time a little of his arrogance slipped. Twisting
around, he looked over his shoulder at the sky and
gasped in a perplexed voice. "I don't know . . . I don't
know where it went."

"A joke is a joke, Loki," Thor spat, "but this has gone
far enough. Where is Mjollnir?"

"I told you. I don't know. Stealing your precious
hammer was not part of my plan." With this Loki's face
turned red and his haughtiness returned.

"You know what that hammer means to us, Loki.
Without it we have almost no defense against real frost
giants," Thor growled through clenched teeth.

A wave of outrage and anxiety swept through the
crowd of giants and they all began to speak among
themselves. Some said that Loki was lying and that he
should be made, by whatever means necessary, to reveal
where the hammer went. Others shouted that he should
be quickly and severely punished. Loki stood apart, his
face even paler than usual. With a furious bellow the

giant without a right hand yelled, "Let's sew his lips together as we did the last time he betrayed us!"

A murmur of approval erupted from the crowd. A rope was found and, with clenched fists, several of the gods, led by the one-handed giant, began converging on Loki.

"Wait, Tyr!" shouted the noble giant. "Don't do this!"

"Be quiet, Balder!" snarled Tyr. "Must you always whimper on behalf of the weak and wicked?"

"But Tyr, if anyone can find Mjollnir, it's Loki," pleaded Balder. "We need his help."

"You've been eating toadstools!" spat Tyr. "How can we trust him after what he's done? And why would he help us anyway?"

Suddenly, the female giant with the golden hair spoke. "I say, let Loki find what he has lost. If he finds the hammer quickly, then no punishment should come his way. If, on the other hand, he turns up empty handed, then he should be brought before Odin for judgment."

Most of the giants nodded assent to this idea, and Balder turned a questioning look to Thor. "I would prefer to wring Loki's neck without delay, but, alas, this suggestion makes more sense," Thor grumbled.

"What do you think?" Balder asked Loki.

"Why bother asking me? What choice do I have?" Loki answered with his arms crossed and a look of bored irritation on his face.

Suddenly, Tyr raised his stump, pointed at the bushes where Samuel and Rag were hiding, and shouted, "Who are your lackeys, Loki? Make them show themselves!"

At the sound of Tyr's voice, Samuel went pale with fear and stood rooted to the ground. Like a loyal guard, Rag drew nearer to Samuel. Thokk, on the other side of the clearing, edged quietly and unobtrusively into the branches of the evergreen on which he was perched.

"Come out, you cowards, or we'll come in and get you," barked Tyr.

Slowly, with Rag pulling at his blanket, Samuel crept out from behind the bushes and into the clearing. Shivering with fear, he stood knee deep in the snow, too frightened to speak.

When Tyr saw Samuel and Rag he sneered, "Can you find no better companions, Loki, than a dirty, whimpering thrall and a moth-eaten bird?"

Loki, without even looking at Samuel or Rag, just scoffed, "They're really not mine. I found them wandering in the forest, trespassing on our sacred ground. I saw no harm in putting them to work. They're just weird little nobodies, savages really. They claim to have never even heard of the Aesir Gods. We're all strangers to them, even Thor. They say they're from a place called Earth, wherever that wretched place might be."

A murmur of surprise and indignation ran through the crowd of giants. Most of them wrinkled up their noses in disgust. Loki continued with a shrug of his shoulders. "I couldn't care less what happens to either of them now. Do with them as you want."

An ominous growl rippled among the giants. Samuel began to fear for his life.

"Wait," interrupted Balder. "There's more here than meets the eye."

Separating himself from the rest of the gods, Balder walked over to Samuel, crouched down, and peered into his eyes. A long moment past. Finally he asked Samuel, "Do you really not know who we are?"

Samuel dumbly shook his head.

"Don't be afraid. I am Balder and I have a gift of seeing into human hearts. I perceive only truth and innocence in you. What is your name?"

"Samuel."

"Now, Samuel, I will not let anything bad happen to you. Do you understand?"

Samuel nodded, still clutching the blanket tightly around his shoulders. For a few seconds more, Balder continued to examine Samuel and then, in a loud voice said, "You don't have much kindness in your heart, do you, Loki?"

"Well, I could have left him to freeze when I found him, but I didn't," Loki retorted.

Balder stood up and faced Loki, and said, "If you have no more use for this thrall, then perhaps you will let Nanna and me have him."

"Your soft heart will be the end of you, Balder," scoffed Loki. "He's yours to keep."

"Hold on, Balder," Tyr hissed. "This is not the end of the matter. Justice has not been served. That young man has taken part in a great evil. A human must not be allowed to go unpunished for such an offense. When we return to Asgard, I will demand that he stand trial before Odin."

"Do as you must, Tyr. But, to me, to even suggest such a thing seems vicious and petty," answered Balder.

"Speaking of traitors, where is that other raven, the one who led us here in the first place?" growled Thor. At this all the giants began to look around for Thokk until the god with the empty scabbard shot up his hand and shouted, "There he is, hiding in that tree."

"You there! Come here!" roared Thor.

Blinking and shaking with fear, Thokk eased out of the tree and flapped reluctantly over to Thor. He landed with a thump, his legs buckling under him.

In a high-pitched squawk, Thokk whined, "Hey, hey, hey, give me a little pity. I just did what Loki told me to do. I mean, what choice did I have? He said he was going to send me to Hel if I disobeyed."

"Silence!" roared Thor. "Your actions seal your fate. You could have warned us. You knew Loki was tricking us. One word of truth and none of this would have happened. You have betrayed us all to deadly danger. If I still had my hammer, I would pound you to pulp!"

Thokk's eyes bulged with terror, and he gulped several times. Fortunately, salvation arrived and it came from an unlikely source.

Loki cleared his throat and said, "It's not my place to keep you from doing such a foolish thing as killing one of Odin's sacred birds, Thor. But before you pluck poor old Thokk for a pie, I have a suggestion. It will be difficult for me to find Mjollnir alone out there in the trees and snow. I could use a spy and messenger. Since Thokk seems to fit that bill rather well, perhaps you could spare his mangy hide, at least long enough for me to put him to good use."

Thor glared at Loki and then back at Thokk. "Fine, fine. The two of you are made for each other."

With a chuckle, Loki said, "Come here, Thokk." He crooked a finger in the raven's direction and Thokk reluctantly hopped over to his side.

Samuel, who was standing close by, leaned over and whispered to Thokk, "I'm sorry. I am sure things will turn out okay in the end."

Nervously, Thokk replied, "How do you know? Can you see the future? All I know is that I wish I were back at the Geyser Inn. I would be, too, if you and Rag hadn't been so obsessed with that ring pin of yours. Next time, leave well enough alone." Here Thokk turned away from Samuel and looked straight ahead.

With a wave of his hand, Balder cleared his throat and said, "Let's move on to more pressing matters. We had better make some plans before Loki sets out."

Tyr and the giant with an empty scabbard nodded their heads, and all the gods, including Loki, gathered in a large circle next to Thor's sled. Their conference was out of earshot of Samuel and the ravens. As the gods talked, Samuel huddled miserably in the snow, his blanket stiff from frost. The ravens fluttered up and perched on the shoulders of the ruined snowman. The giants conferred for a long time, sometimes arguing and shaking their heads. At one point, Tyr began shouting, pointing at Samuel, and then threw down his helmet and stalked off in disgust.

After a while, Loki separated from the group, motioned for Thokk to join him and began marching back to his camp in the forest. He was no longer grinning. Instead, his jaws were clamped shut with suppressed anger. Thokk rose from his perch and reluctantly flapped along behind. Just before he disappeared into the forest, Thokk turned, looked at Rag and Samuel, and uttered a plaintive "caw" goodbye.

After a few more minutes, Balder walked up to Samuel and said, "Loki has left to search for Mjollnir. The rest of the gods and I are going back to Asgard. You and your friend," here he pointed to Rag, "must come with us. To save time, I will carry you to Thor's sled."

Balder picked up Samuel and carried him across the clearing to the sled. In one deft movement, Balder swung aboard the sled and found an open spot on which to stand. He then lowered Samuel to the sled's floor where Samuel was just able to peer over the side.

As the other giants crowded around, jostling for positions, Samuel peered up into their imposing faces. Most were arrogant. Some were fierce. One or two were bitter. Few of them would meet his eyes; none smiled, and most stared straight ahead. Their armor glinted in the sun or sparkled with inlaid jewels. Their tunics and cloaks were made of silk, richly dyed wool, fur trimmings, and magnificent embroideries. Samuel felt very small as he glanced down at his own grimy clothes, faded and torn, and his skin blackened by ashes and grime.

Thor mounted the sled last and worked his way up to the front. He picked up a set of reins and snapped a whip above the goats' heads. The sled leapt forward with a lurch. In a broad arc, it cut across the clearing and re-entered the forest at the same spot from where it first appeared. As it raced onward, following a narrow path, the wind caught Samuel's hair and brushed it softly across his forehead. He soon became mesmerized by the endless rows of spruce and fir as they flashed past in a flickering succession of light and shadow.

Under Balder's protection, Samuel felt more secure than at any time since leaving the Geyser Inn. All the tension of the past three days began to melt away and was replaced by an overpowering exhaustion. He soon slumped down on a pile of furs that had been thrown in a corner of the sled near Balder's feet. His eyes began to droop and he nodded off to sleep. Samuel saw one last thing though, before he slipped into unconsciousness. It was Rag, perched on the side of the sled with the wind ruffling his feathers. He was staring straight ahead, and there was a brilliant spark in his eyes.

Chapter 9

Samuel awoke to find himself wrapped in Loki's blanket, lying on a feather-filled mattress. At first he thought he was in a vast, dim cave, but after his eyes adjusted to the light, he saw that he was at one end of a huge chamber, the walls of which were pierced by a few high windows. The openings let in long narrow beams of golden light, each ray dancing with thousands of dust motes. The air was suffused with a faintly acrid odor of fish, oil, old wood, smoke, and leather.

As Samuel continued to look about, he saw that running the entire length of the chamber were two parallel rows of wooden pillars. Each individual pillar was carved in the shape of an enormous, ugly gnome. These gnomes held above their heads a heavy crossbeam, which, in turn, supported a structure of rafters and, ultimately, a dense thatched roof. Piercing the ceiling at regular intervals were smoke holes through which Samuel could glimpse the blue sky beyond. All surfaces not sculpted in the shape of some creature were painted or incised with the same intricate ribbon pattern that graced Thor's sled, Loki's cot, and the raven's ring pin.

The floor under the mattress was of rough-hewn wooden planks. A trench, perhaps ten feet wide, split the floor the entire length of the room. In this depression were several long, narrow fire pits, each surrounded by a stone hearth and a packed clay floor. In the nearest pit a small pile of coals sputtered fitfully. Neatly stacked nearby were numerous iron and bronze kettles and other cooking utensils, all blackened from soot and ash. Scattered about the upper wooden floor were a few enormous tables and benches. All were nicked and notched by heavy use. Along the outer walls were stacked the disassembled sections of many more pieces of furniture.

Samuel sat up and rubbed the sleep from his eyes. As he did so, he noticed numerous tapestries scattered about the hall, hanging between posts and draped from the ceiling trusses. Sewn on each were cheerful celebrations of daily life—people feasting, herding cows, threshing wheat, or spinning wool. These scenes featured broad, simple figures embroidered with bright thread on coarse cloth. As Samuel gazed at these banners, his eye caught a flicker of movement. There, perched on a nearby beam, was the sleeping figure of Rag.

Except for the raven, the hall appeared to be empty, but as Samuel began to stir, a dim shape at the far end of the room rose and half walked, half waddled toward him. As it neared, Samuel perceived it to be a great black bird with a white chest. Its head swung back and forth in a slow arch as it shuffled forward. It had a heavy black beak—narrow near the face and ballooning to a bulbous tip—inscribed along the sides with narrow white lines. Strikingly, the bird had extremely short wings, mere stubs, nestled at its sides. It seemed ancient and tired as it limped along on short legs and webbed feet. Suddenly an image formed in Samuel's mind—a drawing he had seen while searching for information on the ring pin in the Inn's encyclopedias—a pen and ink sketch of the Great Auk that had once lived in Iceland, but was now extinct.

"Hello, hello. Are you feeling better?" said the auk in a rich old voice, modulated to a singsong.

"Yes, very much so; but where am I and who are you?" Samuel asked, smiling at the old bird's silly accent.

"I'm Kvasir, Balder's servant. You are in my lord's home in Asgard. But, come, come—no more questions now. First you need a bath, some food, and a change of clothes."

Kvasir led Samuel to a nearby door hidden in the shadows. Inside was a large room without a floor or foundation, the walls being constructed around several poles thrust into the earth. Cold draughts of air gusted through large gaps under the walls. The ground was a rough uneven surface of yellow and white rock, scraped clean of dirt. The structure had several windows of what looked like gray frosted glass. Samuel later found out that these panes were really thin sheets of mica. Even though small, the windows infused the atmosphere with a pale illumination. In the center of the room was a large steaming pool, fed at one end by a trickle of boiling water. This rivulet emerged from a glistening yellow and red terrace of opalescent stone that inter-mittently spewed forth a furious froth of bubbles and a miniature tidal wave. The pool itself was perfectly clear and cast with a faint blue hue. Not far from Samuel's feet an outlet stream ran down a moss-covered channel and disappeared under the nearest wall. A faint whiff of sulphur infused the air.

Kvasir said, "Now, my little herring, get in the pool here at the outlet and don't go near the inlet; the water is scalding. Call me when you are through."

After three days out in the cold, sleeping in grimy clothes and being smothered by smoke and dusted with ashes, bathing in the hot pool was a sublime expe-rience for Samuel. The heat was terrific at first and his skin prickled with pain. But slowly, as he sat in the pool up to his neck, his body adjusted and he could feel the bite of cold, which had remained in his toes and fin-gers, slowly melt away. He splashed water on his face, vigorously rubbed his cheeks, wrung his hands and scraped the black dirt from under his nails. Finally, he just lay back and let the warmth of the water seep into his bones.

After awhile, Kvasir returned with a bundle of clothes under his stubby wing. He set down the bundle on a wooden stool next to the door. "Come on, you lazy thrall, get dressed; your breakfast is ready."

Samuel emerged reluctantly from the pool; the warmth had made him drowsy and the air was a chill shock to his skin. He was shivering by the time he had dried himself off.

In his haste to stay warm, Samuel paid little attention to the garments he was pulling on. But when the job was through, he looked down at his new clothes in amazement. His artificial down jacket, jeans, rubberized snow boots, T shirt, and nylon-covered gloves were all gone. He was now wearing a pair of loose, plain cloth trousers and a heavy woolen, collarless tunic that reached below his knees. The tunic was dyed blue and secured at his waist by a broad leather belt. On his feet were wool socks that made his toes itch and burn. Over these were what appeared to be moccasins, secured at the ankle by a single loop clasped over a simple button made from a knot of leather. In his hands he held a pair of fur mittens, which he stuffed in his belt for future use. On his head was a conical fur hat, below which his hair barely peeped out. Everything was too big, but with much cuffing and folding, Kvasir and Samuel managed to make the outfit comfortable. As a final touch, Kvasir draped a faded blue cape around Samuel's shoulders. As he was about to fasten it together with a bronze ring pin, Samuel said, "Wait! I already have one of those."

"You have a brooch? I didn't see a cape among your things," answered Kvasir.

From the pocket of his old coat, Samuel retrieved the raven's ring pin and showed it to Kvasir. The auk stared at it for several seconds, his eyes wide with amazement. In a hushed voice the auk said, "This is a very special brooch. It's much too precious to wear for every day. When you get a chance, you must show it to Balder. But for now, let me tie a strap to it and put it around your neck. Hide it there for safekeeping. Let's fasten your cloak with this ordinary pin."

When all was done, Kvasir stepped back and admired his handiwork. "You look like a regular blue-toothed Norseman now. Yes, you do," he said with a chuckle.

Next Kvasir lead Samuel back to the main hall and to a small bench positioned close to the fire. Here a tray was set out loaded with food. Samuel eyed it with delight. On the tray were half a loaf of coarse heavy bread and two soft-boiled eggs—gray, speckled, and set in little wooden cups—a small fried fish on a soapstone plate, an apple, and a leather tankard of buttermilk. All these things Samuel ate with relish, hardly stopping to breathe. He did have to ask Kvasir how to eat the eggs (with a little spoon straight out of the shell).

As he was gulping down the last of the buttermilk, Samuel suddenly remembered Rag. He quickly looked up and about and saw that his friend was missing. "Where is Rag?" he asked Kvasir, concern edging his voice.

"You mean your raven friend? Don't worry. Balder just took him for a walk. They'll soon be back," Kvasir answered.

"Will Balder give him something to eat? I am sure he's very hungry."

"Of course, of course! Balder always takes good care of those in his charge," Kvasir answered with a smile.

Just then the front door opened, letting in a bright shaft of white light. Samuel and Kvasir turned and saw Balder walk through and stamp the snow off his feet. Behind him Rag hopped past the threshold. Both then came across the room to where Samuel and Kvasir were sitting. Balder pulled up a bench and Rag hopped onto a nearby table.

In a quiet, even voice Balder asked Samuel, "Are you all right? Did you get enough sleep?"

Samuel nodded and, as he put his dishes back on the tray, said, "I feel much better now. Thank you for breakfast and thanks for letting me stay here. I feel all right for the first time in a long time. Being with Loki was not fun."

"I can well imagine that for you, it must have been very strange and frightening to be Loki's companion. He has little compassion and is often erratic and vengeful. Even his fellow gods do not know whether his actions are for good or evil, " Balder replied.

"I am still mixed up by what happened back at the clearing. Whatever was Loki trying to do with that snowman of his? He told me it was just a joke but it seemed much more than that to me."

Balder sighed and answered. "Loki likes to keep the cauldron bubbling—a trick here, a prank there, anything to keep the rest of us off balance. Apparently the snowman was, just as he claimed, a little mischief meant to scare and humiliate us. Unfortunately the joke got out of hand and Mjollnir was lost."

"What exactly is Mjollnir? I know it's Thor's hammer, but why is it so special?" asked Samuel.

Here Balder frowned and looked long and hard at Samuel. A flicker of the same disbelief and amazement that had so often crossed Loki's face now appeared in Balder's eyes. Slowly he said, "Mjollnir was made a long time ago by two dwarfs named Brokk and Eitri, as a gift for the gods. It has two amazing properties. The first is that it will destroy anything against which it is thrown. Nothing can withstand a blow from Mjollnir. The second is that it will always return to the one who throws it. Thor was given Mjollnir to defend us, the Aesir gods, from our enemies, principally the frost giants of Jotunheim."

"Frost giants? What are they?"

"The frost giants are a race of creatures made of stone and ice. They are, for the most part, cruel and greedy, although once in a while a wise one is born. These demons haunt a land of glaciers and barren mountains called Jotunheim. Occasionally they invade Midgard and Asgard, spreading chaos and destruction in their wake. They forever aspire to scatter the Aesir gods, destroy Asgard, steal its riches, and rule in our place. Many frost giants have tried to conquer Asgard. Most have been destroyed by Thor with the help of Mjollnir. Loki's snowman appeared and acted exactly like one of these monsters."

"Why do you think Thor's hammer didn't return this time?"

Balder shrugged and said, "I can only guess. I think that when Thor threw Mjollnir at the snowman, he did so with tremendous force. He thought he was trying to pierce steel and crush stone, to slay a granite devil. When all Mjollnir met was a thin crust of snow, its momentum must have carried it away beyond the point from which it could return. It must have landed miles and miles away from the clearing. In any case Mjollnir must be soon found, especially before the real frost giants learn of its disappearance and take advantage of our misfortune. Odin is very concerned."

"Who is Odin? I keep hearing his name."

Here Balder looked genuinely startled and his mouth dropped open in surprise. In an incredulous voice he said, "Loki mentioned that you were extremely strange and now I truly believe him. To be ignorant of Odin is to be unknowing of the sun or the moon, to have not seen the sky or walked on the ground, never to have breathed air or tasted your mother's milk.

"He, along with his two brothers, created the nine worlds of our universe, built Asgard and brought man and woman to animation from driftwood. He is the wisest of all of the Aesir gods, our greatest poet and lawgiver, warrior and leader. He is the 'All Father,' the 'Terrible One,' the 'One-Eyed King.'" Here Balder paused and fixed upon Samuel a long and curious stare. He then slowly said, "Odin is known to even the smallest child in every corner of every world. How is it that you know nothing of him? This is not to mention your apparent ignorance of every other Aesir god and goddess.

Where do you really come from? Name this land that has never heard of Odin."

Samuel swallowed hard and looked up at Balder looming above him. "I'm from a place called Earth."

Balder frowned and said, "I have never heard of Earth. Is it a village or a town or a kingdom?"

"It's a whole world. Millions, actually billions, of people live there."

Balder's expression became a grimace and skepticism showed in his eyes. "Perhaps we should take a different track. When Loki found you in the clearing, you were indeed trespassing on our sacred ground. How did you get there?"

"I'm not sure. We were sort of sent there by this ring pin." Here Samuel retrieved the brooch from around his neck and showed it to Balder.

Balder took the ring pin with a look of astonishment and stared at it for a long time, rubbing the runes with his fingers tips much like a blind man reads braille. Finally he looked up and said, "This is a very special brooch. How did you come to own it?"

"It's not really mine. It's Thokk and Rag's. They just let me use it," answered Samuel. "Thokk told me that Rag found it in a hole near the Geyser Inn last summer. I'm sorry, but that's all I know about it."

Balder continued to examine the brooch and then, without looking at Samuel, asked, "Is this Geyser Inn your home then?"

"Yes, I guess so."

"Are your parents innkeepers?"

"Sort of. My dad takes care of things and makes everything work."

"And you were at the inn when the ring pin transported you to our world?"

"Yes, that's right. To the clearing where we met Loki."

"What exactly happened after you first met Loki?"

"He took us back to his camp and we spent the night there. The next day he made us help him build the snowman. The day after that he summoned you all to the clearing."

Balder nodded and then asked, "Did Loki mention stealing or hiding or somehow making Mjollnir disappear? This is very important, so please think carefully."

"No, I don't think losing Mjollnir was part of the joke. I believe he was just as surprised as the rest of you when it didn't come back. "

Balder ran a hand through his hair and then said, "Well, sometimes it's very hard to read Loki's true emotions, but I think you're right in this case."

Suddenly, somewhere in the distance a rooster crowed and Balder looked up at Samuel and then at Kvasir. A flash of anxiety filled his eyes.

"Samuel, it is now noon and you must go with me to Odin's palace. I meant to speak with you more about the ring pin but there is no time now. Take it and keep it safe, for indeed it is extremely valuable."

Balder handed the ring pin back to Samuel, and said in a stern voice, "As I told you, I am a good judge of the human heart. You have a bright and honest soul. You are telling me the truth, without hesitation, concerning your time with Loki. I know that you are not responsible in any way for the disappearance of Mjollnir, but unfortunately, you are still in very serious trouble. What Loki and his snowman did put Asgard and all of the Aesir in horrible danger. There is much anger over this. Even though it was against your will, you helped Loki. Many gods are as furious at you as they are with the lord of fire. As a result, you must go to Odin's palace and stand before him and be judged. All the Aesir gods will be there. Many feel that you deserve severe, even extreme punishment. A few of them will say some very frightening things. But don't lose hope. I will be there and I will speak for you. All will turn out well in the end."

Chapter 10

Balder and Samuel didn't leave immediately for Odin's palace. Instead, Balder took Kvasir aside and gave him a long list of whispered instructions. He then disappeared for a time into another room, from which his and a female voice could be heard. While Balder was gone, Samuel pondered his upcoming meeting with Odin. The longer he thought about it, the more alarmed he became. Finally Balder reappeared and motioned to Samuel that it was time to leave. With a lump in his throat and with Rag at his side, Samuel stood up and followed Balder outside and into the sunlight.

Samuel was dazzled by what he saw. He was on the edge of a wide circular courtyard surrounded by twenty or more great halls and mansions. Their wood and stone façades shimmered in the midday sun with bright paint and gilt metal. Each was like a magical toy festooned with dragon heads, weather vanes, flags, and banners. Each structure had its own character—grim and forbidding like a fortress, opulent and flamboyant like a palace, or plain and humble like a peasant's cottage. Samuel saw that Balder's hall fell into this last category.

It was the simplest and smallest building in sight and the only one with a thatched roof.

Running along the boundary of the courtyard was an avenue paved with the felled trunks of slender trees, each log laid crosswise to form a corduroy surface. All along the walkway's length, the snow had been brushed aside and mounded into two parallel drifts. A row of giant oaks bordered each side of the sidewalk. All were now leafless and barren, their branches casting a dense net of sticks against the blue sky. Samuel and Balder quickly walked down the path while Rag flapped slowly behind.

As they proceeded, Samuel saw a low hedge of evergreen holly at the exact center of the courtyard. It, in turn, surrounded two extraordinary trees. One was a spindly old apple tree, burdened with deadwood and discolored by disease. From its gnarled branches hung brightly shining fruits, red as drops of blood and glimmering like jewels. The other tree was an ash and as Samuel gazed upon it, he shook his head in disbelief. For even though it was the dead of winter, this tree was covered with leaves. Great rafts of green foliage flickered and rustled in the breeze. It was also huge, towering over the courtyard like a circus tent.

"That tree—the big one—it still has its leaves!" Samuel exclaimed.

"That's because it is the world tree, the holy Ygdrassil. Until the end of time it will never lose its leaves," answered Balder, in a voice full of reverence. "Ygdrassil's tap root reaches into every one of the nine realms ruled by Odin. Like the spine of a man, it binds these worlds together into one universe. Everything that lives owes its breath to that tree. It is the source of all life. The driftwood that Odin used to fashion the first man and woman were but broken twigs from Ygdrassil. All the animals that roam Midgard and the plants that grow in its soil are the fruits of Ygdrassil. Suckers of the world tree sprout in every corner of Midgard and Asgard, like holy shrines, never to whither or die."

"Is there also something special about that apple tree?"

Balder smiled and said, "The Aesir gods are very fond of that tree. Its fruit gives us eternal life. Without it we would all soon die. But enough questions for right now. We must hurry."

Balder led Samuel quickly along the log highway, which for such a main thoroughfare seemed strangely empty. After a few minutes a large cobbled space came into view. In it was a tremendous boulder upon which a grisly scene was carved and painted. Three warriors were dismembering a huge giant; one was setting its skull in the sky, another was forming its bones into mountains, and the third was filling the ocean with buckets of its blood. Samuel grimaced as they passed this gruesome memorial.

Looming above the sculpted stone stood Odin's palace, a towering cathedral of wood, paint, and gilt. Its front thrust upward like a great cliff, broken only by a huge doorway and several high windows. At the façade's pinnacle a falcon's head, painted black and gold, loomed like a monstrous watch dog. The rest of the building was shaped like an upturned boat, its roof crest humped like a whale's back. Down from this arched spine, the gables sloped nearly to the ground, each covered by countless wooden shingles cut to the shape of scales. The entire building was stained a tar black and stood stark amidst the snow-covered landscape.

Samuel then saw something which he could scarcely believe. Out of the sides of the roof, near the rear of the building, projected the limbs of a gigantic oak tree. Its branches hovered about the hall like a gray cloud. Where each limb exited the roof, the shingles had been carefully cut to fit. In the tree roosted a tremendous flock of crows, rooks, blackbirds, grackles, ravens, and starlings. The air was filled with their incessant calls and the roof was stained white with their droppings.

Samuel and Balder walked on. Soon the outer doors of Odin's hall filled their vision. These portals were at least twenty feet tall, made of polished silver and adorned with an eagle and wolf twisted in mortal combat, their bodies enmeshed in a frenzy of violence. A murmur of harsh voices emanated from behind the doors, like the tuning of a discordant orchestra. Samuel felt an overwhelming sense of dread as he neared this fearsome passageway.

Like the leaves of a book, the heavy doors opened and Samuel stepped, knees knocking, into a chamber of stunning proportions. It was an immense, gloomy space, three times as tall as Balder's hall. A tremendous ceiling beam, like the backbone of a whale, stretched over his head. Pinioned to it, with pegs as wide as a man, were timbers as thick as redwoods. These rafters stretched, rib-like, all the way to the ground and formed a great arched cavern. Everything was blackened by soot and age. Wisps of smoke hovered about like storm clouds.

Halfway between the ground and the ceiling, a series of crossbeams stretched across the room. Attached to them were rows of round wooden shields. Each circle was painted black and yellow and adorned with a silver boss at its center. Hanging below were huge embroideries of wool and silk, bright and stark in the murk. Stitched in a simple blocky style, they illustrated, in graphic detail, a great panoply of battles. Huge monsters, many-headed trolls, and loathsome serpents were all dispatched by gods in shining armor. Fierce warriors, astride great horses, traded blows with sword and ax while below dismembered and decapitated victims were stripped of their armor by thieves.

Lining the hall on each side was a single row of ornate wooden pews. These benches had tall backs and were boldly carved with friezes of snakelike animals. On each sat several giants, rigid and unsmiling. As one, they stared at Samuel as he passed. Some looked bored. Others glared with open contempt. Only a few seemed kind or in any way compassionate.

As Samuel glanced away from this gauntlet of stony faces, he noticed that the floor was of hard-packed clay, every footstep sending up a faint puff of dust. Several stone fire pits were scattered about the room and in one a large fire blazed and crackled. Its light flickered on the faces of the gods and made the walls and tapestries dance with shadows. Above all, this flaring flame illuminated a scene which Samuel would never forget.

At the far end of the room was the enormous trunk of a tree, the one whose branches sprang from the roof outside. The trunk was deeply furrowed like the face of an old man, and the bark scarred by the hacking of blades. At its base was carved, into living wood and covered with sheets of beaten silver, a great throne. Around this royal seat was gathered a dense crowd of warriors and upon the throne sat a giant, taller than any Samuel had yet seen.

For a moment Samuel's heart leapt with joy, for the figures gathered at the base of the tree were human. But as Samuel neared, his new-found hope was dashed. From under iron helmets and behind wooden shields, these men stared out at him malevolently. Suddenly, a wild man dressed in a bearhide cape sprang from their ranks and began stomping the ground in front of the others, sending up a cloud of dust. With a jerk, he tore off his cloak and began swinging an axe above his head in a huge circle. His eyes were mad and white foam flecked his lips. A wild hiss went up from the mob, and they all began to beat their weapons upon their shields.

Samuel stumbled a step back, and Balder grasped his shoulder to steady him. Rag edged closer, his beak nervously clacking together.

Suddenly the mob parted and a woman, taller than the tallest man and dressed in mail, stepped forward and cried, "Enough!" The din ceased in a second but the ranks of warriors continued to growl and stare like caged dogs at Samuel and Balder. The woman then turned to the three of them and said in a frosty voice, "All who come to this throne must bow before Odin, the All Father."

At this Balder knelt on one knee and bent his head forward three times. Samuel, not knowing what else to do, copied Balder's actions as best he could. As Samuel's head rose for the third time, he took in the great figure on the throne above him. Odin wore a tunic of fine silver mail that reached down to his knees. Around his waist was a wide black belt, pierced with silver studs and inlaid with rubies as large as walnuts. His legs were encased in bright yellow trousers that billowed like pleated balloons above his low boots. About Odin's shoulders was a cape of heavy black wool, edged with white fur, lined with red silk and embroidered with gold thread. Around the biceps of his left arm was coiled a snake of twisted gold and on his fingers were numerous rings. In one hand he held an enormous spear with an oaken shaft, its broad point inlaid with silver tracery. On the arms of the throne were perched two enormous ravens, twice as big as Rag and Thokk. Lying on the floor at Odin's feet were two silver-gray wolves, their alert eyes tracking Samuel's every move.

Slowly Samuel peered up into Odin's face, and gasped at what he saw. It was a noble face, handsome in detail with an aquiline nose and a jutting, beardless chin. Long blonde hair framed a broad forehead and strong cheekbones, but one detail overpowered all the rest. He was missing an eye. The surviving orb was a sharp glacier blue, piercing in intensity, a diviner of truth. Where the other should have been was a gaping hole, a dark ugly pit. This disfigurement marred the beauty of the face and lent it an unparalleled fierceness.

Odin looked at Samuel and Balder impassively as they rose from their knees. Slowly he turned his head and nodded to a nearby bench. Tyr, his face twisted into a sneer of contempt, rose from his seat and said in a loud and angry voice, "Here is the savage that helped Loki betray us—a coward that has brought evil luck and drastic danger to us all, a wretch who claims to be ignorant of the glorious Aesir, even though such a thing is impossible. Do not let such an evil imp hide in the folds of Balder's cloak. I call now for justice. I demand that he stand trial by fire."

A murmur of anger and agreement ran along the benches and from the rabble of human warriors. Samuel's heart fell and his stomach constricted. He looked at Balder and the god reached down and reassuringly touched his head.

Balder looked at the one-handed god and in an even voice replied, "Tyr, no one is braver than you. You are Asgard's greatest swordsman and most valiant son, quick to avenge any affront to our pride and honor. But, I beg you, let your virtues be tempered by compassion and justice. Don't let your anger over the loss of Mjollnir cause you to lash out at the innocent. We all know that Loki, and Loki alone, is the cause of our current distress. This human was an unwitting and unwilling slave of Loki's. When Loki found him, he was lost and desperate, freezing in the wilderness. He had no choice but to go with the lord of mischief and do his bidding. We cannot expect a mere human to stand up against the will of a god. This young man was not a party to Loki's plots, only an . . . "

Here Odin raised his hand with a jerk and interrupted Balder. "Silence. I have heard enough." Odin's voice was haughty and touched with irritation. "This matter is not worth my time. The savage is yours, Balder, do with him as you wish. Except that I now make you responsible for the things that he has done. His guilt in the loss of Mjollnir now becomes yours. If Loki returns empty-handed, or is not soon successful, then you must join the search for Thor's hammer yourself and labor on until it is found."

"Oh, great father," Tyr hissed through clenched teeth, "what example does this set? A human has transgressed against the gods and receives no punishment? He should bear the consequences of his actions. At least decree that he should attempt to set right that which he has done. Why shouldn't this son of man not come to the aid of the gods? Isn't it his honor, duty, and glory to do so? He looks capable to me, at least his body appears sound."

"You speak with the conviction of truth, Tyr," Odin exclaimed. "I will change my judgment. If Loki does not return within a week with Mjollnir, then it is my will that the skraeling also join the hunt. He is condemned to suffer and endure all the hardships and dangers that might ensue, no matter the cost. Is that understood, Balder?"

Balder cast down his eyes and replied, "Yes, All Father."

"Good," said Odin. "We will wait one week for Loki to return. After that Balder and the savage must leave Asgard and begin their quest."

Suddenly there was a cough from the back of the hall. A rustle of clothes and scraping of feet filled the space as everyone turned to see its origin. There, standing up from his seat, was Thor, dressed in his armor, but without a helmet. His great red hair shone in the dim light and his tremendous beard hung from his chin like a crimson waterfall.

"Oh, what a brave judgment, Odin," scoffed Thor. "Mjollnir is lost and all you're going to do is send 'Balder the Mild' and a simpering skraeling out to look for it. Doesn't this disaster demand a stouter response? Shouldn't all the strength of Asgard be gathered to meet this challenge? Why can you not join the search yourself? Are you crippled or incapacitated in some way, or do you fear the drudgery and danger of life outside of the comforts of Asgard?"

Without hesitation Odin answered, "It is my place to rule, not dirty my hands. That is why I am up here and you are down there. That is why I wear the crown of Asgard and you sit at the back of the hall. Remember who you are. For all your power and glory, you are still nothing more than my royal retainer, bound by oath to do my bidding. Instead of bothering your limited wits about what I should do, think instead of who lost Mjollnir, who carelessly cast it away. Was it I or was it you? Is it not more your duty than mine to aid in its recovery? I have not heard you volunteer to join the search."

To this Thor seemed at a loss. He opened his mouth to reply but no words came. His cheeks turned a bright red. He turned to Balder and said in a hoarse voice, "If you and the skraeling must go, I will come with you. Mjollnir is mine and I want it back more than anyone else."

"Your help is always the best kind. Thank you," replied Balder.

With that the trial broke up and the gods returned to their palaces. As Samuel walked with Balder back across the courtyard, he noticed his protector seemed both anxious and distracted—as if pondering a garbled and distressing message. In spite of his curiosity, Samuel held his tongue, afraid to hear the god's fears (and his own) spoken out loud. In the end, Balder and Samuel did not have to wait a week to learn their fate, for Thokk returned four days later with dire news.

Chapter 11

Thokk returned to Asgard windblown, battered, and alone. With his last reserves of strength he limped to Thor's doorstep, feebly rapped on the door, and then collapsed in an exhausted heap. His usually glossy feathers were torn and dirty, and one eye was swollen shut. Upon finding him, Thor hurried to Balder's hall, carrying the semiconscious bird. They laid him by a fire where, after awhile, he regained enough strength to speak.

In a cracked and irritable voice he began. "The lords of Asgard owe me big for what I've been through. Just look at my eye!" He strained open his puffed-up eyelid and revealed a brilliantly inflamed eyeball.

"Yes, yes, we can all see that you have suffered bravely," Thor said impatiently. "But where is Loki? Where is Mjollnir? What have you been doing for the last six days?"

"Hold on, hold on, let me start at the beginning," protested Thokk. "Let me think."

Slowly, and with many more bitter complaints, Thokk began his story:

As you know, after the fight with the snowman, I returned with Loki to his lean-to. He was in a terrible mood—let me tell you—constantly grumbling and muttering to himself. He quickly jammed his belongings into that huge pack of his, and then stamped off into the forest, yelling at me to keep up.

The going was rough, especially for Loki. He was constantly having to send me aloft to scout ways through tangles of deadfall and deep snowdrifts. At one point we had to backtrack about half a mile to avoid an impassible ravine. It was then that Loki began to curse out loud. He damned the hammer, me, the snow, and everyone and everything else. More than once I felt like flying off and never looking back.

As we proceeded, the forest became gloomier, the trees taller, and the undergrowth thicker. Once or twice I saw wolves among the branches. Fortunately, they paid no attention to me and gave Loki a wide berth. Eventually, we camped by a frozen pond and spent a miserable night huddled by a small campfire. The next day was more of the same until we suddenly came out of the trees and found ourselves on the edge of a steep rocky slope overlooking a narrow body of water.

This lake, or whatever it was, seemed to go on forever in opposite directions. I smelled salt on the air and Loki informed me that it was a fjord, an arm of the ocean thrust deep inland. Across the fjord, perhaps a half mile away, the land climbed steeply to a high plateau. The *lower slopes of this tableland rose directly out of the water and were covered with clumps of trees and steep meadows. Near the base of one clearing, a great gash was torn. Loki and I could see freshly crumpled rock and upturned earth, like a vivid scar against the surrounding snow and brush. A rock avalanche originating at the crater had plummeted debris all the way down into the water below. Loki was immediately interested in this wound and his mood brightened. It was obvious that the hammer could have struck the ground at this point. Loki quickly began picking his way down to the water.*

We soon reached the fjord's edge. Here Loki stopped and frowned with frustration. The crater was so close that it seemed you could reach out and touch it. Unfortunately we, or I should say Loki, was facing a dilemma. How was he going to cross the water? A boat came immediately to mind, but there were none in sight and Loki didn't want to take the time to find one. I suggested that he could just swim over. To this he answered that "in his present form," the water would be too cold and he would get all his clothes wet. I asked him what he meant by "present form" and he took this as an opportunity to brag about his shape-shifting abilities. How he could ". . . in the flash of an eye, change from a mouse to an eagle, from a minnow to a salmon, from a uniped to a dragon . . ." He ranted on for an extraordinarily long time about this magnificent skill of his. Finally I asked,

"Well then, why don't you just turn yourself into a bird and fly over the fjord?"

"And leave all my food and supplies over here? No, I don't think so. I might need them," Loki answered me impatiently. At this point I decided that it was probably best to just leave him alone.

Loki had not been overly generous with his breakfast rations, so I was more than a little hungry. Tentatively I began to pick about for something to eat. As there was nothing nearby, I asked if could fly up the shoreline in hopes of finding a dead fish or stranded crab. With a wave of his hand Loki approved.

First I flew one way, saw nothing, and then flew the opposite direction. Suddenly, as I rounded a slight curve in the fjord, I forgot all about food. Tied up to the shore was a giant boat, at least 150 feet long, and hidden from Loki by a bend in the shoreline. It sat high in the water with one great mast at its middle. Its sail was a giant sheet of green and white stripes with an octopus at its center. The bow and stern curved gracefully up from the waves and the prow ended in a snarling dragon's head. All along its high sides, perhaps eight feet off the water, were the holes for forty or more oars. A bronze weather vane was set on the stern post and everything was covered with carvings. I usually find things made by men to be ugly, but this boat was something else. I almost found it to be beautiful. . . .

As I circled around, someone on the boat must have seen me. A commotion arose on the deck and an arrow *flew in my direction. Being the conscientious bird that I am, I swooped around and flew straight back to Loki, who was still chewing his knuckles about crossing the fjord. I had just gasped that I had seen a ship when around the bend whirled a huge flock of seabirds, mostly gulls. Loki went pale and told me rather rudely to be silent. The birds flew up and around us like a snow squall and alighted with a great commotion of squawking and screeching. Out of their midst stepped a large black cormorant who said, "What business do you have here?"*

"It's private—so go away!" replied Loki.

"Really!" said the cormorant. "Private business way out here in the wilderness? It must be a particularly important and difficult endeavor for you to have come so far. Perhaps we can help."

"I don't think so. Goodbye," said Loki.

"But I insist. You are obviously travelers far from home. We are honor bound to offer you our hospitality. Is that not the tradition of Midgard? Please come and at least eat a simple meal with us. Our master's ship is just around the corner; he will be very happy to receive you." Here the birds drew closer, ominously clacking their beaks together. The cormorant then added with a menacing glint in his black eyes, "Remember, to refuse such kindness is a serious affront."

"Who is your master?" Loki asked cautiously.

"Oh, just a humble fisherman," answered the cormorant as one of the large gulls grasped Loki's cloak in its beak and began to tug.

"All right, all right, I guess we have no choice but to accept your invitation." Loki muttered reluctantly.

So with half the birds in the lead and the other half following behind, Loki and I walked over to the strange ship. It was anchored next to a high bank. A long timber stretched between the boat and the shore. As we walked across this gangplank, the sea birds rose up in a storm of flapping wings and perched themselves about the boat like so many chickens on a hen house.

Once on board, we were met by several soldiers, the first humans I had seen for a long time. Each was dressed in a tunic and trousers of various colors and patterns, from tweed to stripes. All of them were wearing green woolen capes, and on their heads were leather helmets of similar size and shape. They were all grasping long-handled axes and from their sides hung wicked-looking swords. All these weapons struck me as far from welcoming. They led us to a large tent erected in the center of the ship. This canvas shelter stretched from one gunwale to the other and was supported by crisscrossing poles. One of the soldiers pointed to the entrance and took a step back.

Loki reluctantly opened a flap, put one foot in the tent, and then sprang back as if he had touched a burning coal. One of the men put a restraining hand on his arm. With a savage jerk, Loki cast the hand off and threw the soldier to the deck. As one, the rest of the warriors surged forward into a tight circle around Loki and me, their axes at the ready. For a moment Loki eyed them with a fierce look of anger and defiance. They returned his glare with expressions both of fear and determination. Finally, Loki straighten himself out, and, with as much dignity as he could muster, re-entered the tent. I was forced, by the prod of an axe handle, to follow.

Inside the tent only a single candle flickered in the murky air, but this illumination was enough for us to see the tremendous figure that filled the center of the tent like a wall. This giant was dead-deer ugly, with a bulbous nose, pocked cheeks, matted gray hair, and a huge greasy beard that reached down to his waist. This vile expanse of snarls swarmed with life as hundreds of sand fleas and miniature crabs skittered about in its tangles. Our "new friend" was grossly fat, like a bag of suet with limbs. His whole body shook and jiggled as he moved. He was dressed in a tunic of sealskin that glistened oily black in the dim light. His bare feet were like hooves from growths of callouses, warts, and barnacles. As Loki and I stood before him, he peered at us with wall eyes, one pupil meeting our gaze while the other wandered aimlessly about the tent. This being was so ugly that, if he had been a chick of mine, I would have fed him to the magpies.

As we stood gawking, this monster sat placidly, every breath it took a wheezing rattle.

Next to him was a small table overflowing with dirty, bone-filled plates and upended drinking cups.

Casually, he shifted his weight and tapped his fat fingers on the table. It was then that we saw, resting next to his hand, Thor's hammer. It was glowing faintly.

A gurgling eruption came welling out of the giant when he saw us ogling the hammer. Whether it was a belch or a laugh, I couldn't tell. The creatures in his beard began a frenzied dance, and his belly heaved like a mudflat in an earthquake. Then he croaked, "Loki, my favorite hooligan, welcome to Wave Strider, my home away from home. What brings you wandering about? Are you perhaps looking for something?" Here he put his hand on Thor's hammer and patted it gently. "Is this what you seek? I found it in my nets this morning."

"Aegir," replied Loki in a hoarse voice, "I see that you have found Thor's hammer."

"Is it Thor's?" Aegir opened his eyes wide in feigned amazement. "Loki, Loki, Loki, you know as well as I do that anything and everything that sinks below the waves becomes mine by ancient right. Mjollnir fell into the ocean and is therefore mine to keep." At this he chuckled like a strangled cow.

"Aegir, don't delude yourself." said Loki, "You may be the king of the sea, but Odin is ruler over us all. Ultimately Thor's hammer is the property of Odin. One way or another you will have to give it up. Return it now and I am sure that Odin will reward you well for finding it."

"Where is it written that Odin is my overlord?!" snorted Aegir. "I am no one's servile vassal. I never have

and never will grovel before the so-called 'All Father.'
Besides, I think that pompous old one-eyed devil has sat
on his throne too long. Maybe the three fates have put
Mjollnir in my hands for a reason. Perhaps I should be
king of the Aesir!" Here Aegir straightened himself up,
looking not unlike a giant toad.

Loki, with a glint of threat, replied, "Don't be foolish
,Aegir! Are you really ready to fight Odin and Thor and
the rest of the gods, even with Mjollnir?"

Aegir looked at Loki for a long time, his expression
unreadable. I could hear the waves sloshing against the
hull of Wave Strider as they stared at each other in silence. Finally, Aegir replied, "Perhaps you are right. War
is such a messy undertaking. What kind of reward do
you think Odin would give me for returning Mjollnir?"

"Probably anything you asked for," Loki answered
in a relieved voice. "After all, what is more valuable
than Mjollnir? With a trusted go-between, you might
reap tremendous riches, perhaps even the necklace of the
Brisings?" Here Loki leaned forward, and in a conspiratorial voice continued. "Let me act as your broker. Tell
me your price and then let me return to Asgard. I will
negotiate a very good deal for you."

Aegir stared at Loki for a long time, his eyes rapidly
blinking. Slowly, he said,. "Loki, you are known far and
wide for your cunning. Many tales are told of how you
and Thor have joined forces and together, through trickery and strength, extracted terrible vengeance for the

Aesir gods. Together you have defeated enemies both powerful and clever. If I were to let you go back to Asgard now, you would not return bearing gifts. Instead, you and Thor would come with a plan to bilk or bully me out of what is rightly mine. In the end I would not gain a reward for finding Mjollnir, but instead, lose my head. No, it is much better that you stay here with me as my 'guest' while your servant," here Aegir pointed to me, "returns to Asgard with the news that I have Mjollnir and will return it for a price." This time, Aegir did not laugh.

Loki snarled, "You're making a mistake, Aegir. The Aesir will not tolerate one of their own being held hostage! Take heed of what I say, this will end badly for you."

Aegir just snorted and clapped his hands. Two soldiers quickly appeared, bound Loki's hands with a cord and escorted him out of the tent and back to shore. I never saw him again. I spent the rest of the day perched on the mainsail yard, guarded by a pair of sullen seagulls. I never did see any of that wonderful hospitality the cormorant promised.

Early the next morning I was again brought before Aegir in his lightless tent. For a long time he let me watch as he gobbled down his morning meal, a whole salmon roasted in wine and garlic. It smelled delicious. I had only been given the fins and tail of a day-old cod for my breakfast. Finally, after wiping his lips on the back of his *hand, Aegir motioned that I should come near. With his good eye squinting with concentration, he leaned over, looked me in the eye and said, "Memorize this message and tell it to Odin:*

> *As soon as possible, a representative for the Aesir must be sent to my Royal Hall on the island of Hlesey. This diplomat must be ready to negotiate a generous price for Mjollnir and a fat ransom for Loki's release. If the Aesir attempt to take the hammer from me or to free Loki by force, I will give Mjollnir to the frost giants.*

With that I was turned loose and pointed in the direction of Asgard. Unfortunately, a violent storm blew up on my second day out. I was blown in circles and became completely disoriented, blundering about like a witless fledgling. I even managed to scratch my eye on a twig. Finally, at dawn this morning, after flying all night, I saw the lights of Asgard in the distance.

Like it or not that is the news I bring. Now, if you don't mind, I deserve a little rest. Good night!

With a sigh, Thokk tucked his head under his wing and closed his eyes. As Thokk drifted into oblivion, Balder turned to Thor and said with a look of grave concern, "I am sure that Odin will select Samuel and me as the emissaries to be sent to Aegir's hall. The road to Hlesey is hard and dangerous. If your offer still stands, we could indeed use your assistance."

Thor nodded and said, "I am always true to my word."

Chapter 12

After Thokk finished his story, Balder and Thor went to Odin's palace to discuss Aegir's ultimatum with the king of the gods. Samuel was left behind with Thokk and Rag and spent the day wandering about in Balder's hall.

As the morning turned to afternoon, Samuel began to feel very hungry. Usually two meals were served in Balder's Hall, a late breakfast, and a main meal after dark. Because of Thokk's arrival, breakfast had not been served. Samuel was just at the point of finding Kvasir and asking for something to eat when a magnificent female giant appeared with a tray full of food. With a graceful bow, she set the tray down on a bench and introduced herself as Nanna, Balder's wife. Behind her came Kvasir, waddling along on his short little legs and carrying an additional platter of dishes.

Nanna was unlike any of the other female gods Samuel had seen. He had glimpsed Odin's wife Frigga, Thor's wife Sif, and numerous other female gods at his trial. Almost without exception, they had been blond-haired, blue-eyed, beautiful, and forbidding. None had even looked at him as he had walked past their seats. Many of them had worn mail coats and carried weapons just like their husbands. In contrast, Nanna was tall, slender, and intelligent. She also had dark eyes and hair. She was clothed, not in the garments of war, but in a dark blue, overlapping dress, held up at the shoulders by two egg-shaped bronze brooches. Around her neck was a band of amber beads, like chunks of frozen honey, and on her head was a simple cloth scarf. Her movements were graceful and precise and her voice soft and pleasant. Samuel felt both awed and yet secure and welcome in her presence.

She brought food for everyone—nuts and bread, apples, cream, butter, and honey. Everything was delicious; even Thokk woke from his slumbers to take a little food.

Between bites, Nanna and Samuel began to converse. She asked him about his trial before Odin's throne and he related Tyr's fierce words and the fear he felt as the king of Asgard had glared down at him. Nanna shook her head, grimaced, and exclaimed, "It's beyond the bounds of reason to put you on trial for the actions of Loki. Only vicious fools would do such a thing." Samuel found it very easy to like Nanna.

As time went on and after Kvasir had removed the empty trays of food, Samuel found himself talking about his old life back at the Geyser Inn. Nanna seemed genuinely interested in the ordinary activities that filled his life. Soon, without his realizing it, Samuel began talking about his mother and father. He described the coldness that seemed to exist between them; how they never talked or laughed or even seemed to like being in each other's presence anymore. Samuel glanced up suddenly and saw a look of concern etched on Nanna's elegant features. Startled, he went quiet, averting his eyes and blushing.

Nanna reached over, patted his shoulders, and said, "It's all right to speak of your fears, Samuel. Never be ashamed of being open and straightforward. It's when we deny the thorn in our heel that we end up having to cut off our foot." With that Nanna excused herself and left Kvasir to keep Samuel and the ravens company.

As Nanna retreated out of view, Samuel remarked, "What a nice lady."

"Oh yes. She certainly is. My favorite for sure," responded Kvasir, "But you know, just between you and me, she doesn't quite fit in with the rest of the gods."

"Why not?"

Here Kvasir smiled sadly and said, "You have to understand, Nanna is the goddess of home and hearth, kindness and motherhood. Glory and pride, attributes which the other gods value above all else, mean little to her. But, here now, let's not gossip. Do you know how to play chess?"

Late in the afternoon Balder returned with a worried look on his face. He slumped down on a bench next to Samuel and Kvasir and let out a deep sigh.

"What is the news?" asked Kvasir.

"Tomorrow Samuel, Thor, and I leave for Aegir's palace. We have been directed by Odin to negotiate the release of Loki and retrieval of Mjollnir by whatever means necessary and as quickly as possible," replied Balder.

Kvasir shook his head and said. "Must Samuel, a stranger to our world and a mere mortal, really go on such a perilous mission?"

"Yes, I am afraid so. Odin has decreed it. The rest of the gods feel that he should not escape without some kind of punishment. It was also decided that Thokk and Rag must likewise accompany us. They will be our messengers and lookouts. I suspect that Thokk will find acute displeasure in this outcome."

"What!?" Thokk squawked. He had been secretly listening, only pretending to be asleep. He now shook himself fully awake and stared at Balder with blurry, bloodshot eyes. "If this isn't a rancid deal, I don't know what is! I've already paid my debt to society, haven't I?"

Balder just shook his head and shrugged slightly. He then looked directly at Samuel and said, "The journey to Aegir's Hall will be long and hard, and once we are there things will only become more dangerous. But don't lose hope, you will be traveling with Thor, Asgard's greatest warrior, and me. You will never be alone and with luck, all will turn out well."

Samuel swallowed hard and nodded, then asked, "Where is Aegir's Hall?"

"It is on an island called Hlesey, in the middle of the great western ocean. It will take us many days sailing to get there. But first, we will go to the home of Njord, lord of calm waters and friendly winds. His home is on the coast. Hopefully he will lend us a ship and a crew and they will take us to Aegir's home. Our journey might last as long as two months, but I hope that it will be shorter. We leave tomorrow at dawn."

Here Kvasir broke in and asked, "What will happen when you reach Hlesey? Certainly Aegir will not just hand you Thor's hammer and release Loki with a pleasant *fare thee well.*"

A wan smile crossed Balder's lips and he replied, "Formally, Odin has instructed us to bargain for the return of Mjollnir and the release of Loki. He has put it upon our shoulders to negotiate the smallest price possible. Unfortunately, he expects something completely different. He really wants us to win back Loki and Mjollnir for free, by either force or trickery. He implied—in no uncertain terms—that this task should be simple if Thor and I were but clever and brave enough."

Kvasir's eyes bulged a little and he sputtered, "Good god, Odin expects the sun and the moon from you, doesn't he!"

Balder just sighed and shook his head.

The next morning, in the bitter chill before dawn, Kvasir awoke Samuel gently. The auk had brought him a simple breakfast of bread and cheese. A single candle flickered on a nearby table, like a star in a cavern. Glumly, Samuel rose and dressed, mentally preparing himself, the best he could, for the upcoming day. As he slipped on his shoes, he heard rustling noises from the far end of the hall. In the dim light Balder and Nanna were organizing blankets and food parcels and packing them into a number of large wicker baskets. Samuel finished gathering up his few belongings and walked over to where the two gods were working.

Balder was wearing a sleeveless coat of plain steel mail, which reached down to his knees. Under the armor, he was clothed in a heavy brown leather tunic. Around his waist was a thick belt and from his right shoulder was slung a sheathed sword hanging from a baldric. His movements were stiff and awkward and the sword was constantly getting in his way. Over his shoulders he wore a tremendous woolen cape, edged with gray fur and embroidered with stars sewn with silver thread. He looked distracted and anxious as he labored over the supplies.

If Balder looked lost, Nanna's face was filled with frozen fury. Her actions were full of anger and aggravation. She violently yanked on a strap, intending to pull it tight. Instead, it snapped in two with a twang. In one furious movement she hurtled the cord off into space and spat, "Surely, Odin must know that you are no warrior. It is folly to send you and Samuel out on so dangerous a mission. Did you not discuss these things with Odin, or did you just bow and scrape like you always do?"

To this Balder made a feeble attempt to defend himself and the other gods, only to be harshly interrupted by Nanna. "Don't defend that mob of goblins; they're just a pack of self-righteous, arrogant, trumped-up trolls. Why doesn't Odin get off his gaudy throne and go wring Aegir's neck himself? Answer me that!" Balder was wise enough to only nod dumbly as Nanna turned to savagely punch a leather sleeping bag down into a basket.

All at once a rumble and clatter, which made the floor boards tremble, erupted outside the hall. Thor's sled had arrived and it stopped with a thump in front of the door. His two goats, Toothgrinder and Toothgnasher, could be heard snorting and pawing the ground. Thor's voice pierced the wall like a trumpet, "Balder, the sun is nearly up, our journey must begin."

Nanna looked up at Balder, her features softened, and she reached out and touched his face. With a break in her voice she said, "Take care and come back quickly." She then turned and rapidly walked away, her dress rustling softly. Balder watched her leave, worry and regret clouding his face. Like the beating of a drum, Thor banged at the door and yelled, "Come on, Balder, we must be off."

Spurred on by the irritation in Thor's voice, Balder and Samuel came out into the gathering light. The air was brittle with cold and Thor was stamping his feet to keep warm. His giant goats moved restlessly in their harnesses, puffing out clouds of vapor. Balder heaved a basket aboard, lashed it down, and then told Samuel to sit on top of it. From this seat, Samuel could see all around and rest his arms on the sled's upper edge. With a flutter of wings, Thokk and Rag appeared. As they alighted on the sled, Thokk glanced quickly at Samuel and gave him an evil look.

Thor boarded next, brushed past Samuel, and made his way to the front of the sled. He seemed jovial, as if this were the start of some merry adventure. A large bundle of supplies were stowed next to his feet. Included in this pile were several weapons: spears, an axe, and a huge sword. Thor had also brought a tremendous shield, round and as big as a cart wheel, with a blood-red boar's head painted on its face. At his feet were several bags of grain for the goats.

As the sled creaked and groaned with the weight and movement of the gods as they shifted supplies about, Thokk could be heard muttering complaints. Thor suddenly straightened up and with a broad smile said, "Oh, be quiet, Thokk, things could be far worse." Thokk just sneered in reply, said something inaudible and then tucked his head under his wing. Thor chuckled, pulled tight one last remaining knot and took up the goats' reins.

Finally Balder heaved the last basket of supplies aboard, gave Samuel an extra blanket and found a comfortable place to stand. He then nodded to Thor. The thunder god turned, adjusted his gloves, and cracked a whip over the goats' heads. The sled lurched forward with a jangle, as the rattle rings suspended above came to life. Without further ado, Samuel, Thor, Balder, and the two ravens, in one reluctant company, set off in the direction of Aegir's hall.

Chapter 13

From his perch atop Balder's pack, Samuel watched the halls and palaces of Asgard flash by in the early morning light, their stone or wood façades tinged the purple gray of dawn. At this hour there were no lights, sounds, or activities to disturb the predawn quiet; everything was as still as a mausoleum. They rounded a corner and there in the distance a tremendous wall came into view.

When Samuel first entered Asgard, he had been asleep on the floor of Thor's sled. As a result, he had not seen the outer fortifications that surround the home of the Aesir gods. Here they now loomed, soaring sixty feet into the air, enormously thick and separated into three levels. The first course was of rough-hewn granite blocks, unmarked and unadorned. On top of this was a layer of snow-covered sod that sloped up and gently inward. The final level was a palisade of tree trunks, sharpened to a point and weathered to a stone gray. No sentries patrolled the walls; only solitary black and gray jays whirred and fluttered about its nooks and crannies.

As Samuel looked upward, he saw a man slowly walking along the base of the palisade casting grain in a sweeping motion. Balder leaned down and said, "The walls of Asgard are unguarded, except for the jays. If any danger were to approach, they would warn us. For their vigilance, the gods feed them."

As they drew close to the walls, Samuel saw two huge oaken doors, bound by iron hinges and carved in low relief with an intricate pattern of intertwining snakes, dragons, and warriors. As the sled slowed and came to a stop, the doors opened with a creaking groan, revealing a long dark tunnel. With a harsh shout and a snap of his whip, Thor urged his goats into the damp blackness. The doors shut behind with a boom and for a moment the sled careened forward in total darkness, the rasp of the runners on bare ground loud in Samuel's ears. Then, like a false dawn, a sliver of illumination appeared at the far end of the tunnel and another set of doors swung open.

The sled burst forth onto a small platform surrounded by a low rock wall. Thor halted his goats with a hard tug on the reins, and the doors behind closed with a thump. In front of the sled was an immense chasm, perhaps a quarter mile wide. Below Samuel's horrified eyes the earth fell away in one sheer cliff, a thousand feet deep, a dizzying drop that made him clutch the sides of sled tightly and constricted his stomach to a ball. Across the gulf, a fractured face of ice rose nearly to the level of the ledge on which they now stood. It glimmered blue and green in the gloom. To their right and off the ledge ran a narrow path along the base of the fortifications. Gingerly, Thor urged his goats onto this catwalk.

As the morning light strengthened from slate gray to amber yellow, the surrounding landscape took on shape and form. Samuel saw that Asgard was built upon a high, flat-topped mountain, one pinnacle in a long chain of peaks. A hundred or more crags arced away on either side, modulating from brown and gray to blue as they grew faint in the distance. From the gentle curve of their path, Samuel guessed that the walls of Asgard were circular. It also seemed that the city of the gods must be completely surrounded by cliffs or formidable slopes. As the night shadows receded even further, Samuel saw that the great wall of ice across the canyon was, in fact, the start of a tremendous glacier. This river of ice tumbled and flowed out and down a long U-shaped valley, its pale face riven with countless fissures. At the very end of the ice field, miles away, an area of giant boulders and treeless slopes opened up. These ended abruptly in a wall of evergreen trees. The forest, pale and mute in the distance, seemed to go on forever.

Cautiously Thor nudged the goats along the path, the wall on one side, a chasm on the other, the trail ahead barely wider than the sled's runners. Clumps of snow, disturbed by their passage, tumbled into oblivion like lost souls into the darkness below. Samuel stared around mesmerized, hardly able to comprehend all that he was seeing. Yet, one more amazing sight awaited his eyes. Slowly, like the drawing back of a curtain, a magnificent bridge was unveiled from around the curve of the wall. It leapt across the abyss, from city to glacier, in one magnificent arch, both beautiful and breathtaking. Like a spotlight being switched on, the sun peeped over the horizon and a flood of brilliant light revealed the span in all its glory. It was constructed with a dazzling montage of colored stones, agate and quartz, amber and amethyst, serpentine and travertine, onyx and lapis-lazuli. These stones shimmered in the clear morning light like the scales of a wet and slithering snake.

As they neared the bridge, Samuel saw a lone giant sitting by it on a wooden throne. He was old and weatherbeaten, his skin tanned to a walnut brown by exposure. His clothes were faded and frayed and in one hand he held a great horn, its bell curving above his head like a cobra ready to strike. Thor hailed the giant as they approached and he in turned raised a hand in recognition. But as they passed, Samuel noticed that no welcoming smile crossed the lips of this giant and he never diverted his watchful gaze from the landscape. Later, Balder explained to Samuel that this god was Heimdall, the watchman of Asgard, ever vigilant and never resting.

With a harsh clatter, Thor's sled ran onto the rainbow bridge. As they climbed over the arch, Samuel peered downward into the night-shaded depths below. The pit beneath was a shadow land of shattered boulders and avalanches of scree. Great icicles and flows of frozen water clung to torturous walls or cascaded down talus slopes. A river of chalk-blue water churned in a rocky channel, only to disappear into a subterranean tunnel. Everything was broken or shattered, a desolation of ice, stone, and gloom.

With a bone-jarring thump, the sled trundled off the bridge and onto the glacier beyond. A well-worn trail had been etched into the ice, its boundaries marked with cairns of stone. The sled rocked from side to side as the path wove around sinkholes and crevasses, and switchbacked across the face of the glacier. They descended at a perilous angle and speed, and sometimes Samuel felt they were simply careening out of control. As the sun rose higher, his eyes began to sting from the brightness of the snow and he was forced to shield them with his hands. Once or twice the shrill cry of a hawk split the silence. Samuel twisted about looking in vain for the bird, never quite spotting it among the crags.

Slowly, after several hours, they reached the end of the ice field and the sled rumbled onto the bare slopes that lay between the glacier and the forest. Asgard had receded till it seemed a mere toy perched atop a distant peak. Their progress became faster. Clumps of wind-tortured firs, mummified with snow, flashed past. Suddenly the forest loomed up, a dense green curtain of evergreens, weighted down with overcoats of snow. With a rush, the sled plunged into the trees and the hiss of the runners over the dry snow and the grunts of the goats as they labored became louder, echoing back from the encroaching pines and firs. The path narrowed and wound itself around massive tree trunks, through deep shadows of blue and under tunnels of overhanging branches. Occasionally, a glade or clearing would open up and Samuel could glimpse a broad stretch of sky, now deep blue and cloudless, or, rising in the distance, a rocky summit.

On and on the sled raced. Periodically Thor adjusted the reins in his hands or cracked a whip above the back of the goats. Balder stood staring pensively ahead, his mind lost in thought. Thokk and Rag, their heads drooping, appeared to doze. Samuel drew his knees up to his chin, and tried, as best he could, to stay warm.

They did not stop until twilight. In the gathering dusk, Thor halted the goats in a glen where a frozen stream lay buried beneath blankets of frost, its course marked only by a depression in the snow, like the trail of some subterranean animal. They were so tired that Thor and Balder didn't even build a campfire. In the gathering gloom, the travelers ate only a cold meal packed the night before by Kvasir. Fortunately for Samuel, whose teeth were chattering with cold, Thor had filled a corner of the sled with fur pelts. Samuel burrowed into them like a mouse in an old blanket and quickly fell asleep. Thor and Balder spent the night sitting at the back of the sled with their feet on the ground and their capes drawn close, quietly discussing the journey ahead. Rag and Thokk remained on the sled's rails, ruffling their feathers against the frigid night air. The last thing Samuel remembered before he dozed off was the mournful hooting of an owl somewhere off in the shadows of the forest, a spectral sound in an otherwise silent landscape.

In the wee hours before dawn, Samuel was jolted awake by yipping and howling. This racket filled the forest but seemed to come from no one place. Both Balder and Thor were standing, quiet and expectant, one at the rear of the sled holding a spear and the other comforting the goats. The landscape was bathed in brilliant moonlight, so bright that the trees cast sharp black shadows across the still clearing. Finally a lone wolf appeared in a break between the trees, its eyes glowing faintly in the moonlight. It stared at Balder and Thor for a moment, violently shook its head, and then wandered off. The mournful wailing of the wolves quickly faded and Samuel slept again.

Samuel was awakened the next morning by the jolting and jostling of the sled as Balder rearranged supplies and Thor harnessed the goats. The sun had just risen and the light was dazzling. Neither Thor nor Balder were in a good mood and both seemed preoccupied with their own thoughts. Breakfast was bread and dried apples. The day passed much like the last, endless ranks of trees interspaced with an occasional meadow. Near evening the sled entered a large clearing through which a small river ran. Most of the stream was covered by thick ice or a blanket of snow. But here and there small pools of clear water were visible, like black mirrors set into the snow. At one end of the clearing there was a tremendous boulder. On its face a great stone eye was carved, and painted in black and yellow. Surrounding the orb was a band of runes chipped into the rock, highlighted with blue paint. A regular road emerged from the forest nearby and ran up to the stone. It was marked by a regular depression in the snow and by a few half-buried sled tracks.

"Where are we?" Samuel asked Balder.

"We are at the edge of the world of the gods. Beyond this boundary is Midgard, the realm of man. No human may pass this point, unless invited by one of the lords of Asgard. We are going to camp here for the night."

The next day they again rose early and covered many miles. The going was much easier, as they were now on a real road instead of a mere trail. A wide swath of trees had been cleared on both sides, banks were cut and occasionally a marker stone was set on the road's edge. Even so, it was obvious that the road was little used because few tracks marred the surface of the snow. At dusk they came to a crossroads. A tumbled down cabin stood nearby, lonely and forlorn, its roof partially caved in. A few fresh tracks could be seen on the intersecting road, one set of horse tracks even turning off in their direction.

Near the cabin was a ring of exceptionally large spruces, soaring towers of thick emerald foliage tapering to points high above the surrounding forest. Their dense canopy of overlapping branches created a large roomy space underneath, nearly free of snow and underbrush. Only a light sprinkling of frost covered the ground. It was obviously a regular camping spot because a fire ring of stones was set in the middle, and between two trees a log had been lashed to tether horses.

After having an initial look around, Balder began to dust off the fire stones while Thor took out a hatchet and began chopping off a few low-hanging boughs and laying them in a neat pile next to the fire ring. Thokk and Rag awoke from their perch on the sled and fluttered over to investigate. Samuel looked on as the giants worked, unsure of how to help and not wanting to be in the way.

After a few minutes, Thor stretched his back, looked at Samuel and said, "Young man, I have a task for you. You can collect some kindling for us. If you look about, you will find patches of moss growing on the shadow side of many trees. Scrape it off and bring it to me. Just don't wander too far away. These woods can be dangerous."

Samuel nodded and began looking around, happy to have something to do. He saw a few clumps of yellow green moss, like bristly tufts of hair, attached to the north side of a few trees. Unfortunately, most growths were above his head and those which he could reach clung tenaciously to the bark. After much labor, he had collected only a small handful. Gradually, he was forced deeper into the woods in search of more promising clumps of moss. He tried to keep Thor and Balder in sight, or at least stay in hearing distance of them. After a long time of nearly fruitless effort he spied a great mass of shaggy lichen clinging to the upturned side of a newly fallen tree. Unfortunately, it was quite a long way off, much deeper into the forest than he felt comfortable going. Anxiously he hesitated. But then, with a reluctant look back toward where he knew his friends were, he headed off toward the toppled tree. Slowly and carefully he picked his way through downfall and drifts, often wading up to his hips in deep snow.

Finally, after a good deal of effort, Samuel reached his goal and began to gather great gobs of precious moss into his arms. As he labored, twilight began to fall, shadows darkened and everything took on a gray pallor. Suddenly, as if brushed by a chill breeze, the skin on the back of his neck prickled and he stood bolt upright with a jerk. There, not two yards away, like an apparition, was a girl, ankle deep in the snow. She was Samuel's age, blonde haired and pretty. She wore a purple dress, leather boots, and clutched a white shawl over her shoulders. Her skin was so pale it almost glowed in the falling light. A puff of vapor came from her mouth. She smiled and took a few steps backward, her feet leaving only faint impression in the snow. Samuel gasped and his arms went limp. All the moss he had collected dropped to the ground. The girl giggled and gestured for him to follow. As if in a trance, Samuel obeyed. He was bewitched by the girl's friendly face and by his own curiosity. She glided over the snow like thistledown over a summer meadow. She never quite turned her back to Samuel or seemingly even touched the ground. Samuel stumbled after like a clumsy draft animal, tripping over hidden branches, slogging through snow banks and wheezing for breath. On and on they went, deeper into the forest, and then, all at once, from behind a tangled pile of deadwood, a blaze of golden light burst forth like the sparking of a match. Samuel's eyes were seared and he instinctively threw up has arms as a shield. As he slowly withdrew his fingers he saw the mouth of a cave. Inside was a long, smooth tunnel, lined with finely cut stone and lit by torches. Everything glowed bright orange and red, like the embers of a fire. At the passageway's end, Samuel glimpsed, deep underground, a field of waving grass bathed in sunlight. The fragrance of flowers, grass, and cows wafted out of the passageway. The joys of summertime flooded through Samuel's mind. He imagined himself running barefoot, without a shirt, through knee-high grass and thousands of dandelions. The hot sun was on his bare shoulders and the air was moist and warm. Tears came to his eyes and a sharp pain burned at the back of his throat. He gazed at the girl and in return she smiled and spoke, her voice sweet and inviting, "Come along, come along." Completely dazzled, he took a step toward the door.

All at once there was a rush of black wings and Samuel was knocked from his feet. The girl screamed and dove into the tunnel. Just as she turned, Samuel saw a tail, long, black, and tufted at the end, protrude from her dress and swish in the air. The passageway shut with a snap and Samuel was left in the dark with Rag pecking at his sleeve.

It was a long way back to the campsite, and Samuel would never have found his way if it hadn't been for Rag. His footprints seemed to have disappeared or have been covered up and he had no idea in which direction the ring of spruce trees lay. Rag guided Samuel through the maze of trees by flying up and around to locate a trail in the near darkness. Even so, it was a long time before Samuel saw the ring of spruce trees in the distance. By that time his feet were numb and his shivering uncontrollable.

As Samuel got closer to the campsite, he could hear Balder calling out his name, his voice echoing among the trees. Samuel was too exhausted to answer, just trudging along required all his energy. With a lurch, he stumbled out of the shadows and into the light of a blazing campfire. He was dead tired, in shock and his clothes sodden with snow and sweat. Thor jumped up, a stern frown on his face. He opened his mouth to scold Samuel, but when he saw the boy's face, he shut it with a snap. Balder, who had been standing just beyond the light of the fire, rushed over to Samuel's side. He knelt down and with a voice edged with anxiety asked, "What happened? Where have you been?"

In a rush, Samuel told the two gods of the girl, the passageway and how Rag had intervened at the last moment to save him. As he spoke, he stared blankly at the fire, his eyes distended by fright.

"Was there anything strange about this girl?" asked Balder.

Samuel thought back to the moment when the tunnel closed and replied, "She had a tail, a cow's tail."

Balder quickly looked up at Thor and both frowned. Balder spoke. "There are many weird and dangerous things in Midgard and you have just escaped, by the skin of your teeth, from one of the strangest. The girl you met was a Hudler child. The Hudler are a race of people who live underground, much like trolls and dwarfs. Unlike those other races, though, their abodes are places of beauty and peace, giant caverns lit by magic fires. Their homes are always carpeted by luxuriant meadows where herds of fat cows roam freely. It is always summer in their caves and the Hudlers live an easy and pleasant life. Just one curse mars their existence. Only daughters are born to them, never a son. They must therefore find mates in our world. This they do by luring young men into their underground homes. They especially prey upon those who wander in lonely places. Once inside their caverns there is no escape, no way back. For a while the men trapped in this way lead lives of comfort and pleasure. But slowly, over many years, their limbs grow thick and their features heavy. Then one morning grass sprouts on their back. Then their eyebrows turn to moss, mushrooms grow from their ears and their feet turn to stone. Finally they can no longer move. Earthbound and motionless, they transform into featureless and lifeless mounds of sod. That is the fate of all men who enter the world of the Hudlers."

150

Samuel shivered and looked up at Balder's kind and worried face. A cold spasm of fear shook his body as he considered how close he had come to this terrible and strange fate. Balder reached out and put his arms around Samuel's shoulders and said, "All is now well. But in the future, you must always stay close to us and never wander away again. Remember, our world is very dangerous."

Samuel dumbly nodded his head. Suddenly he felt very thirsty.

Chapter 14

After Samuel returned from escaping the Hudler girl, Thor and Balder kept the campfire blazing all night long. Everyone, including the ravens, was unnerved by Samuel's close call. When it was finally time to go to bed, Thokk and Rag unceremoniously found the nearest branch to the fire on which to roost.

Samuel and the gods slept in leather bags covered over with sheep and goat pelts. The mound of spruce boughs Thor had so painstakingly cut earlier kept them from lying directly on the frozen ground. They awoke the next morning dry and reasonably warm. Once out of his sleeping bag though, Samuel started shivering violently in the frigid morning air and didn't stop until Balder lit a fire.

Everyone was anxious to leave the crossroads, now seemingly haunted by the events of the night before. In their haste, they ate only a simple breakfast of cheese, stale barley bread, and water, then hurriedly reloaded the sled and reharnessed the goats. Just before they left, Thor piled a small cairn of stones next to the fire ring.

On the highest rock he scratched several runes with his knife.

"What are you doing?" asked Samuel.

"I'm leaving a warning. Now anyone who stops here will know that there are Hudlers about. Perhaps it will save some poor soul from an evil fate."

Finally, after a few more tasks, they were ready to leave. As they moved away from the ring of spruce trees and the smoke from their smoldering campfire disappeared behind a bend, Samuel felt an enormous wave of relief. The rest of the day passed slowly, one monotonous hour inching into the next. The forest seemed to go on forever. The only change was that late in the afternoon the trees began to grow taller and a few birch and maples appeared, intermixed with the evergreens. The travelers camped at a lonely and desolate spot that night and slept in the back of the sled.

Although the next day dawned bright and clear, cirrus clouds soon rolled in from the west. Late in the afternoon they were replaced by a heavy gray overcast sky. A stiff, raw breeze picked up and the air became more humid. By evening the snow on the ground became thinner and no longer were the trees weighted down with lumps of snow. Patches of bare earth showed here and there under trees and on slopes facing the sun. Once or twice Samuel was nearly thrown from the sled when it hit a lightly covered pothole. As evening fell, the undergrowth became extremely thick. Brambles and vines nearly blotted out the sky. Had it not been for the road, their progress would have been impossible. All at once the forest gave way and the sled rumbled out onto a beach.

A sharp, cold gust of wind caught Samuel's hair and ruffled it back across his scalp. He could taste the tang of salt and sea on his lips. A large bay, surrounded by green headlands and dotted with islands, filled his eyesight. A patchy haze hung over the choppy water. The crashing surf was so loud that Samuel had to shout to be heard. A tremendous profusion of driftwood, from huge logs stripped of bark and bleached white to ragged piles of sticks, was scattered along the strand. All at once, the setting sun found a gap below the clouds and its slanting rays bathed everything with a brief, luminous, fire-orange glow. In this light Samuel saw, far in the distance, a group of timber buildings close to the shore. A few twinkling lights shone in the sea mist and gathering darkness. Thor, after a moment's pause, turned the goats toward the village.

Night had fallen by the time the sled pulled into the hamlet. It was just a small collection of huts and storage sheds built around one large central hall. Everything was constructed of wood and stained a dark beetle-brown. Rickety racks for drying fish were scattered about and the unfinished shell of a large boat rested on wooden blocks. The main house was perhaps two hundred feet long and rectangular in shape. Its roof ridge bowed up in a gentle arch. The gables reached nearly to the ground, and were covered with a thick thatch of reeds. The foundation was constructed of rough-cut stone. A few modest carvings of sea creatures projected from beneath the eaves and immediately above the main entrance.

As Thor reined in his goats, a small group of humans emerged from the hall and gathered about the sled. Thor leaned over and asked, "Is Njord here? If so, tell him that Thor has come to call."

Before anyone could answer, a gruff but welcoming voice boomed out from the doorway. "Thor, you old glutton, have you come to empty my larder and drink me dry again? The last time you were here, my people went hungry for a year!"

Out strode an old but handsome giant dressed in a blue-green tunic and pale gray trousers. His gray hair was streaked with white and his face lined with faint wrinkles. He had a hawk nose, wind-burned skin, and watery blue eyes. He took one look at Thor's slightly startled expression and laughed a great booming roar. Then looking over at Balder and Samuel he said, "I see that you have brought help this time! My pantry really is in trouble. However, on second glance, I must say, your cohorts look rather puny."

Thor, picking up Njord's jovial mood, remarked, "Alas, they're the best I could find. Samuel here used to be a great god, as big as you and me. But then he took up listening to his wife and dithering about Asgard and look what happened. He's shrunk to a wee shadow of his former self. On the other hand, I think Balder here is salvageable, but only time will tell."

Njord scratched his chin, stared at Balder, and replied, "I don't know. He seems pretty hopeless too." Both Thor and Njord laughed, winked, and shook hands.

In a tired and formal voice, with more than a hint of testiness, Balder said, "The lords of Asgard need your help, Njord. Can we please go inside?"

"Of course, of course, let's all go in," Njord replied.

Everyone, except for the ravens who remained perched on the sled, went into Njord's hall. Inside, a cloud of warm and smokey air buffeted Samuel. Large whale oil lamps set on tables or attached to columns suffused everything with an amber glow. One long rectangular fire crackled in the center of the hall and its smoke spiraled out of a hole in the ceiling. A great steaming cauldron and several spits weighted down with flounder, cod, and other fish hung over the fire. Numerous tables and benches stood on the wooden floor and in the sand around the fireplace. Colorful banners and flags hung from the ceiling beams. The hall was crowded with people. They stared curiously, but kindly, as the visitors walked past. Njord led them to his table at the front of the room and motioned for them to sit down.

After they were seated, leather tankards of beer appeared. Samuel nodded to the middle-aged woman who served them. She was clothed in a two-layered dress held together by two bronze brooches positioned just below her collarbones. From one of the brooches hung a set of keys, a small pair of scissors, and a blue amulet. Her hair was intricately braided and she smiled as he took a tankard from her. Samuel began to feel more at ease than he had felt for a long time. He grimaced though, as he tasted the beer, the first sip of alcohol he had ever had in his life. It tasted bitter and stale, and he would have much rather had a plain cup of water. Fortunately a great platter of roasted salmon and bowls of a fish stew, seasoned with cumin, were placed before everyone and Samuel was able to politely ignore his drink.

After a while Njord turned to Thor and said, "What adventure brings you our way?"

Thor finished chewing a chunk of salmon. With a thoughtful look, he answered. "Loki has got himself into some trouble with Aegir. We are on our way to negotiate his release."

Njord looked surprised and said, "What terrible thing has the lord of fire done to cause Aegir to hold him prisoner?"

"Oh, you know Loki. He's always stirring up trouble where he shouldn't, and usually getting himself in a fix while he's at it."

"Yes, that's true. But what exactly did he do?" Njord asked with a cautious note in his voice.

Thor looked uncomfortable and shifted in his seat. "I'm not sure . . . He probably tried to pull one of his vicious pranks on Aegir," Thor answered evasively.

Njord grimaced and said, "I know Aegir. He would never dare hold one of the Aesir gods prisoner unless he had suffered a terrible insult or had . . . how can I say this . . . a great deal to gain. There is something here that is not being revealed."

"Look, Njord. The lords of Asgard have a problem with Aegir. That's all I can say." Thor blurted, his patience at an end.

A frown creased Njord's face and he looked away from Thor and stared at the table in front of him.

Balder quickly said, "There is indeed more to this than a little mischief on Loki's part. Unfortunately, the situation is far too delicate for us to discuss freely. Perhaps if we were in private, we could speak to you more openly. For now, please trust us in this matter."

Njord glared at Balder and said, "Anything can be discussed without fear in my house. My people have been with me since they were children. None would ever betray me or the Aesir."

Thor and Balder looked at each other for a moment and then Thor slowly shook his head ever so slightly. Balder spoke. "I'm sorry, Njord—it's just too dangerous. I can't give you any more details right now. I'm sure . . . "

Here Njord interrupted, his voice sharp and twinged with sarcasm, "Enough fishing with blunt hooks! I can well see where this is leading. What is it that the lords of Asgard want from me this time? To marry off another one of your problems?"

"No, no, just a boat and some of your thralls for rowers," answered Thor, his expression impenetrable.

Njord glanced at Thor and then stared at Balder, real anger flickering in his eyes. Balder looked down at the table, his cheeks colored.

Slowly, and in a voice thick with fury, Njord said. "I have no slaves. The humans who live in my hall are my family. We have endured winter gales and summer calms, shipwrecks and famine together. Every baby born to one of them is like my own son or daughter, ever more precious since I myself will never have any children. I do not risk them lightly and especially not for unknown reasons. A ship is mere wood and iron bound to rot anyway. You may have a ship for your mission, but not even one of my sailors. You can row yourself to Aegir's Hall." With that Njord stood up, bowed to the room and left through a nearby door. The room fell deadly silent. All of Njord's people averted their eyes from Samuel, Thor, and Balder.

When dinner was finished, Thor and Balder were shown to small alcoves off the main hall. Each contained a bed and was separated from the rest of the building by a heavy woolen curtain. Samuel was given a pillow and blanket and told he could sleep on the floor next to Balder's compartment. It wasn't that Njord's servants had suddenly become rude, but the friendliness that had first greeted them had evaporated.

Before Samuel went to sleep, he asked Balder, through the curtain, why Njord could not have any children. Balder sighed and answered, "Once a giantess, named Skadi, had a claim against the lords of Asgard that they could not pay. In exchange for the original debt, the giantess agreed to take a husband from among the gods. She desired me but was tricked into taking another. That unwanted mate was Njord and the marriage was a total failure."

"Why?"

"Because Njord is the lord of calm seas and gentle breezes, whereas Skadi is the goddess of ice, snow, and bitter winds. Njord cannot bear to leave his people or the seaside and Skadi is unable to abandon her high mountains and ice fields. Their union was and remains an ill and barren match."

With these sad words Samuel fell asleep. He tossed and turned the entire night, waking several times with a start, confused and unable to remember exactly where he was. Once he called out in alarm, only to be answered by a hiss. Finally, morning came and the interior of Njord's hall was infused with a blue-gray light filtering in from the high smoke holes. Women and children appeared and began to make preparations for breakfast in the pallid and smoky gloom.

In spite of his anger and distrust, Njord was true to his word. Late in the morning he showed Samuel and his friends a boat which they could use for their journey. He had even regained some of his good humor as he led them to a quiet inlet near the village. Here a small fleet of boats had been drawn up on the sand or moored to a single pier. Most prominent was a magnificent ship, 150 feet long, resting on rollers and protected from the weather by a roofed structure. It was embellished with carvings and painted blue and green. Along its side were the holes for numerous oars. From its bow a great, snarling falcon head soared straight up into the air and from the stern, an equally high tail rose to a delicate curl. This ship was a thing of beauty, graceful and serpentine, a royal yacht fit for a god. It was also not the ship Njord was going to lend his uninvited guests.

Instead Njord showed them quite another boat, much smaller and without paint or gilt. It rested directly on the sand and showed the scars and wear of heavy use. It was also an elegant ship, but in a more humble and functional sense. It was forty feet long, with a hull nine feet high and a beam of ten feet. Seen from above it had the shape of an almond, tapering to points at each end. The sides were constructed of long planks overlapping each other and bolted together with iron rivets. These planks, or strakes, as Thor corrected Samuel, were held to the interior ribs by tree roots lashed through cleats. Everything was built around a very stout keel that had been carved from a single oak tree. Unlike the previous ship, only a simple figurehead rose from the bow, and the stern was nothing but an unadorned post. Curiously, only the front and the back of the boat had a deck, the middle was left open all the way to the keel. Samuel learned later that this space was used as a hold to carry livestock. Two T-shaped crutches rose from the deck, one fore and one aft. Also positioned about the deck were a small auxiliary boat, a stack of oars, and a small post near the stern of the boat. A large, paddle-like rudder was fastened to the right side of the stern. It had been pulled up out of the way and was lashed to the top strake.

A number of men were working on the boat. Several, with ropes and poles, were raising a mast to a central position, fitting it into a massive block at the bottom of the hull. Two men were fastening a row of shields along each side, binding them to a light frame. Still others were securing rigging and caulking seams with hot tar and strands of wool or splicing frayed ropes. But even as these men labored and sweated on his behalf, Thor stepped forward, frowned and said, "I say, Njord! This is hardly the vessel for two gods. It's a merchantman, a mere knarr. I would prefer a proper drakar—even a longship would do."

"Those vessels need a large crew and many rowers. Unless you have them tucked away in your sled, you have none of those," Njord answered with a wry smile. "This knarr can be sailed or rowed by the two of you. It is also steadier in rough seas and can hold more supplies. Trust me, this is the ship you need."

Balder nodded his head, but Thor just stared at the boat and put his hands on his hips. Finally he grumbled, "It's a bad omen when the junton of thunder is forced to go about in a farmer's wagon instead of a chariot."

Provisioning the knarr and preparing it for sea took the entire day. Samuel spent some time wandering up and down the beach, watching the rollers crash along the shore and collecting sea shells. Rag and Thokk were his constant companions, hopping along in his wake. For a while he returned to the inlet and watched Njord help Thor and Balder become familiar with the knarr. He listened intently as they discussed the best route to

Aegir's home and what perils, storms, monsters, and adverse currents they might encounter along the way. To Samuel's inexperienced ears, their impending voyage sounded nearly impossible, fraught with terrible dangers. When the gods were finished talking, Samuel drifted away and sat down to rest at the base of a nearby dune. He lay on the warm sand, dreaming of home and listening to the surf roll in from the ocean.

The next morning Samuel was awakened before dawn by Balder. There was an urgent edge to the god's voice. "The wind is right and the tide is going out, we must set sail before the sun rises and the wind shifts."

With as much haste as he could muster, Samuel pulled on his clothes and hurried to where their ship was beached. It was still dark and the ocean seemed strangely quiet. When he arrived at the inlet, a mob of men were heaving and shoving the knarr into the water, their legs splashing in the sea. With one final push the ship came alive, gently bobbing up and down. Ropes were thrown, the boat was drawn to the pier, anchored and a gangplank positioned. Kegs, boxes, and bags of supplies were hustled aboard.

Close by the pier, a large bonfire of driftwood had been lit. It snapped and popped with fierce abandon and cast an orange glimmer across the inlet. By its light, Thor was receiving last-minute advice from Njord. The thunder god nodded his head and stroked his beard in the frosty morning air, while Njord spoke and pointed vaguely off into space. Balder was busy unloading Thor's sled, which had been drawn up to the beach.

Baskets, blankets, pelts, and Thor's weapons lay in a pile on the sand, ready to be transferred to the knarr. Several men were unhitching Toothgnasher and Toothgrinder from their halters and leading them away to pasture.

"Hey, Samuel, ever been on a boat on the open ocean before?"

Samuel twisted around and there were Thokk and Rag, perched on a nearby log. He could have sworn that Thokk had a malicious glint in his eyes. "No, why do you ask?"

"Oh, no reason, just curious," Thokk said with a cackle.

Finally, all was ready for their departure. With a wave, Balder gestured for Samuel to join him on board the knarr. Reluctantly, Samuel edged his way across the gangplank, arms outstretched for balance as the dark water below sloshed against the hull. With a hop he jumped down into the boat. It pitched ever so slightly as he landed. A woozy sensation crept up from his stomach.

With a stab of anxiety, Samuel realized that he was about to do something that he had never even dreamed of doing. He was going to sea in a small boat for a very long time. His mouth went dry and he felt both afraid and excited at the same time.

All at once there was a great pounding on the gangplank and Thor came trotting across. With a thump, he jumped onto the deck. The gangplank was lifted up and shoved on board. There was a shout, and then first one and then another walrus-skin rope came snaking through the air to land on the deck. Both ropes were quickly coiled into neat piles. Balder and Thor then grabbed two long oars and began pushing and shoving the knarr away from the pier. As knarr and pier parted, a hurrah went up from the beach and Balder and Thor waved in return. With a whirr of wings and a single caw, Thokk and Rag alighted on the mainsail yard.

Balder and Thor quickly set to work. They sat down amidship, each to a side, their giant legs disappearing down into the central hold. They slipped their oars through the sides and, with powerful, back-bending strokes, began to row. Not knowing what else to do, Samuel sat down on a chest near the back of the boat. Quickly the bonfire on the beach became small, its glow fading away in the growing light of dawn. Somewhere out ahead Samuel could hear the surf crashing on a line of rocks.

Gracefully the knarr skimmed across the sheltered bay and through a narrow passageway. All at once it was buffeted by a swell, rocking upward and then plunging downward in one surging movement. Samuel's stomach dropped to his feet and a giddy grin froze on his face.

They had entered the open ocean. As the boat bobbed over the crest of another wave, Samuel was reminded of a carnival ride he had once taken. For the moment, the sensation was exhilarating.

Like the hand of Midas, the sun rose above the horizon and filled the air with a golden glow. High above, a fragile tracery of wispy clouds dyed a frosty pink filled the heavens. A cold breeze brought tears to Samuel's eyes and set his cloak flapping. Green waves, spattered with whitecaps, undulated endlessly into the misty horizon. The wind whispered, the oars creaked, and a passing fulmar squawked. For a magical instant, the world seemed newborn, without stain or danger. Samuel, as he looked about, felt a fierce joy fill his soul.

Chapter 15

Shortly after the knarr left the shelter of Njord's harbor, Thor set a huge square sail from the boat's single mast. This great sheet of wool was patterned with an alternating design of blue and white diamonds and crisscrossed with stout leather straps for support. Its top was bound to a wide yard and its bottom secured to the hull with numerous shroud lines. The yard itself was attached to the main mast by a ring of wooden rollers. Samuel saw that this clever design allowed the yard to be positioned at any angle and to be run up and down by simply adjusting a single rope. This rope, or stay, ran from the yard up to the top of the mast, through a block and then to the stern of the boat where it was firmly anchored. When Thor raised the yard on the first morning of their voyage, the sail quickly unfurled and filled with air, billowing out like the lungs of a living animal. The shroud lines snapped taut and the knarr stirred to life.

According to Njord, Hlesey lay nearly due west from his small settlement. Unfortunately the wind was from the north and was pushing the little knarr south, contrary to the direction it needed to go. Unfazed, Thor, with the deftness of experience, adjusted ropes and rigging so that the yard pivoted and the sail caught the breeze at an angle. And then, at Thor's signal, Balder heaved on the tiller and the knarr lumbered around, settling into a heading crosswise to the wind and nearly in the right direction.

It was at this moment that Samuel's stomach began to rebel. First, he felt only a mere queasiness as the knarr dropped into a particularly deep trough. But then with each successive wave his head grew hotter and his nausea stronger till he felt sicker than he had ever felt in his life. Soon he could no longer stand. He lay down on the deck, his knees curled up to his chest. Every new swell was an agony to be endured; every sway or roll of the knarr was a curse. He felt like he was dying.

As Samuel moaned and groaned, Balder moved him to a dry spot on deck and covered him with a blanket. He then tried to feed him some dry bread and cold salted fish. Samuel quickly waved them away, their very smell repugnant. First hours, then days went by, and Samuel showed no improvement. Sleep was his only respite and that came in fitful intervals and only as a result of sheer exhaustion. Thor just rolled his eyes at Samuel's plight and muttered to Balder, "This skraeling is like an untempered sword, ready to shatter at the first hard blow."

In contrast to Samuel, Thokk and Rag seemed to enjoy the voyage. They clung to the yardarm high above the deck and let the breeze ruffle their feathers. Periodically they would launch themselves into the wind and let it carry them aloft like kites in a stiff breeze. Then they would return, with laboring flaps, to their original perch. On the fourth day out Thokk called down to Samuel with a chuckle in his voice, "Aren't you enjoying our little cruise, Samuel, my boy? Perhaps next time you'll listen to me when I tell you to leave well enough alone. I'm sure the Geyser Inn doesn't buck up and down so much." Thokk only stopped when Rag gave him a sharp shove with his wing.

With the mention of the Geyser Inn, Samuel was overwhelmed by homesickness. A great lump formed in his throat as he thought about his home and his parents. Questions raced through his mind. What were his mother and father thinking and doing now? Were they still searching for him, panic stricken and desperate, or had they already given up? Would he ever see them again? Was it even possible for him to find his way back to the Geyser Inn?

In his misery, Samuel tried to imagine his old home, to conjure up every last detail. He pictured himself sitting at the small table in the hotel's break room where he sometimes did his homework and his family ate their meals. A single incandescent lamp attached to the wall above the table was lit, bathing everything with a mellow, orange glow. His father was watching the evening news on television while his mother bustled about in the kitchen making dinner, humming a quiet tune to herself. The wind was moaning outside, making the break room seem all the more snug. The smell of roast beef and potatoes drifted through the air and his father laughed and shook his head at something flashing by on the TV screen. His mother set the table, setting out glasses of milk, little jars of butter and jam, and a bottle of ketchup. Plates and silverware clinked as they met the yellow linoleum top of the table. Samuel felt warm and comfortable as his mother removed from the oven a pot roast surrounded by braised carrots and onions. Suddenly, a jet of ice-cold water drenched Samuel's face and he was jolted awake.

Everything had changed for the worse. The wind had turned to a freezing arctic blast. The sky was a glowering melee of swirling clouds, scudding banks of mist and bursts of gravel-like sleet. The sea was no longer a landscape of even swells, but a furious tumult of mountainous waves roaring toward the knarr, one after another. Up watery slopes the boat would be swept, and then down like a toboggan it would rush into seemingly bottomless troughs. Water erupted like a geyser over the side and set kegs and chests in the hold spinning in a swirling tide of sea water. The wind howled through the rigging, moaning like a vengeful ghost. The sun was gone and everything was bathed in a gray half light, shades of slate and green, slashed with white.

Samuel stared about in shock. Balder was standing in the hold, frantically bailing with a scoop. Thor, with great difficulty, strained at the tiller, endeavoring to keep the knarr heading into the waves. One false move on his part and the ship would either roll over sideways

or be swamped. The sail, which had been partially
furled, alternately flapped or strained violently in the
wind. Thokk and Rag were no longer on the yard but
were cowering in the very back of the boat under the
stern post.

A giant wave towered over the knarr and Thor began
to scream something to Balder, his words torn away by
the wind. Balder twisted around, his face a mask of bewilderment. In confusion he jumped out of the hold
and cupped his hand to his ear. With the rumble of an
earthquake, the wave snatched the knarr and lifted it to
its crest. At the roller's very pinnacle a gust of wind
caught the sail and twisted the knarr sideways. A wall
of water came hurtling over the sides. The wooden
block securing the sail in position was torn asunder
and several shroud lines snapped. Like an unleashed
monster, the sail completely unfurled and began to
flap and flail unhindered in the gale, the heavy woolen
cloth sodden with rain. With one snap it knocked Balder
off his feet and he fell stunned to the deck.

Like a wounded whale, the knarr spun and wallowed
through the raging sea. Another tremendous swell
caught the boat and water cascaded over the gunwale,
covering Samuel in a great gushing, ice-cold bath. He
was swept toward the side, hitting his shoulder on a
chest, his eyes blinded by froth and foam. Only the
fragile shield wall caught and saved him from being
washed overboard.

The light faded and Samuel glanced forward. Another giant wave, dark and menacing, was rushing toward

the stricken boat. Samuel was horrified as this green wall approached. He froze in place, barely able to move or breathe. In panic he glanced back at Thor and saw that the thunder god was desperately hacking with his knife at a rope. With a crack the rope parted and the yard plummeted to the deck. The sail floated after, covering the stunned figure of Balder like a shroud. Thor dropped the knife and grabbed the tiller, just as the wave caught the knarr.

Again a wall of foam and spray engulfed Samuel and he was barely able to stay on board. He clung desperately to a loose rope as the water cascaded over him. Coughing and sputtering, his hair plastered to his forehead, he rose to the surface and stared at the wreckage about him. Sea chests were rolling about the deck; several planks were missing or lay splintered against the gunwale. Most of the shields on the right side of the boat had been torn away. But worst of all, the mast had been snapped in two, its stump pointing at the sky like a splintered femur. Through the open hold, Samuel could see the hull, its planking flexing ominously. Rivulets erupted between the boards in vicious little spurts.

In despair, Samuel turned on his back for what he was sure would be his last look at the sky. Frigid eddies of water gushed about his body and down his back. As he glanced upward, he saw Thor heaving at the tiller, his face pale and grim with teeth bared in fear and concentration. Through the deck boards Samuel could feel the next wave gathering under the keel, buffeting the thin strakes of their knarr like a tremendous body blow. But then, ever so slowly, the knarr spun completely around and instead of meeting the crest of the next wave broadside, the slim stern of the knarr sliced through it with grace. Only a crashing spray doused the knarr and its crew.

A groan came from under the sail and Balder appeared on all fours, his face white as ivory, with a huge purple welt on his forehead. Feebly he brushed strands of bedraggled dark hair out of his blurry eyes. He gazed at Samuel with a befuddled look. Suddenly, Thor shouted in a furious voice, "Come on, you lazy rats—to the buckets! We're not out of danger yet!"

Jolted to action by Thor's voice, Balder grabbed Samuel and nearly pushed him into the hold. With a splash, Samuel landed up to his waist in frigid water. Balder followed and began frantically scooping out the incoming sea. Crates and kegs, which had been so carefully packed before, bobbed about or banged against their ankles. Both Samuel and Balder stumbled and reeled as the knarr rocked upward and then dove backward over another wave. With numbed fingers Samuel grabbed an empty keg that floated by, its top having been knocked away. With great effort he filled the keg half full of water, hoisted it over his head and poured it over the side. For every bucket Samuel managed to bail, Balder scooped out ten. Yet, in spite of all their efforts, the knarr wallowed deeper. Every new wave brought a fresh rush of water into the hold and the knarr's seams were leaking like open wounds.

As Samuel became colder and colder in the icy water, he began to despair. His teeth were chattering and his hands and feet felt like blocks of wood. Every other wave cast him on his back or knees as he lost his footing on the slippery wood. Very quickly his senses went numb and his mind grew foggy. Soon all he wanted to do was just lie down and gently float away.

As if in a dream, he imagined himself drifting face up, arms outstretched in a placid stream. Green branches were above his head and beyond them a blue sky full of meandering clouds. Everything was warm and bight with sunlight. Suddenly Balder was over him, shaking his shoulders and shouting into his ears, "You can't give up, Samuel! You have to keep going!" Without knowing it Samuel had collapsed against the side of the hull. He was slowly sinking into the water. Dazed, he stared blankly at Balder. Even his teeth had stopped chattering. Balder shook him again. In a trance, Samuel rose to his feet and picked up his keg. Mechanically, he began to fill it with water and hoist it over the side.

Minutes, then hours passed slowly. Samuel felt like he was in some fuzzy nightmare, horrible but distant. His arms felt like dead weights and his hands like disembodied talons. He no longer felt pain or cold. Dark images, half recognized, flitted across his fading vision. Night fell and the world constricted to a shadow land of shrieking wind, icy water and splintered wood.

After what seemed like days, Samuel's bucket began to scape against the bottom of the boat. Startled, he glanced about and saw that it was daytime and that he was alone. No longer was there an armada of kegs and boxes floating about. They were all shipwrecked in battered heaps around his feet. All that remained of the swirling ocean that had once filled the hold was a shallow pool. The knarr's sides oozed instead of gushed and waterfalls no longer cascaded from the deck above. Cautiously he set down his keg and stumbled to where he could pull himself out of the hold and onto the stern deck.

A keen east wind smote Samuel as he scrambled up out of the hold. He immediately began to shiver. The sky was crystal blue and the sea choppy. The breeze was ruffling the wave tops into a spume of white froth. Miserably, he pulled a sodden blanket from where it lay wadded against the gunwale and draped it over his shoulders. Its wool provided a little protection from the piercing wind. His breath came in faint puffs.

As Samuel peered about, he saw Balder and Thor stumbling around like automatons, their faces gray with fatigue. They had somehow saved the yard and it lay lengthwise on the deck. The sail was thrown nearby in a crumpled heap. Stacked in one pile were all the crates, barrels, oars, blankets, and other supplies that had broken loose, but had not been washed overboard. Several deck boards had been smashed in, leaving gaps like missing teeth. A number of rigging ropes and tackle blocks hung overboard and trailed in the water.

As Thor and Balder labored at saving what they could, the knarr bobbed aimlessly in the wind-raked sea. No one had the strength or time to mind the tiller.

Thokk and Rag were perched on the gunnel preening their feathers and looking no worse for wear. Dumbly, Samuel stumbled over to where they stood. Idly, Thokk turned his head and glanced at Samuel. In a casual voice he said, "Well, at least your sea sickness is gone."

They drifted for two days. Thor and Balder collapsed in an exhausted sleep soon after the ship was out of immediate danger. Both slept for nearly twelve hours straight. Samuel dozed fitfully as the gods snored, often waking with a start when any unusually large swell rocked the knarr. He wrapped himself in as many blankets and pelts as he could scrounge. When warmth finally returned to his body, he began to ache from countless bruises and cuts. A tremendous black and blue welt, edged with yellow, covered his entire right shoulder and he had trouble lifting his arm above his head.

Once Balder and Thor awoke, it took them a long time to get the knarr underway. There were a hundred pressing repair jobs: ropes to be spliced, leaks plugged, and the tiller repaired. All their stocks and equipment needed to be dried, resorted, and restowed. This job was relegated to Samuel. He soon discovered that they had little left to eat and even less to drink. Only two kegs of water had survived the storm. The most distressing damage though, was the broken mast. Without it the knarr could only creep along. Despite some half-hearted efforts at improvising a mast, neither Thor nor Balder could rig a temporary sail. Samuel and his friends needed to find a replacement mast, especially before their meager supplies ran out.

The storm had blown the knarr so far and so fast off course that Thor and Balder found it nearly impossible to reckon where they might be. A tense argument erupted between them as to which way they should head. Thor pressed to go southwest toward Hlesey. Balder said go straight east and back toward Asgard and safe havens. In the end they compromised, turning the knarr's prow northward, the direction in which they both agreed that land was the closest.

Without a mast, Balder and Thor were forced to row. This they did for two straight days. Soon their hands were covered with blisters and sores. Their muscles ached with fatigue. By the evening of the second day, Balder especially seemed near exhaustion. Their relief was great when Thokk, from his perch atop the stern post, saw land the next morning.

This landfall appeared dim and hazy to the north-west, a purplish range of mountains rising above the waves. With renewed vigor Thor and Balder began to row as best they could in the direction of these hills. After a quick lesson from Thor, Samuel was put in charge of the rudder. Having something productive and obviously important to do lifted Samuel's spirits. As the knarr sped toward apparent safety, some of the excitement returned that Samuel had felt that beautiful first morning as they sailed away from Njord's home.

As they neared the coast, Thor became grimmer and grimmer. A shoreline slowly emerged from the sea mist, a long jagged palisade of rocks being continuously assaulted by ranks of white-crested rollers. Springing immediately from atop these sea cliffs was a dense ever-green forest and, in back of that, rose the mountains Thokk had first seen that morning. Dominating the range was a tremendous peak, much higher and more massive than the surrounding crags. This enormous citadel of black granite, cleaved by glaciers and riven by landslides, was an ugly hump of shattered rock. Thor began to curse under his breath as the summit sharp-ened and came into clear focus.

Balder frowned, put down his oar and asked, "What's the matter, Thor? All the blood has left your face."

In a choked voice, Thor answered, "I had no idea that we had been blown so far west and north. If I had, I would have gladly rowed us all the way back to Njord's harbor myself. We are being washed upon a most horri-ble place. Ahead is Nastrond, the land of the dead."

"How can you tell?" Balder asked with a gasp.

"That mountain there, the great ugly one, is Hel-bjorg, the capstone to Hel. I would recognize it any-where. Below its roots live all that is dark and dreadful in our world. The goddess Hel herself lives there, in a hall walled with writhing snakes. Surrounding Helb-jorg is a haunted forest where all the souls of men not condemned to Hel but not blessed to enter Valhalla wander till Gimilli's gates are opened to all. Its trees are the ones we now see. The ghosts who live there are bit-ter with their fate and envious of all that lives." Here Thor paused and bit his lips, and then continued. "Also there is Nidhogg, a great monster that stalks the forest, guarding it and Hel against any invaders. It takes many shapes, sometimes a tremendous serpent, at other times a great white bear. Whatever its form, it is as pale as death and as fierce as a berserker. I am loath to enter this place. To even speak its name strikes my heart cold." With that Thor went silent and stared grimly at the distant shore.

"But do we have any choice?" asked Balder. "Our mast must be replaced. All we need is one good tree and an hour to chop it down. By the looks of it, there are many tall trees in that forest that would suit our purpose well. Nastrond looks huge. Certainly Nidhogg would not notice such a trifling intrusion."

Samuel could see many tall and well-shaped pines rising up through the forest. Trees ideal for making a mast, yet below them an impenetrable gloom, like a black fog, encased the ground level of the forest. Perhaps it was just his imagination or the wind, but Samuel thought he could hear a moan drift out from the forest. A shiver ran down his back. He began to hope that Thor and Balder would, in the end, just decide to row away.

Slowly Thor answered Balder. "Unlike you, Balder, I have been on many journeys and seen much of the world. I am not mocking you, but it is rare that you leave the gates of Asgard. I know how cruel and wicked the outside world can be. I have heard that Nidhogg is loath to let any living thing set foot in Nastrond. He is jealous of every stunted tree and every clod of earth. He drives even birds and squirrels away. You do not know what we are in for if we enter that forest, no matter how brief our visit."

"Well then, we should leave as quickly as we can. Surely there are other forests nearby."

Thor responded, "Unfortunately, there are not. Nastrond is surrounded by the wastes of Jotunheim. There are only mountains and ice fields for hundreds of miles in all directions, all haunted by frost giants and trolls. If we were to find a tree, it would be a scrub willow and in no way suitable for a mast. In order to reach Aegir's hall, or even to return home, we must have a new mast. The trees we see out there are the only ones available."

Balder frowned and said, "Then our course is set. We must risk entering Nastrond."

Thor nodded his head reluctantly. "The tide is certainly carrying us in the right direction. We will soon be driven on hidden reefs if we are not careful. I hope that we can find a place to land on so rocky a coast. If we do get ashore, Samuel and the ravens must remain in the boat. Nastrond is especially dangerous for them. You and I will go into the forest alone and cut down the nearest tree we can find. We will drag it to the boat, branches and all. It can be stripped and peeled once we are back out to sea. After the new mast is on board we must paddle like Angerboda herself is after us." Here Thor paused and looked up. An anxious, haunted look filled his haggard face. He no longer seemed the mighty god of thunder and lightning. Slowly he stood up and said, "Beware, this is the most desperate and dangerous thing we could ever imagine attempting. It will be far more perilous than any storm."

Chapter 16

Thor, Balder, and Samuel paddled along the haunted shores of Nastrond for several hours, looking in vain for a place to land. Nothing looked right. Either half-submerged reefs barred their way, the tide was too violent, or the shore too rocky. Finally they found the outlet of small river running into the sea, a fast milky cascade full of glacial sediment. In desperation they decided to row up this stream in an attempt to bypass the treacherous shoreline. Unfortunately, the river's current was too powerful to paddle against. Balder and Thor were forced to jump into the icy surf and tow the knarr up river with ropes. The gods stumbled and heaved for a long time, making little progress against the frothing water. Numerous times they fell headfirst into the swirling current and came up gasping for breath and clutching for handholds. Samuel was left aboard to manage the tiller as best he could. After an hour of frantic actions, curses, and hard labor, the knarr was finally brought to a spot where it could be moored against a high bank. Thor tied it fore and aft to tree roots and set out the gangplank. Hours had passed since they had first seen the shores of Nastrond in the morning light. The sun was low in the sky—a pale, watery disk even now sinking behind the trees on the far side of the river.

As Samuel peered into the surrounding forest, all he could see were the enormous boles of spruce or fir trees, receding in rank upon rank into ever-deepening shadow. Near the ground these trees were covered by gray denuded branches emerging from the bark like porcupine quills. Higher up, they disappeared into an impenetrable ceiling of evergreen foliage. Not even the smallest ray of sunshine penetrated this clotted mat of green. The ground was level and bare and covered with a thick carpet of brittle brown needles. Sunlight quickly faded to inky blackness in the forest's depths. The whole impression of the place was that of a basement held up by countless pillars and without illumination or exit stairs.

Samuel shivered as he looked at this eerie landscape. Then he noticed something else. Everything was smothered in silence. There was no rush of air through high branches, no bird calls, no squirrels chattering in annoyance, no distant surf, even the river swirling below the knarr seemed muted and faraway. It was as if someone had stuffed his ears with cotton. In surprise Samuel blurted out, "Why is it so quiet?"

His voice boomed in the silence, like a shout in a small room, and both Balder and Thor jumped in alarm. Angered, Thor whirled around and violently motioned for Samuel to be quiet. Balder quickly took

Samuel aside and whispered, "From now on you must be absolutely silent. We have to do as little as possible to attract attention. Whisper and then only if you have to. Do you understand?"

Embarrassed and not a little afraid, Samuel nodded his head. It occurred to him that if merely speaking out loud was dangerous, then this forest must certainly be a very evil place indeed. In fear, he gulped, "You have to let me go along to find a new mast! I can help carry things. I just can't stay here on the boat alone."

"No! Absolutely not," Thor growled. "It is far too hazardous. You must stay here." He than added with a stern look, "Samuel, you have been a man for three years now, act that way."

Thor and Balder quickly began gathering up ropes, an axe and other tools and fabricating torches in preparation for the task ahead of them. As the two gods labored, Thokk and Rag nervously edged up to Samuel, like two fawning beggars. Thokk leaned over and in a barely audible hiss said, "You don't believe in ghosts, do you?"

Samuel stared at Thokk, amazed that he could be sarcastic at a time like this. But then, with a shock, he realized that his old friend was dead serious. Thokk and Rag were both wide-eyed with terror, their bodies trembling with fear. "What's the matter?" Samuel gasped.

"We saw something," chattered Thokk.

"What? What did you see?"

"That tree branch over there. Someone or something brushed it out of the way; only there was no one there."

"Maybe it was just a squirrel," Samuel said in a hoarse voice, desperately trying to keep his courage up.

"A squirrel?" spat Thokk, his eyes bulging. "I don't think so! The only squirrels in this forest are little pale zombie squirrels. I tell you, someone or something is out there watching us. I, for one, am going to find somewhere to hide."

As Thokk and Rag scuttled away, Balder knelt down next to Samuel and put a hand on his shoulder. He then looked him in the eyes and said, "We are leaving now, so be careful. No matter what you see, or hear, do not leave the knarr! If you enter the forest, you will be lost forever, doomed to endlessly roam under its lightless eaves or, worse yet, meet up with Nidhogg. Stay in the boat!"

Samuel said that he understood. Even so Balder continued to stare at him for a long moment as if to emphasize the importance of his words. A tight knot of fear hardened in Samuel's stomach. Finally, Balder stood up and looked at Thor. The two gods then picked up their tools, thumped across the gangplank and disappeared quickly in the gloom. Samuel was left alone in the thick silence on the deck of the knarr. Unceremoniously, Thokk and Rag had decided to crawl under a blanket—two lumps scrunched against the gunwale.

Samuel sat down on a barrel and put his head in his hands. A long time passed and nothing happened. In the morose light everything appeared gray and without color. The boat gently rocked at its moorings. All was quiet. In spite of imminent danger, Samuel's eyes began to droop and his mind went hazy. The days of seasickness, nights of restless sleep, and the ordeal of the storm had left Samuel exhausted to the bone. Now in the twilight, on the swaying boat, he fell asleep.

Suddenly, Samuel sat bolt upright. Something or someone was behind him. He spun around. Nothing was there, nothing had moved and nothing was out of place. Yet as he stared, a deck board close by emitted a long and pronounced creak and he felt as though someone had run an icy brush through his hair. He stood frozen in place and completely bewildered. Somewhere in the far distance he heard, or thought that he could hear, the chopping of wood.

Something crashed to the deck behind Samuel and he whirled around. A silver cup rolled across the planking and bumped against the gunwale. A moment of silence followed.

Then the lid of a nearby sea chest flopped open with a bang. A wooden plate levitated out, hovered for a second and then hurtled off into the forest. A faint laugh, harsh and defiant, came to Samuel's ears. Petrified, Samuel staggered backward and tripped over the barrel he had just been sitting on. With a rumble, the keg went rolling across the deck, the noise shattering the smothering silence. Samuel barely regained his balance, grabbing onto a sail crutch for support. For several minutes all was quiet and nothing moved. Samuel exhaled a great sigh of relief, only to have it catch in his throat. A sharp staccato tapping began in the forest. It was the rap of a stick against a tree; Click, Click, Clickclickclick. On and on it went.

Samuel stared about him—eyes wide with terror. The light grew dimmer as the sun set out beyond the forest. Nothing moved. Nothing stirred. The rapping droned on like Morse code. Barely discernable above it, Samuel heard the hollow thunk of an axe against wood.

All at once the clicking stopped. There was a splash and a stick floated past the knarr, spinning and whirling in the river's current. Samuel stared back into the forest, afraid of what he might see. Everything was still and peaceful. He gave a little gasp of relief. But then, at the very edge of his vision, in among the trees, the forest floor began to rustle in one great disturbance. A swelling and spreading shock wave of up-thrown needles and sticks rushed across the ground like a sea flood swirls over a tidal flat. A faint chorus of groans and wails drifted through the air.

Samuel glanced desperately around the knarr, the blanket where Rag and Thokk had been hiding now lay flat and empty upon the deck. In wild panic he grabbed the silver cup and hurled it at the advancing wave. It sailed through the air, only to be knocked aside and trampled underfoot by the unseen horde. Faintly in the distance, Thor's axe kept up its steady beat.

Samuel stumbled back as the ghostly phalanx charged nearer. It seemed to his horrified eyes that the knarr was about to be swallowed up in a raging tornado of vengeful spirits. They were all around now, surging toward the boat. Tree branches whipped about or snapped with vicious pops. A hollow moan, like wind through a cave filled the air. Here and there faint wispy shapes, like shreds of mist, congealed into spectral arms and legs or bodies, only to dissolve again like melting frost.

Samuel could not bear the horror of this advancing sea of wraiths. He desperately looked about for some place to run or hide. Behind him rushed the frigid river, impossible to wade or swim. Then, like the tick of a clock heard through a nightmare, the faint sound of Thor's axe came again to Samuel's ears. Panic-stricken, Samuel lunged across the gangplank and toward this slim beacon of hope. This frantic escape route led Samuel straight at the advancing army of ghosts. As he burst into their ranks, his arms and legs were grasped by a hundred fingers of ice. He struggled and thrashed as if drowning in an icy sea. A leering face, skin pulled tight across a pallid skull, floated by like a cloud of smoke. He turned and twisted desperately, fighting his way through. With one final squirm he freed himself and ran unhindered across the forest floor.

Samuel raced toward the sounding axe, heedless of trunks and low-hanging branches. He glanced back, and to his horror saw the wave of needles and sticks race after him. An ominous crackling, like the onrush of a forest fire, came to his ears. Samuel raced on, his breath coming in tremendous gasps. His lungs felt on fire. Sticks caught at this clothes, and he heard his cape separate with a rending tear. Deeper into the forest he sped, the band of light that marked the river becoming more and more obscured by tree trunks until it was lost all together. Soon he was in near blackness, guided only by the sound of Thor's axe.

Suddenly, the chopping of wood stopped. There was a cracking pop followed by the rush of branches and a dull thump. All was silent. Samuel could not hear a thing except for the laboring of his own breath and the crunch of his running feet on the ground. Suddenly, he hit a tree head on and fell stunned to the ground. Dazed he staggered to his feet, horrified by what he thought was still following him. Heedless of direction he sprinted on, only to run into another tree in the darkness. This time he halted to listen. He no longer heard the pursuing rustle of needles. Everything again was smothered in silence. Wobbly, he regained his feet, pinpricks of light danced in front of his eyes. Blindly he grouped for the next tree. He was enveloped in a thick blackness, nearly impenetrable to his tear-clouded eyes.

Samuel tried to call out, but all that emerged from his throat was a harsh rasp. His lungs felt rubbed raw and his breath came in great heaves. Blood was on his face; a low-hanging branch had sliced a great gash across his forehead. He sobbed with despair and pain. Like a blind man he felt ahead with outstretched arms, fingers trembling, until he reached the next tree. Everything was fading to nothingness; he could barely even see the ground below. Worst of all, he had lost all sense of direction.

On Samuel floundered, wildly looking around for any kind of landmark or glimmer of light that might point the way back to the river or to where Thor and Balder might be. He began to feel nauseated. Even his sense of up and down was being distorted by the lack of light. He paused, strained his eyes and stared off into the impenetrable night, hoping against hope to see some spark of light, some faint glimmer. Desperately he gaped about, slowly turning around in a circle. Suddenly he froze. Fear welled through him like an electrical shock, every muscle in his body was paralyzed.

Through distended eyes, Samuel saw a giant bear drifting silently among the trees. Its fur was bleached the sickly white of a cave creature. Like a great cloud of fog, it wove silently in and out between trunks, pale and luminescent amid the darkness. Its mouth was a vivid slash of blue-purple. The bear was larger than Thor's goats, as big as an elephant. Bulging muscles rippled like knots of iron under a loose coat of fur. It sniffed the ground, bared two long rows of yellow teeth, and emitted a thunderous purr. It stopped and raised its muzzle high above the ground. Slowly the bear swung its head back and forth, searching the air for scent. It was then that Samuel saw its eyes. They were frosted over with a gray glaze, like sand-blasted glass. This disfigurement divested it of any soul or spirit, other than one of unparalleled fierceness. In spite of its blindness, Samuel knew, with a cold spasm of fear, that this monster was well aware of his presence.

Samuel slowly stumbled backward. His feet seemed glued in place, every muscle numbed by fear. A twig snapped under his foot and the bear froze in place. Samuel opened his mouth to scream, but no sound came. With a growl like a rolling drum the bear swung its head toward Samuel and took a step in his direction.

Suddenly, an icy hand gripped Samuel's shoulder from behind in a vice-like grip. He was swung violently around. Emerging from the darkness was a milk-white face distorted with terror. Something behind the head fluttered and flapped. A dull haze passed over Samuel's eyes and he passed out.

When Samuel regained consciousness he was being carried under Balder's arm like a rolled-up carpet, his own limbs flailing wildly as the god raced through the trees. Above the crackle of needles under Balder's feet, Samuel could hear the rush of wings and the tread of something much larger following behind. This pursuer was shaking the ground, splintering branches and brushing aside trees. Slowly the light began to grow, shapes sharpened and emerged from the clinging darkness. Suddenly, there was the hollow thump of Balder's feet on the gangplank and Samuel was violently cast upon the knarr's deck. He tumbled to rest next to a heavy pine log. As he lay sprawled in a dazed heap, Samuel saw that Thor was already on board and was hacking with an axe at the ropes anchoring the boat to shore. Samuel started to rise, but Balder screamed at him to stay down. The sound of shattering wood and heavy footfalls grew in Samuel's ears like the rush of a locomotive. With a crash the knarr began bobbing and moving in the river's current as the ropes finally parted. Balder yelled at Thor, who whirled toward shore, his eyes growing wide with fear. With a mighty heave he hurled the axe. An angry screech erupted like a trumpet, piercing the muffling silence and drowning out the sound of the river. Thor took a step back, picked up an oar and brandished it over his shoulder, his face pale with desperation. At that moment the knarr was caught by the river's current. It swirled around, gathered speed and rushed down the river, out of the forest, and into the waiting ocean.

Like a toy, the knarr bobbed and pitched in the tangle of waves and currents that rippled and eddied where the rushing river met the pounding ocean. Both Balder and Thor stared at the shore as if gripped in a trance, holding their breaths. Suddenly, there was a tremendous splash; the bear had entered the water. Both gods grabbed their oars and began to row violently, their shoulders straining and bulging with every stroke and their heads bowed in total concentration. Samuel felt nauseated with fear and shock as he lay panting on the deck. All at once even holding his head up seemed an overwhelming task, a labor too great to bear. His eyelids fluttered closed and he fell into a deep impenetrable slumber. His limbs were cast aimlessly amid the clutter of the deck and the branches of the felled pine.

In the end, Samuel and his friends escaped the bear. It turned back about a mile from shore, trailing a slick of blood. Samuel slept for several hours. When he awoke, all that he heard was the gentle lapping of water against the hull. The knarr rose and fell above a gentle swell. The air was cold, but there was no wind. A half moon had risen over the eastern horizon and its pale face bathed everything in a cool gray light. Someone had put a blanket over Samuel and its coarse fabric rubbed against his cheek. He rose and saw Balder and Thor standing nearby, next to the freshly cut log now lashed to the deck. They were conversing in a low tone.

Samuel stood up and stumbled over to the gods. In a cracked and hoarse voice he said, "I'm sorry. I'm so sorry. They were after me, thousands of ghosts. I had to run."

Both Thor and Balder looked at Samuel for a long time, their faces veiled by shadow. Finally Balder said in a quiet voice, "That was a horrible place, beyond reason and courage. Even for Thor and me to have set foot in there was folly. For a mere human such as yourself to have survived is a miracle. Especially since you aroused the interest of Nidhogg. We were desperate and we did a desperate thing. By fantastic luck we came through unscathed. Feel no shame and try to forget your hours amid those trees."

Samuel nodded his head dumbly and then gasped, "Where are Thokk and Rag? We didn't leave them behind, did we? Please say that they're all right."

"They're fine. They're up on the stern post," answered Thor.

Glancing back, Samuel caught sight of his friends, calmly preening their feathers in the moonlight.

Thokk raised his head and in a calm, deadpan voice said, "Finally come around, have you? We thought you might be dead, scared to an early grave. In any case, I'm touched that you think so keenly of us."

"What happened to you? One moment you were there, under the blanket, and the next you were gone," said Samuel.

"Well, you see," said Thokk, "the blanket seemed a flimsy shelter, especially when that graveyard of ghosts came wailing through the trees. Being the ingenious fellow that I am, I found a nice stout barrel down in the hold to crawl inside. Rag wanted to stay up top and help you out, but I was able to convince him (for once) that discretion was the better part of valor. We stayed in our little bolthole for a long time, listening to you whine and whimper, wondering why you didn't find your own barrel to squeeze into. Then, like someone deranged, you went screaming off into the forest. Of course Rag started feeling bad—why I'll never know— and decided to go chasing after you. By some miracle he was able to find both you and Balder. He then led Balder back to where you were blundering around—just in the nick of time as I understand. Good thing for you that we ravens can see and hear exceptionally well."

Samuel looked at Rag and in a quiet voice said, "Thank you. You've saved me once again."

"Rag is quite a bird, Samuel," said Balder. "He's braver and certainly more loyal than most people. Keep him well."

As Rag ruffled a wing and looked impassively at Balder, Samuel replied, "I don't think that I own Rag. He's really more of a friend than anything else."

A faint smile crossed Balder's lips and he replied, "He is indeed a very good friend. But then, ravens are special birds, and Rag, under those rumpled feathers of his, is certainly more than he seems."

"Yeah, more trouble than he's worth," Thokk mumbled under his breath.

After a while, Thor and Balder began rowing again and continued throughout the rest of the night. By morning Nastrond and Helbjorg were completely out of sight. After a short rest and a breakfast of cheese and smoked herring smeared with butter, they set to work constructing a new mast. Having lost most of their tools in the storm, they were forced to remove the pine's branches and bark with a sword. This was dangerous work and both Thor and Balder cut their hands badly in the process. After that, it was still a long and laborious task to size and shape the log. While they worked, the knarr wallowed aimlessly in mid-ocean. They hoped the tide would not carry them back to Nastrond or that some other disaster wouldn't strike.

As the hours ticked by, Samuel tried to help as best he could. Thor set him to work tidying up the hold, bailing out the bottom of the boat and keeping the deck clear of shavings. These tasks only took up a few hours, and soon Samuel found himself sitting on a sea chest, idly watching the two gods labor. As a day came and went, his boredom turned to depression and he began to brood. He fretted about their shortage of water and the supplies they had lost in the storm. Every dark cloud became the harbinger of a new gale, every shadow on the northern horizon materialized into the evil shores of Nastrond. In particularly dark moments, his thoughts returned to the haunted forest and the giant white bear with its sightless eyes. Only with a shudder could he dispel the image from his mind.

Finally, with great effort the stump of the old mast was unstepped, cast overboard, and the new mast was raised in its place. Ropes were re-rigged, blocks replaced, the sail repaired, and the main backstay secured. When all was at last ready, the yard was hoisted and the sail unfurled.

Like a horse let out of its stall, the knarr came alive. The sail billowed with air, the prow heeled over, and the boat began to speed forward. Thor turned the helm south and west, straight toward Hlesey. As the bow sliced through a sea of mounting swells, the waves thumped against the keel. A shower of glistening spray erupted over the gunwale with each swell and doused the deck with clear green water. Sea foam clung to the figure-head like saliva from the mouth of a charging stallion. Samuel's spirits rose as the knarr dashed before the wind, the sharp breeze bathing his skin with salt and mist. His black mood evaporated. Hope was restored.

Chapter 17

For many days the knarr was pushed south by a brisk arctic wind. With this favorable breeze, Samuel and his friends were soon close to their original course to Hlesey. The weather was bitter and Samuel was always cold. A coat of white ice formed on the deck and gunwale. It made the boat appear as though it were covered with white icing. Samuel was given the job of chipping off the worst accumulations.

Although they were now making good time, the expedition's situation was grim. Samuel and the gods were down to two cups of water a day and mere scraps of salted herring, ground oats, and bits of cheese. Worst of all, the knarr seemed to be falling apart. The deck, especially in the front of the boat, was in terrible shape; planks were missing, the crutch had been broken away and most of the shields were gone. The sail itself was ripped and frayed and several rigging ropes were lost. Even a few of the spruce root cords that bound the hull boards to their supporting ribs had parted. Balder spent most of one day trying to repair leaks. He succeeded in stanching the worst hemorrhages with wads of wool. Even so, the hold had to be bailed out every few hours, in what soon became a tiresome routine.

Thor and Balder were near collapse. The days and nights of unending labor required to sail the knarr, tend its wounds, and man the tiller had taken their toll. The gods struggled through their chores as if in a daze, hardly speaking to each other or to Samuel. Thokk and Rag were equally worn out. They spent most of their time sleeping on the yard, heads drooping and feathers unpreened.

Samuel, himself, felt as though he had been through a savage fight. He was constantly exhausted and his whole body ached. One afternoon he looked down at his hands and was shocked by what he saw. They were red, chapped, and bleeding. A nail had been torn off and one knuckle was ominously black and blue. Samuel, like the knarr and its crew, was reaching the limits of his endurance.

Then one morning Samuel awoke to find Thor and Balder kneeling over a curious device set up near the stern of the boat. Samuel had many times seen the plain wooden pedestal emerging from the deck near the tiller. He had always imagined that it had something to do with rigging. But now, to his amazement, Thor had fastened a flat disc to its top. This plate was marked along its rim with thirty-two evenly spaced notches. By each indentation were inscribed several runes. In the center of the disc was a movable pointer, like the hand of a clock. The whole contraption looked like the spinner in a child's board game. As Samuel came closer, he noticed that one notch was aimed straight at the sun, now just peeping over the horizon. He also observed that the pointer hand was directly aligned with the bow. In a sleepy voice, he asked the gods, "What's going on?"

"We're trying to get ourselves back on course," Balder said. His voice was tired and edged with irritation.

"Try nothing! We are back on course, like an arrow to its target. Just look at the bearing wheel," Thor crowed with obvious delight. "I'm a better sailor than you, Balder my friend, think I am. We'll be at Aegir's Hall in no time; just you wait and see. Be an optimist for once!"

"I guess the wheel isn't lying," Balder said hesitantly. "But after all we've been through, I begin to wonder if we are not cursed. It was supposed to be a straight shot from Njord's harbor to Hlesey. Yet so far we've had to weather a storm, survive Nastrond, and fix a broken mast, and now we're nearly out of food and water."

"Bahh! Those things are all behind us now. What else could go wrong?" scoffed Thor.

"Plenty," muttered Balder. "Plenty."

Later in the day Balder was given the grim satisfaction of seeing his words proven true. As the sun sank to the horizon, the wind ceased and the sea became calm and unruffled. Slowly and irresistibly, a thick bank of fog rolled over the knarr like a slow-moving avalanche. The air became damp and chill. The last rays of the sun were blotted out in a clammy mist. Soon the sail was hanging from the yard like a wet rag and puddles of drizzle formed on the deck. The ends of the boat became distant shadows. As night fell, a gray darkness enveloped the boat. Balder sank down on the deck, put his head in his hands, and moaned, "How many misfortunes must we endure?"

"Come on, Balder," Thor cajoled. "It's not as bad as it seems. By my reckoning Aegir's island is very close, perhaps only one or two days away."

"What good is that? There's no wind and we can't row. If we tried to move, we would only end up going in circles. Hlesey might as well be a thousand miles away in this fog," snapped Balder in a bitter voice.

"Come, come, Balder, don't be such a bellyacher," answered Thor. "Stop mewling like an orphaned calf."

That was too much for Balder. He jumped to his feet, threw up his arms, and yelled, "And why shouldn't I complain? I am not some jolly adventurer or experienced campaigner. I should be at home with my wife and son. Tyr should be here—or Odin himself—not me. They are hardened to the rigors of war and questing. They would laugh at this fog and wait it out for a hundred days. I am already sick of it. Sick to the point of madness. I'm also sick of poor food, sick of no water, sick of danger, sick of this boat, and sick to the point of death with your blithe, unfounded confidence."

As Balder raved, Thor crossed his arms and stared impassively off into space. When Balder, his voice hoarse and gasping, finally finished, Thor quietly said, "You're correct that we cannot row right now, but let us wait until morning and perhaps then our luck will change. We all, especially you, need a good night's rest."

Balder groaned, shook his head, and stalked off toward the front of the knarr.

Usually Thor and Balder kept watch at night, trading off around midnight. That night, however, they cast their fate to the wind and lay down to sleep along with Samuel. They all crawled into their leather sleeping bags, covering themselves with as many pelts and blankets as they could scrounge. They even wrapped themselves with a tent awning that had been stowed away under the aft deck. Even so, Samuel woke often, the damp gnawing at his bones. Balder did not sleep much either. He seemed consumed with worry. Whenever Samuel glanced his way, the god's eyes were wide open and his teeth clenched shut like a trap. Only Thor slept the night through, his tremendous snores echoing like a broken horn.

A little before dawn, Samuel awoke with a start. Both gods were already up and moving about. Balder was mixing the last of the dry oats with a little water to make a sticky paste for breakfast. Thor was standing at the back of the boat near the bearing wheel.

The fog still enveloped them in a dismal cloud. Samuel had long ago lost all sense of direction. There was no way of telling north from south or east from west.

Suddenly Thor said, "Forget breakfast, Balder, let's row!"

"Why would we do that?" Balder answered, his voice thick with irritation. "We'll just expend the last of our strength or run ourselves upon some rocks."

"Just trust me," was all Thor said, suppressing a smirk as he turned his back to Balder.

Wearily, Balder covered the bowl of ground oats with a cloth and picked up an oar. When both he and Thor were in rowing position, Thor pointed off to one side of the boat and said, "We will go in that direction. Try to follow my stroke."

"Whatever you say Thor. But, if you ask me, this is a fool's gambit."

"Just row and hope the sea is kind to us," Thor answered with a smile.

Thor and Balder labored for several hours, pulling their oars across the smooth sea. It was unnerving to go forward into the unknown. More than once Samuel imagined rocks or reefs suddenly materializing out of the mist. All at once, Thor called, "Stop." Then, as the knarr drifted, he proceeded to do something extremely strange. He sat very still and stared at the palm of his right hand for several minutes. Ever so slightly he would adjust, back and forth, the angle of his hand.

Finally, when he could take it no longer, Balder demanded in a tired and frustrated voice, "What are you doing Thor? Have you contracted a mind fever?"

Thor just shook his head and waved down Balder's complaint. As he did so, Thokk called out from the back of the boat, "I didn't know you were a palm reader, Thor. What does your hand say? I'll wager the news isn't good. Perhaps your life line has grown a little shorter?"

Thor ignored Thokk's jibes and continued to gaze studiously at his hand. Finally he looked up and pointed out a new direction for the ship to head. He also instructed Samuel to lean slightly on the tiller and keep a light, but even, pressure on it. Again Balder and Thor began to row, bowing their heads with every stroke.

The hours passed, unending and dreary. Samuel sat on a chest next to the tiller and sneezed as condensation ran off his hat and splashed on his nose. The top of his pants, soaked with rain, clung to his thighs in a chill embrace. Trickles of ice water ran down his neck and back and into his shoes. His hands were raw and red on top and wrinkled and white underneath. Blurry with fatigue, his eyes itched and burned. His toes were numb with cold. Samuel had never been as uncomfortable in his life as he was now. Yet, on and on they went in this sodden, vaporous world, without landmark or horizon. Samuel's shivered and wondered if he would ever see the sun again.

Suddenly Thokk gasped. "Look! The mist is lighter up front—there by the figurehead."

Indeed, the bow of the knarr was bathed in a sharper light. The fog was turning from a woolen gray to milky yellow. Fatigue and despair were cast off like old clothes. With great thrusts at the oars, Balder and Thor heaved the knarr free of the clinging mist and out into the sunshine of late afternoon. A few rags of vapor clung to the mast, only to be swept away, like cobwebs before a broom, by a fresh breeze. The sail filled and the boat gained speed.

Thor let out a cheer and even Balder smiled. Samuel nearly cried with relief. The sun had never seemed brighter or more welcome to Samuel. As he savored their escape from the fog bank, Samuel looked out across the gentle seascape. He saw a few distant clouds to the south, and, then something else. A mere smudge on the northwest horizon. "Look, look, over there! What is that?" he shouted.

Thor sat bolt up right, letting his oar trail in the water. He shaded his eyes and then proclaimed in a loud and happy voice, "We made it! Ahead is Hlesey, Aegir's island home. Tomorrow we will be there."

Balder and Thor cast aside their oars and danced with joy upon the deck. Samuel let go of the tiller and gave a shrill whoop. Even Thokk was happy, dipping his head up and down with excitement. Rag flapped up above the knarr, stared at the island and then swooped down to land on the deck.

When quiet returned, Balder turned to Thor and—in an envious voice—asked, "How did you do that? How did you know in what direction to row?"

Thor glanced at Balder slyly and replied, "Just an old sailor's secret."

"Come on Thor, why did you keep looking at your palm?"

"I wasn't looking at my hand. I was looking at this."

Thor held out a small flat rock, which shone slightly iridescent in the sunlight. Balder took the chunk, gazed at it skeptically, and asked, "What's so special about this?"

Thor replied, "Turn the flat side away from the sun and tell me what color it is."

"Pink."

"Now angle it toward the sun."

"Incredible! Now it's tinged with blue."

"That's right, and it does that no matter the amount of cloud or fog hiding the sun. Njord, who gave it to me, called it a sunstone. All that time you thought I was going crazy staring at my hand, I was turning the stone until it faced directly into the sun. Once I knew where the sun was, I knew which way to row. I told you that you didn't give me enough credit as a sailor."

"I guess I was wrong to mistrust you," Balder admitted ruefully.

Thor laughed and said, "Of course you shouldn't have doubted me. But no matter, things have turned out well." Then in a more serious tone he added, "Let's get to work, we need to adjust the sail and get ready for our arrival tomorrow in Aegir's Hall. That's when things will really get sticky. We had better be well prepared."

On through the few remaining hours of daylight the knarr sailed toward Hlesey. The breeze increased as they left the fog bank behind. Soon they were charging through a choppy sea. Once the sail was set, Balder fixed a meager dinner of salted fish and water. In spite of the harsh, oily taste, Samuel gobbled his portion down. They had been on half rations so long that any food was now savored like a banquet. Water was ladled out like rare honey.

As they ate, Balder turned to Thor and said, "Well, tomorrow we finally confront Aegir. How should we handle it?"

Thor frowned and looked at his fish. "I don't know. The battle tomorrow will be a war of words, not axes, delicate negotiations instead of brute force. I'm not good at such things. When Loki and I go out on our adventures, I always leave the talking to him. He's the one with a quick tongue—not I."

"Loki would indeed be the perfect man for this situation," Balder said with a sigh, "Unfortunately, I doubt that Aegir will even allow him to speak. I am afraid it's all up to us. We had better have a good plan."

"Well, perhaps you could come up with a solution for once," Thor growled irritably. "Remember, this is your mission after all. Odin sent you and Samuel to retrieve Mjollnir, not me. I just came along to help. Don't expect me to bail us out of every tight spot on this trip."

Balder's face colored and he replied, "Of course, of course; you're absolutely right. It's just that I thought that you might have something in mind." Here he looked out to sea and said slowly in a worried voice, "To tell you the truth, I feel quite out of my depth. I am not at all skilled in diplomacy. Worse yet, I'm not at all sure what we are trying to achieve. Are we here to parlay a fair settlement for Mjollnir and ransom for Loki? Or is our mission to simply demand their immediate release? Odin seemed to direct us to do one thing while implying that we should do another."

"I am as muddled as you are concerning Odin's instructions," replied Thor. "On the other hand, I know exactly what Aegir will do. He will haggle with us for Mjollnir and Loki. He will begin by demanding a fantastic price, probably the sun and the moon with the stars thrown in. Whatever we do, we can't take his first offer. We must whittle his price down and pray that luck is on our side."

"Surely our negotiations will not be reduced to petty bartering!" Balder said incredulously. "Mjollnir is the most mighty weapon under the sky, Loki is an Aesir god, Aegir is the Lord of all oceans, and we are the sworn representatives of Odin, the All Father. A war between Asgard and Hlesey hangs in the balance. I cannot believe Aegir would reduce such matters to the level of crude deal making."

"Balder, don't be so naive," scoffed Thor. "Aegir is a bandit, after all that he can get. Hlesey is far worse than the meanest trading post back in Midgard—just you wait and see. Aegir will lie, cheat, and exploit any weakness on our part to his advantage." Here Thor leaned forward and in a stern voice continued. "When we speak to Aegir, we must be aggressive, full of iron and salt. We must stand our ground. If we back down to him at all, even for the most minor or trivial reason, he'll soon have us both under his power. Pay Aegir no homage or respect, no bowing or scraping before his throne, no fancy titles or address, no 'My Lord' or 'My Majesty.' Mark my words, if we humble ourselves at all, we'll not only fail our mission but we'll end up Aegir's prisoners, just like Loki. We must be sly, ready to pounce if Aegir makes a mistake or lowers his guard. Give him no mercy. If we can cheat Aegir out of his treasures, all the better."

Balder shook his head and blurted, "I can't act as you describe; it's not my way! I am neither fierce nor cunning enough. Besides, I think our best hope lies in reasoning with Aegir. Let's hear his side of the story. Perhaps he has a case against the Aesir that needs to be fairly addressed. He was, after all, the one who found Mjollnir. Surely with all that is at stake, a good and reasonable solution can be found."

Thor rolled his eyes and groaned. "If you believe any of that, then we are lost already. The only way for us to prevail tomorrow is for you to stiffen your spine and help me stare Aegir down. Only then will we have any chance of winning the release of Mjollnir and Loki. For once in your life, Balder, don't be a mouse."

Balder stiffened and replied, "I know myself, and my strengths. I will not squabble like a toothless merchant or threaten like a berserker crazed by toadstools. I will speak the truth and argue for reason; it's the best that I can do."

With a jerk, Thor threw up his hands and stalked off, muttering as he went. Balder stared at Thor with a look of injured dignity. Samuel finished his dinner in silence.

Soon darkness fell and the long winter night began. Not wanting to overshoot the island in the dark, Thor ran down the sail, threw over the anchor and let the knarr drift. The gods, exhausted from their long day of rowing, retired to their sleeping bags on the deck. Thokk and Rag alighted on the yard and tucked their heads under their wings. Only Samuel remained awake, sitting on a sea chest near the tiller, his mind drifting aimlessly.

As Samuel sat listening to the waves slap against the hull, he stared out at the dark ocean, a landscape of rolling swells. A full moon, bright and cold, rose above the sea haze, into a crystalline blackness. Sea foam glowed luminous in the lunar light. A chill breeze caressed his windburned cheeks. Stars filled the sky, pinpricks in a black velvet tent. As he gazed at the moon, he remembered something he had once read about ancient Egypt, that the pharaohs believed the moon to be the eye of Thoth, the god of the night. It was easy for Samuel to imagine the moon as a giant eye, the orb of some remote, omnipotent being, staring down on his sleeping creation.

As Samuel pondered the silvery disc, half-formed thoughts flowed across his consciousness like water over a smooth rock. "What a god that would be, to have the moon for an eye. He would be larger than the earth, remote and ethereal, a vast cloud in space. Could he see everyone and everything with that single eye of his? How could he? He would only be able to see great events, earthquakes and tidal waves, wars and epidemics. To him I would only be a speck, a bit of dirt in a dusty world. How can you really care about that which you cannot see?" Here Thor let out a great snore and turned over in his sleep. Balder mumbled something and his face twitched. Samuel looked at them with affection and thought, "Here are two gods, I guess. I've yet to see them do anything that my father couldn't do, yet I would choose them over the moon any day."

The next day the sun rose in a clear sky, banishing the stars behind a blue curtain. Hlesey had drifted off to the north, its rugged shore now gray green and more distinct. After breakfast, during which they drank the rest of their water, Balder and Thor set the sail and slowly maneuvered the knarr toward Aegir's home.

Hours passed and it was slow going against a contrary wind, but finally Hlesey filled the horizon and Samuel could hear the surf crash against its shore. Aegir's island was a broken land of high, steep mountains, monstrous cliffs, and black gravel beaches. No trees grew upon its slopes. They were covered instead with either tundra, boulders, or snow. Surrounding Hlesey were several islets. Stone tusks jutting out of the ocean, jagged and hundreds of feet tall, their sides stained white with bird droppings. As the knarr passed, vast clouds of birds erupted from their craggy sides, to go whirling about: silver-gray Kittiwakes, black-and-white puffins, and white, yellow-billed gulls.

Thor and Balder furled the sail and began to row. Samuel was again put in charge of the tiller. As the gods labored, concentration knit their brows. They were now in dangerous and tricky waters. Thor, his voice edged with anxiety and his eyes ever scanning for hidden reefs and sand bars, would abruptly bark directions to Samuel. Slowly they worked themselves around to the western rim of the island. There, like the opening of a gate, an extremely narrow fjord appeared. It penetrated deep into the island like an immense crack, its sides lined with steep and unclimbable cliffs. Purple shadows filled the cleft and the water shone black within. At the fjord's mouth, the sea boiled and rippled in a confluence of currents, a field of warring whitecaps and vicious waves broken by patches of strange flat water, smooth as sheets of marble. The shore was lined with a huge rill of pillared basalt, columns of which had broken lose and toppled into the sea. These jagged shards lay half submerged like broken jaws amid the thundering waves.

Carefully the gods guided the knarr toward the entrance to the fjord. Suddenly, the knarr was caught by a savage riptide and began to wildly twist and buck about. With a violent jerk, the tiller was torn from Samuel's grip and he was thrown to the deck. The knarr was picked up and rushed toward one side of the fjord, as if grabbed by an unseen hand. A gnashing row of rock teeth loomed out of the water, awash in a froth of foam and driftwood. Samuel froze as these pitiless fangs loomed inexorably closer. Thor screamed at Balder, who dropped his oar, lunged across the deck and grabbed the tiller. In one mighty heave he jammed it against the gunwale. Thor, in a frenzy of desperate and frantic motions, rowed backward with his lone oar. Just in the nick of time, the knarr whirled around and spun away from the mouth of stone. Thor continued to paddle, first one way then the other, until the knarr was under control and pointing in the right direction. Everyone sat wheezing for breath, shattered by how close they had come to shipwreck.

With shaky hands, Balder raised the tiller and locked it in place with a leather strap. He then retook his seat next to Thor. Nether he nor Thor looked at Samuel or said anything to him. For a long time Samuel sat silently at the back of the boat, stunned by shame and fear. He looked at his hands and saw that a great blister had formed on his right palm. This wound was now torn open and a flap of yellow skin hung loosely to one side. He held his hand tightly to ward off the pain.

In a rush of feathers, Thokk and Rag, alighted next to Samuel. Rag pecked at his sleeve and Thokk, in a conspiratorial tone, whispered, "Don't feel too bad. I don't think our two wonder giants, if they were your size, would have done any better back there than you did. You're just a half-pint, after all. What do they expect?"

Samuel smiled weakly; somehow Thokk's clumsy attempt at sympathy was comforting. With the back of his hands he rubbed his eyes, sniffed, and then looked up and about.

They were now gliding through a narrow, shadow-cloaked canyon. The sky, like a blue snake, slithered above their heads. The air was bitter cold like an icebox, and it bit at Samuel's ears and fingers and made his eyes water. Sheer cliffs of volcanic rock rose directly out of the water and soared hundreds of feet into the air. The stone was streaked black, brown, and gray, and mottled with lichens. Scattered here and there were tufts of tundra grass clinging to ledges. Each clump was dusted with snow or encased in crystals of frost. Like fluted columns, frozen waterfalls tumbled into the sloshing sea. Slides of shattered rock choked narrow ravines. Flocks of birds whirred and soared above the knarr and filled the canyon with a chattering, squawking din. Rag and Thokk flinched and crouched as a skua, beak agape, wheeled low overhead. A seal poked its head above the waves and stared at them with dog eyes. Suddenly, they rounded a bend, the passageway widened to a bay, and the knarr shot out into the sunlight. Ahead lay Aegir's hall. They had reached their goal at last.

Chapter 18

Aegir's hall lay at the far end of a broad expanse of water. Surrounding this bay were wide gravel strands bisected by outcrops of lava slag and tongues of ice. Rafts of ice floated in the blue-black water or were washed up onto the beaches like stranded whales. Above the water's edge the land rose steeply in broad steps to rocky crags that lined the horizon like broken teeth. The hillsides were swathed in a thick coat of snow, torn here and there by avalanches. At the far extremity of the bay, one sharp peak rose above all the rest. This mountain was almost completely covered by glaciers and snowfields, except at its summit, where patches of black rock showed stark against the snow. A frail column of steam rose like the breath of a sleeping dragon from the mountain's very top.

Balder and Thor rowed slowly and the knarr glided gracefully across the calm waters, leaving hardly any wake. Samuel gawked with upturned head and open mouth at the fierce and desolate landscape. Even Thokk and Rag looked about in wonder.

Slowly the sun peeled back a blue haze of shadow cloaking the western face of the highest mountain. Like a conjurer's trick, a single shaft of light broke through a cloud and illuminated a tremendous cliff that rose straight out of the water. A narrow expanse of this sheer rock face, perhaps two hundred feet high, had been polished to a smooth surface and shaped to an arch. The worked rock shimmered in the sun, dazzling Samuel's eyes with its brilliance. High up, a few windows pierced the arch. At its base was a huge double door in a shallow niche. Surrounding the door was a façade of pillars sculpted from the living rock. Issuing out from the portal, like water from a spring, was a broad stone staircase. These steps cascaded down several flights, widening as they went, until they reached the waves. This, in all its glory, was the entrance to Aegir's royal home.

Below the stairs, at the water's edge, was a large quay. From it projected several smaller piers. A large fleet of ships and boats was secured to this dock or anchored nearby in rows. Mighty drakars—dragon ships—dominated this jumble of humble knarrs, proud longships, and tiny fishing boats. Some crafts were as small as canoes, while others were more than a 150 feet long. A few ships glinted with fresh paint and silver adornments, but most were battered scows with ragged sails and splintered wood. Many had rows of overlapping shields lining their gunnels, and racks of spears set on their decks. Countless flags and banners flapped and spun in the breeze. It was if a great host had gathered for immediate battle, but there were no sailors to be seen, not even a single guard or sentry. Only fulmars and kittiwakes wheeled and swooped overhead.

Towering over the armada was one great drakar, longer and higher than all the rest. The shields lining its side were all painted with a writhing white octopus on a green field. Samuel guessed that this must be Aegir's own flagship, the one on which Thokk and Loki had been imprisoned. He glanced up at Thokk, perched on the yard above, and pointed to the ship. Thokk nodded in understanding and affirmation.

The knarr glided to a stop next to another enormous warship whose sides were punctured like a sieve with oar holes. It was obviously built to carry a whole company of warriors, perhaps a hundred or more. Red and black shields lined its sides. Its prow bore the snarling head of a falcon. Great swaths of its woodwork were incised with ribbon beasts, all twisted and wound together into a violent tangle. A bronze weather vane creaked atop the stern post. In contrast to this majestic man-of-war, Samuel's little knarr seemed a pathetic tub, a run-down plow-horse next to a stallion. Thor gazed up at the long ship with undisguised envy as Samuel stared at it in wonder. Balder, on the other hand, was lost in thought and barely noticed the larger ship.

Samuel, Thor, and Balder quickly tied their boat up to a piling and hurried across the pier to the base of the steps. Samuel swayed as he walked, the sensation of solid ground strange after so many days at sea. As they began to climb the stairs, the wooden doors above opened and a group of soldiers marched forth in two orderly lines. They wore dark tunics that reached to their knees, patterned trousers, and green woolen capes. Each had a sword about his waist and in his left hand held a round shield overlaid with a green leather cover. They all had plain, close-fitting leather helmets. Only a few wore shirts of mail. They were big powerful men. Even so, the largest was dwarfed by Thor and Balder.

The two parties met in the middle of the stairs. Samuel and the ravens hung a few steps back. The crowd of soldiers parted and one, taller than the rest, stepped forward. He wore a tunic of fine, shiny cloth and his cape was embroidered along the edges with silver thread. In a loud and commanding voice he said, "Halt! I am Eldir, servant of Aegir. You are trespassing."

"Trespassing!" scowled Thor. "How can we be trespassing when it was your master who sent for us? Don't you know who we are?"

"I know well who you are, but I have been told to consider all those who land unannounced in the sacred bay of Hlesey as trespassers."

"But how can we announce ourselves without landing first?" spat Thor.

"You should have sent word of your arrival. Certainly two such noble gods as yourselves travel with a retinue of servants and retainers. One of them should have been sent ahead to clear your passage."

Thor opened his mouth to speak, but before he could, Balder quickly said, "Eldir, we are very sorry that protocol was not followed, but perhaps it can be over-looked this time. We come on a mission of peace, one which is of great interest to your master. You would certainly not want to disappoint him by denying us entrance."

Eldir paused, looked in turn at both Thor and Balder, and said, "Against my orders and my better judgment, I will indeed conduct you to see Aegir. But only with the condition that you leave all your weapons here on the doorstep."

Thor's eyes narrowed and he took a step back and growled, "For a mere mortal to demand the weapons of a god is an insult as black as night. This I will not do!"

Balder gripped Thor's arm and whispered. "Thor, let's not quibble with them. Surly one sword will not tilt any negotiations in our favor. I am not even armed."

Thor glared at Balder, yanked his arm out of his grip and stumbled backward. Samuel, as he attempted to get out of Thor's way, tripped and tumbled to the ground. Thokk and Rag fluttered up in alarm. The commotion unsettled Aegir's already nervous guards. In unison they put their hands on the hilts of their swords and low growls came from their throats. Thor stared at them for a long moment and then with a muttered curse, unbuckled the sword from his shoulder and handed it to a pale-faced soldier.

Eldir turned and motioned for everyone to follow his lead up the stairs. With the exception of two guards who were assigned to walk with Samuel and the ravens, the guards lined up on either side of Balder and Thor.

As they went forward, Thor leaned over and in a savage hiss said to Balder, "See, it starts already, we are being marched away like outlaws. Mark my words, this humiliation will soon be followed by treachery."

When they reached the outer doors to Aegir's hall, Eldir halted, turned to Thor and Balder, and said, "You are now about to enter the royal hall of Aegir, Master of the Deep, Lord of the Great Western Ocean. You must pay my master proper respect, bow when you come into his presence."

In response Thor hissed, "I'll not bow to anyone. Have your master meet us here on the steps." He clenched his fists and glared at Eldir.

Again Balder intervened, saying to Thor in a low voice, "Let's just get this over with and not haggle about a formality. If it could help us end this ordeal, I would bow to Aegir's lowest servant."

"That, you have already proven," snapped Thor. But then with a bitter sigh, he nodded his head and motioned for Eldir to lead them on. One of the leading soldiers swung open the doors and the company passed through.

Samuel caught his breath as he entered Aegir's hall. Here again was a vast long chamber, as big as Odin's. It was warm and damp like a kitchen and suffused with a dim amber light. Samuel was standing on a narrow mezzanine, one level above a stone floor that spread out before his eyes like a field. Several rows of columns sprang up from the floor and soared to a high vaulted ceiling. Each pillar was adorned with carvings of seaweed, corals, or other aquatic growths. Smokey torches hung from black iron brackets, their orange flames quavering, flickering and sending off inky plumes. The small, high windows above the door scattered patches of sunshine about the room.

Down the middle of the hall was a long, narrow hearth in which a large fire burned. The stream of flames sparkled and popped with abandon. Over the fire all kinds of meat, fish, fowl, and wild game were roasting on spits. Numerous tripods, like fire-walking spiders, were intermixed with the spits and from each hung a kettle filled with bubbling liquid. A horde of servants attended the pots, like workers at a blast furnace. Smoke from the central fire rose in a great pillar that disappeared through a flue punched in the roof. The ceiling itself was adorned with a mosaic of open-faced oyster shells, their iridescent surfaces glittering faintly through layers of soot and clouds of smoke. Encircling the ceiling was a necklace of huge bronze kettles. Each cauldron was the size of a bathtub and fashioned from sheets of metal beaten to form and riveted together. Some featured a filagree of decorations while others were plain and unadorned. All hung from large iron hooks screwed into the stone.

A vast crowd sat at long wooden tables close to the fire. In fact, the whole hall seethed with a multitude of all kinds of creatures, sitting, standing in aisles, crowding up to the fire and spilling over into the shadow-cloaked outer passageways. At one table alone sat three identical men with tremendous black beards, dressed in red and black plaid tunics; a knobby old dwarf sitting on a high stool; a huge polar bear, its head swaying to and fro; a tall lanky knight dressed in chain mail so rusty that it looked as if he were wearing plush red clothes; a giant, bare to the waist and tattooed with blue whorls; and, finally, a small, three-headed troll talking to itself.

A deafening racket filled the hall, waves of sound rolled from one wall to the next. Yelling, laughing, shrieking, and shouting mingled together in an ocean of noise. Amid the din an army of servants, dressed in coarse white tunics and gray pants, scurried here and there carrying platters of food or trays of wooden tankards. The room was a sea of motion, creatures were drinking, eating, fighting, gambling, or arguing with one another. In one corner there was a flash, a dense billow of smoke followed by a gust of shrill laughter and angry curses. In another, a knot of men shoved and prodded each other as two weasels fought in their midst.

Eldir, shouting orders, directed his men to clear a path through the tumult. As the soldiers pushed and shoved, resorting to fists, the crowd laughed and whistled and pointed at Thor and Balder. Insults were cast like rocks at a stoning. A piece of crockery whizzed by Thor's head. Out of the corner of one eye, Samuel noticed a small black and white bird standing on a table. This creature, a dovekie, was juggling a set of eel skulls, while tapping his foot and chanting:

There goes Asgard's greatest champion,
the mighty red-haired Thor.
He will boast of his bloody battles
until your ears are full sore.
But now he is my Master's thrall,
led in a slave's parade.
Caught like a cod in a seaman's net,
unable our reach to evade.
Where is your hammer now, O great Thor,
when you need it the most?
Why, it's in my king Aegir's hand,
a fact for me to boast.
So hang your head and swallow your pride
for luck is now on our fair side.

Finally Eldir cleared a path through the press to the far end of the chamber. As the last drunken wretch was pushed aside, Samuel saw a great, fat, gray haired, extremely shabby giant sitting on a large ornate throne. From Thokk's description, Samuel knew immediately that this must be Aegir. He was seated at a broad table covered with platters of food and cups of drink. Dirty dishes lay scattered on the table or cast on the floor. He was laughing and eating a huge joint of meat, its juices running down his chin and soaking his beard.

Prompted by Eldir, Thor, Balder, and Samuel each bowed to Aegir in turn. Samuel noticed that whereas Balder bowed deeply and respectfully, Thor barely tilted his head and continued to glare at the sea god from under his brows. Aegir, for his part, barely nodded his head at each prostration and continued to chew his food with disrespectful abandon.

Immediately behind the sea god was a high stone wall covered with weapons—crossed spears, shields of various shapes and colors, mandelas of axes and rosettes of swords. There were also racks of pikes, rows of halberds, shelves of clubs and sticks, and displays of daggers. A whole armory was hanging on the wall. Yet, all of it paled to the one weapon directly positioned above Aegir's throne. There, set in a wooden holder and secured by leather straps was Mjollnir, now gray and stone cold. When Aegir saw Thor and Balder staring at the hammer, he let out an enormous chuckle. He then turned to his captain and said, "Eldir! I see that you have caught some intruders."

Thor's eyes flashed and he snarled, "How can you say such a thing? You sent for us. Or do you always treat your guests so rudely?"

"Look around," bellowed Aegir. "I treat my guests with the utmost of hospitality."

Thor scoffed, but before he could reply, Balder said, "Aegir. Please, enough of this. Where is Loki?"

"Why he's right in front of you. Don't you recognize him?" Aegir said, pointing to a huge glass bottle setting on the floor next to his table. The jar was filled with water and capped with a leather cork. Inside swam a large, silver-gray fish. It dolefully looked out at Samuel and his friends.

"Is that really Loki?" Samuel gasped. "What happened to him?"

At the sound of Samuel's voice, Aegir looked at him for the first time. In a contemptuous voice he replied, "Scrawny impertinent human! Haven't you heard of Loki's famous ability to change shapes? In the beat of a bee's wing, he can be any animal he wants to be. A fish, a horse, a hedgehog, you name it. Really, it's a performance not to be missed. In fact it was such a clever bit of magic, I had to see it for myself. With a little encouragement, I got Loki to demonstrate this wonderful skill. 'Become a salmon!' I said, and lo and behold he was a salmon, flopping about in my wine water jar. And do you know what? I found that I quite liked him as a fish. No more whining, complaining, and snide comments. It's really quite an improvement." Aegir emitted a great blast of laughter and a stricken look crossed both Thor and Balder's faces.

"Come, come! Don't take it so hard." Aegir chuckled. "Sit down and eat something and then we can get down to business."

Two chairs were pulled up and Thor and Balder were directed to sit down facing Aegir. No chairs were brought for either Samuel or the two ravens. When they tried to approach the table, a guard shooed them away, sneering and saying, "This is the god's table, not a servant's mess. Be gone with you!"

Samuel stumbled backward and bumped into an evil-faced troll who brusquely pushed him away. Unsure of what to do next, Samuel looked plaintively at where Thor and Balder sat. With a jolt, as if remembering a forgotten wallet, Balder twisted around and peered under shaded eyes until he saw Samuel and the two ravens. In a harried voice he said, "Find somewhere out of the way to rest. Just keep close and stay put. Everything will be all right." In spite of this reassurance, Samuel could not help but notice the worried look in the god's eyes and the anxious tone in his voice.

Forelornly, Samuel turned and looked about the hall for a quiet place to wait out the god's negotiations. Like an incoming tide, a surge of sweaty, ale-sodden creatures flowed between Samuel and the table where Thor and Balder sat. Samuel felt as though he was foundering in a sea of bodies. Rag and Thokk labored to keep close, savagely pecking at the ankles of a drunken sailor who blundered between them and Samuel. Suddenly Samuel spied a small raised platform, half-hidden behind a row of columns. It was set against the outside wall and nearly obscured in shadows. It was empty except for a single dwarf laboring away at some task. Pushing and dodging bodies, Samuel headed for this refuge, with Rag and Thokk desperately tagging along behind.

Chapter 19

Jostled and bruised, Samuel threaded his way toward the sanctuary he had spotted in the shadows of Aegir's hall. About him the mob swelled and roared like a stormy sea. Thokk and Rag clung to his side, hissing and spitting at anyone who ventured too close. With one last push, they reached their goal.

Samuel had arrived at a cube of rock several feet high and perhaps fifteen feet wide and deep. It abutted an outer wall and around its top was a rickety wood railing. Along one side, a set of narrow access stairs had been carved directly into the stone. Samuel quickly ascended these steps, followed closely by Thokk and Rag. At the top they stopped and peered out and around the hall.

Samuel could just see Balder and Thor as they sat speaking to Aegir. Although he was too far away to hear what was being said, he could see clearly the god's faces, their expressions, and the movement of their lips.

Samuel's hideout was sunk in a murky twilight. His only company, besides the ravens, was a dwarf laboriously hauling up buckets of water from a well set in the far corner of the platform. This creature was dressed in a coarse white tunic covered by a brown hooded cloak.

A long black tail hung down between its legs. Once it had cranked up a bucket of water, it would then pour the contents into a reservoir attached to the wall. From the base of the reservoir a pipe protruded, which gently sloped down and away along the wall to some unseen destination. Because the dwarf worked with its back to the room, Samuel was unable to see its face.

After a while the dwarf finished filling the cistern and flopped down on a pile of old blankets not far from where Samuel was standing and removed its hood. Samuel nearly choked with astonishment. He had expected an ugly, bearded dwarf. What appeared instead was a mop of blond hair, sharp blue eyes and a pretty white face—a familiar face! There, sitting in front of him, was the very same Hudler girl who had just a few short weeks ago tried to lure him into her underground home. He immediately recognized her, even though her features were now smudged with soot. Rag arched his back and beat his wings in terror and surprise.

The Hudler sprang up and froze against the wall. Samuel stumbled backward and nearly broke through the fragile guard rail. In horror, he stuttered, "Stay away!" Thokk looked at his friend and the girl with an expression of complete befuddlement.

Samuel and the Hudler stared at each other for a long moment. Finally the Hudler said, her voice thick with suspicion, "Who are you? You shouldn't be up here."

"Don't you recognize me?" blurted Samuel. "You tried to trap me in your cave just a few weeks ago."

The Hudler studied Samuel with a frown for a moment, glanced at Thokk and Rag and then said, "Now I remember you. Your raven nearly scared me to death."

"Scared you to death!" gasped Samuel. "Well it served you right after what you tried to do to me."

"What do you mean?"

"You tried to trick me into that cave of yours. You put a spell on me or something. If Rag hadn't flown in your face, I'd probably be a lump of dirt by now."

"Who told you that?"

"My friends."

"Well, they got it all wrong. If you had come with me, you would have lived a very long life of ease and comfort. It would have been a much better existence than any in Midgard, let me tell you! No cold, no hunger, and no war. You would have been rich and happy with herds of cattle and many children."

"Yeah, but . . . " Unnerved by the Hudler's quick response, Samuel sputtered for words. ". . . most people like to have a choice about such things. Anyway, who'd want to live their whole life in a cave?"

Here the Hudler looked down and in a quiet voice said, "I would. My cave was beautiful, acres and acres of green meadows, meandering streams and fields of buttercups and primroses. Our ceiling fire burned as bright as the sun on a warm summer day. We even had a small grove of holly trees."

"Well, if you liked it so well, then why aren't you there now?" grumbled Samuel.

"Because I was kidnapped."

"Really? How?" Samuel's voice changed from disdain to genuine surprise.

The Hudler eyed Samuel reluctantly and then began. "The day after you escaped another small party of men camped at the crossroads. With them was a young man about our age. My parents couldn't believe our good luck because not many travelers stay at the crossroads anymore. For two boys the right ages to come along, so soon after one another, seemed too good to be true. Alas, it was too good to be true. In our excitement we became careless and did not look closely enough at this group of travelers. You see, my parents are very old and are desperate that I find a companion before they pass away. Before long, the young man was sent to fetch water from a stream near the campsite. What my parents and I failed to notice was that several of the other men followed the younger man into the woods. As is our way, I approached the young man and tried to lure him to the entrance of our cave. I should have been warned by his looks. He was an evil-looking brat with black, greasy hair and a broken nose. He only pretended to come along with me, smirking and leering all the way. When we were almost to my home, I was suddenly grabbed from behind. I twisted to see a most awful looking brute with only one eye and a tremendous yellow beard. As I struggled in vain to free myself, I remember the brat crowing, 'Well, well, look here. We got ourselves a slave for the market, and one with a tail, no less. Ha, ha, ha.'

"Away they took me from my lonely old parents, my beautiful home, and back to their camp. They were wicked, despicable pirates; Vikings of the worst sort. Their leader was a small man with gray hair and a thin beard who constantly blinked. He looked me over and then declared that I should be treated very carefully because such a strange creature as myself would bring a good price if I were healthy and whole.

"That night I was put on a stump and chained to a tree with an iron ring around my ankle. They gave me a blanket and a bowl of vile stew—seal meat and garlic, I think. I sat there for hours watching them belch and brawl. Two brutes wrestled over an insult, one nearly killing the other. Late in the evening, the black-haired boy showed me the stone on which was carved your warning. The one saying that Hudlers were about. He laughed in my face and tossed the rock in my lap."

"The next day we left the crossroad, and reached the inland end of a fjord by early afternoon. I was immediately loaded, with many other slaves, onto a great ship with red and black shields. There was never any possibility of escape. We sailed with the evening tide and within a week we were here.

"The Viking leader was right about my value, because Aegir immediately purchased me for several bars of silver. I guess he was amused by my tail. Unfortunately, the novelty soon grew old, and I was put to work here at this well. I have labored here ever since."

"I'm sorry," said Samuel not knowing what else to say.

The Hudler girl just sniffed once and stared out at the seething mob. Finally in a slightly choked voice she asked, "Well, how did you get here? Are you going to be a slave also?"

"I hope not. I came with Thor and Balder over there."

The Hudler's mouth dropped open and she gasped, "You came in the company of gods. Are you royalty?"

"No, not at all! I am just, well . . . their helper, I guess," Samuel said, a little abashed, but also secretly pleased that he had impressed the Hudler girl. He then asked in a friendly tone, "What's your name, by the way?"

"Jetta. What's yours?"

"Samuel."

Suddenly there was a large commotion near the fire hearth. A barrel-chested man was yelling and screaming at a small black-and-white bird perched on the shoulder of a drunken giant. The bird—the same dovekie that had mocked Thor earlier—was taunting the man, its voice shrill and grating above the din of the crowd. The giant was blissfully unaware of the drama raging about him. He could barely stand, his eyes were closed to slits and his body swayed back and forth dangerously close to the fire. With one hysterical curse the man picked up a soapstone tankard and hurtled it at the dovekie, who fluttered effortlessly out of the way. The missile, having missed its target, bloodied instead the ear of the giant. With a bellow of anger and pain, the giant picked up the man in one easy sweep and threw him through the air and onto a table. Crockery, cups, and a pitcher of mead exploded in a horrendous spray. The mob roared with delight. "Does this riot ever end?" asked Samuel.

"No. People and creatures come and go, but the drinking, gorging, and fighting have not stopped since the first day I was put to work in this corner. It doesn't matter whether Aegir is present or not."

"Are all of them as bad as they seem?" asked Samuel.

"Perhaps. They are all selfish and crude and care for no one but themselves. But few seem actually vicious or purely evil."

"It must be scary to be here."

"It is. I would almost rather be anywhere else. I stay hidden up here on this platform. I never leave its safety unless I have to."

As Samuel gazed out at the crowd, his eyes returned to where Thor and Balder were sitting.

Balder was sitting, silent and pale, while Thor, his cheeks bright red, compulsively drummed the table with his fingers. Aegir was obviously making a joke at their expense, for a leer crossed his face and a great guffaw boomed from his lips.

In a voice that squeaked with impatience, Thokk said, "What's happening over there? Why can't they just get this over with?"

Jetta looked at Thokk and said with a slow sad shake of her head, "I am afraid your friends are in big trouble."

"What do you mean? How do you know?" gasped Samuel.

"I've seen this routine many times now. It's all part of a cruel game. First Aegir will mock and humiliate your friends till their pride has been injured beyond endurance, just as he is doing right now. Aegir has a knack for finding the raw spot on every man's spirit. He'll then goad them into a contest, as if he is giving them a chance to redeem their injured dignity. Unfortunately, these challenges are never what they appear to be. Aegir always prepares ahead of time and arranges things so that he has an unbeatable advantage. Sometimes his victims are his own cronies who may—or may not have—displeased him. Usually though, they're some innocent traveler who has, by ill luck, come to Hlesey. Yesterday it was an errant sea captain and a week ago an honest trader blown off course. Whatever the case, Aegir always wins and his victims always lose. If your friends are not extremely careful and clever, they will soon be Aegir's slaves."

"What are the contests like? They must be dreadful," asked Samuel.

"Quite the contrary. They usually seem innocent and straightforward. Sometimes they are a challenge of strength, but usually they are a test of skill or cleverness. One of Aegir's favorite stratagems is a game of riddles."

"Is that what happened to Loki? Did Aegir prod him into an unwinnable contest?"

"Yes, the poor soul. Aegir completely outfoxed him."

"How did he do that? I thought that Loki was the god of cleverness," gasped Samuel.

"That is true, but Loki is also the god of fire, and fire often gets out of control. A roaring inferno does not stop to think. Aegir knew that, and used it to his advantage."

"How?"

"Loki arrived here about two weeks before I did. I heard that he was bound in chains when he was taken from Aegir's ship and into the hall. For the first couple of days he was kept in a lightless cell, deep under where we now stand. But then, shortly after I arrived, he was brought up to dine with Aegir. While they ate, Aegir goaded him mercilessly. He started out by telling him he was a dupe for being captured so easily, and a fool for letting himself be sent out, all alone, on such a difficult quest. Loki was clearly angry over these jabs, but had the sense to keep his mouth shut. Unfortunately Aegir kept at it, hour after hour. Soon his taunts became sharper and cruder. He said that Loki was nothing more than a mere wood spirit, without any magical abilities at all, or just a trumped-up troll with stones for brains, totally unworthy of his place of honor in Asgard. Every dig, every prod would bring a howl of laughter from Aegir's minions. They so loved to see a great god humbled.

"Finally, out of desperation to salvage some of his pride, Loki began to brag about his ability to change shape. Aegir sneered that Loki was just blowing hot air, talking nonsense: '. . . a petty gnome like Loki couldn't possibly do something so fantastic.' That is when Loki snapped. His usually pale face went crimson. He leaped to his feet and screamed at Aegir, daring him to name a creature, any creature, and he, Loki, would immediate take its form. As I said, once lit, a fire doesn't stop to ponder its actions.

"Now Aegir leaves nothing to chance. Sometime earlier, a huge jar full of water had been conveniently, and apparently innocently positioned near Aegir's table. Water from it had been drawn all night to thin wine. When Loki broke and accepted the sea god's challenge, Aegir contemptuously pointed to the jar and dared Loki to become a fish. Loki jumped into the air and became a salmon, flopping in a flash of silver into the jar. Immediately several of Aegir's soldiers leapt out of the crowd, plugged the jar with a heavy stopper, and bound it with iron straps. Loki is completely trapped until Aegir lets him out."

"Do you think that Aegir has some similar trick planned for Thor and Balder?" Samuel asked, his heart in his throat.

"I am sure of it," answered Jetta.

Even as Jetta finished speaking, the hall grew quiet. Samuel saw that everyone's attention was now riveted on Balder, Thor, and Aegir. Balder was talking and as he spoke, Aegir's face lost its look of scorn. The sea god's features became thoughtful and reserved. He began to nod his head gravely and stroke his beard with his hand. A mild and almost compassionate look came to his eyes. Balder was speaking quickly and intently, his gesturing hands upturned. Samuel had a giddy feeling of hope. Something was being worked out after all.

Jetta was wrong. Aegir was not going to challenge his friends to some kind of evil and treacherous duel, but instead had decided to see reason and work out a fair bargain. Even Thor looked hopeful as he cast his glance back and forth between the two other gods. Finally, Balder finished speaking, his face flushed and eyes bright with hope.

Aegir shifted on his throne and began to speak, his whole demeanor belied dignity and equanimity. He looked up at the ceiling and then slowly began to nod his head. A breathless quiet filled the hall. Aegir gestured to a nearby servant and a tray with two silver goblets appeared. One glass was given to Balder and the other to Aegir. The two gods toasted and drank from their cups. Aegir rose, leaned over the table and slowly extended his hand. Balder sprang to his feet, an eager smile on his noble features and shot out his hand to meet Aegir's. Their fingertips almost touched. But then suddenly, Balder, with a convulsive rattle, froze. A gray pallor crept, like a malignant disease, from his lips, across his cheeks, and down his neck until it covered his entire body. He remained standing, stone still, paralyzed, eyes glazed and arm extended. Aegir jerked back his hand and bellowed with laughter. A hysterical wave of hooting, shrieking, and whistling erupted from the crowded hall.

Thor sprang to his feet like a bursting volcano and roared, "Aegir! You vile spawn of a sea slug, what have you done?"

Chapter 20

Aegir's hall subsided into a tense silence as the initial frenzy caused by Balder's sudden bewitchment passed. Samuel stood stunned, unable to believe what had just happened. Then, with his heart in his throat, he rushed off the platform and dove into the crowd. He elbowed and shoved his way through the press, with Rag and Thokk at his heels. From all around he could hear a cruel chorus of snickering. He burst through the mob and ran over to where Balder stood. The god of kindness had a ghastly smile frozen to his purple lips. With quivering fingers, Samuel reached out and touched Balder's hand. It was deathly cold, gray, and damp.

All eyes were now turned to Thor, who was standing with his fists clenched and his face red with anger. Through clamped jaws he growled, "What are you doing, Aegir? Do you want war with the lords of Asgard? You are no match for all of us together, even with Mjollnir."

Smugly, Aegir sat back in his throne and said, "But Thor, you are forgetting, I already have Loki and now

Balder in my power. What other champions do the Aesir have left?"

"I will stand against you!" Thor declared as he pounded his fist against the table in front of him.

The sea god just chuckled and sneered, "What threat can you possibly pose to me? You are neither as cunning as Loki, nor as intelligent as Balder."

Thor took a deep breath and as he did so, he seemed to grow both in height and breadth. In a low snarl he said, "Beware Aegir, for I, Thor, have wrestled the sea serpent Jormungand who encircles the very world, fighting off his armored coils and poisoned breath until he fled wounded into his underwater lair. I alone smote the ice king Thrym and all his evil household, smashing to fragments his frost giant guards. And it was I who, with a single blow, slew the great troll Hrungnir, who towered over the land like a mountain. If I can do all these things, then I can certainly crush you!"

"Yes, yes," Aegir yawned. "I have heard all those stories before and do you know what? They don't prove a thing. In every one of those battles you had Mjollnir and now you don't. In fact I think you're nothing without your hammer. Without 'Striker-Crusher' you're just a plain old bully boy."

Thor's eyes narrowed and his complexion went blue. With a savage swing he plucked a silver cup from in front of Aegir, smashed it against the floor and then stamped it flat. A murmur ran through the crowd and several of Aegir's guards took a step forward.

The sea god tensed and his eyes twitched, but his voice remained calm. "Yes, that's it. I think you're just a common thug. A lout and a glutton who's frittered away any virtue you once had through endless days of drinking and carousing. I wager you're now unable to do anything more than brawl—nothing useful at least. I bet you couldn't even bait a fishing line, plow a field or mend a roof. Chopping firewood is probably beyond your measure."

"I could lay waste a whole forest with my bare hands," snarled Thor.

"Really? With your bare hands you say?" scoffed Aegir. "I doubt that. In fact, I know you can't."

"How is that?" thundered Thor.

"Because I know of a tree—a miserable little twig really—which is quite beyond your power to cut down, especially with your bare hands."

Thor paused and growled, "What are you talking about, Aegir?"

Casually, Aegir pointed to a column near the front of the room. With fumbles and shoves the crowd parted and there at the pillar's base was a pool of sunlight cast from one of the hall's high windows. In the smoky halo of light was a spindly ash tree about eight feet tall and not more than two inches thick. Its leaves were the pale yellow of old fingernails.

In a contemptuous voice Aegir said, "That slender weed has somehow sprouted in my hall. It is most annoying and I would dearly like to get rid of it. I wager though, that you are incapable of disposing of it for me."

"This is a trick," snapped Thor. "You have put a spell on that tree or somehow altered it to make it impossible to destroy."

With an extravagant roll of his eyes, Aegir gasped, "I swear by the Well of Mimir that I have done nothing of the sort. I have not touched that sapling. It began to grow there all by itself, and I have just neglected, until now, to order its removal."

"There is something here that I do not see," Thor said in a low voice.

Aegir's eyes widened and he threw up his hands, his voice became loud and agitated.

"I'm offended! There is no mystery here, no double cross. I really believe that it is beyond your power to either pull up that tree or to snap it off. You are just afraid that my little challenge will unmask you for what you really are, a rotten old drunkard! Whatever strength you once had is now gone."

Thor, his jaws clenched and eyes narrowed, stared at Aegir for a long moment. The hall was hushed, as if waiting for an executioner's blade to fall. Suddenly Thor said in deadly calm voice, "If I bring you that twig, will you give me Mjollnir and free my friends?"

Here Aegir drew in his breath with a whistle and said, "That's not fair! I risk everything and you risk nothing. I cannot accept such an offer."

"What would you accept then?" Thor asked, his voice thick with distrust.

Aegir thought—or feigned to think—for a moment and then said, "I'll tell you what. I'll make a deal with you. If you bring me that twig, I will give you all that you ask for. But, if you fail, then you must become my slave, bound to do my bidding."

Thor looked at Aegir, who sat impassively with his hands clasped over his chest and then back to the tree. An icy silence descended upon the room. Only the crackling of the fire could be heard. Slowly Thor turned and pushed his way through the crowd. He stopped in front of the tree and looked back at the sea god. "Remember Aegir! Oaths are sacred among the gods. The very stones of the earth will rise up to enforce a broken bond. Do I have your vow that you have not cast a spell on this tree or somehow made it impossible to pull up?"

"You have my pledge, Thor. Do I have yours—will you become my thrall if you fail?"

"Yes."

"Then bring me that weed if you can."

With a sigh, Thor turned to his task. He squared his feet and reached out with both hands, grasping the tree where it emerged from a crack in the rock floor. He gave the trunk a wring, intending to twist it off at its base. Unfortunately, the twig rotated with Thor's motion, its fibers twining into a tighter and stronger cord. This was not an old and brittle branch, but a young and flexible sapling made of green, fibrous wood. Thor wrung harder, but the twig only became like braided steel cable. He released the tree with a gasp and then grabbed it again with a different grip, trying to snap it in two with a sudden flick of his wrists. Again he had no success. Desperately, he worked it back and forth but it only bent without apparent harm; the wood possessed an unbreakable suppleness. Thor's face became the color of beet juice and a bead of sweat trickled down his forehead. A ripple of low laughter went through the crowd. A dwarf with a nose like an elephant began to shout, "He's not going to be able to do it, har, har, har."

Thor had only one choice left, to pull the tree up by its roots. He planted his feet astride the tree and grasped it again at its base. With a great roar, he arched his back and gave the tree a tremendous yank. An enormous rumble echoed through the hall and a cry of dismay swept through the crowd. Again Thor tugged and the plates and cups on the tables began to rattle like castanets. Finally, with one last great effort, Thor pulled with all his might. Chips of oyster shell rained down from the ceiling, tables were upset, the floor quivered, columns swayed, and the walls shuddered. A grinding thunderous noise like an earthquake echoed through the chamber. But, alas, with one trembling motion, Thor's hands slid up the length of the twig and flew off into space. The god of thunder then stumbled backward like a punch-drunk boxer and tripped over a bench. With a moan of despair, he collapsed in front of the battered but unbroken tree. In a hoarse whisper he asked, "What trickery have you used to defeat me, Aegir? That is no ordinary tree."

"You're right, Thor. That is no ordinary tree." said Aegir in a voice both solemn and arrogant. "It is nothing less than an offshoot of Yggdrasil, the great ash tree which supports Asgard, Midgard and all the other seven levels of our world. To uproot it you would have had to upend the universe. No one is equal to that task, not even you, Thor."

Thor grimaced with chagrin and mumbled an oath under his breath. Aegir stared at him for a moment longer and then crowed in delight. "If my reckoning is right, I now have a new mule for my stables, a big red one at that. Ha, ha, ha!."

With violent suddenness, pandemonium broke out in the hall. A great gloating cheer rose up from the mob and echoed off of the ceiling. Thor was pelted with cups and broken dishes. Taunts were spat in his face. The god of thunder sat on the foul floor in stunned disbelief, his head hung between his legs.

With a nod, Aegir motioned to several nearby soldiers who quickly disappeared behind a column. Amidst a ruckus of claps and hoots they reappeared, wheeling a tremendous iron cage that towered over the crowd. It was a crude contraption of flat straps, rivets, and hinges. Straw covered the floor, rust coated the bars, and it creaked and groaned as the soldiers pushed it forward. Propped up on the inside was a tremendous flask of wine.

With cruel vehemence, Aegir sneered, "Well, Thor, what do you think of your new home? Does it meet with your approval? I have provided it with all that you might desire." Here Aegir pointed to the flask and a tidal wave of laughter roared through the chamber.

As Thor stared at the cage with a mixture of despair and disbelief, two giant trolls brusquely grabbed him under each arm and yanked him to his feet. They then dragged him through the howling throng and flung him into the cage. The door was shut with a clang and a heavy chain was wrapped about the latch. Once inside, Thor was poked and prodded by sticks and anything long which the mob could grab. The cage was spattered with food and sprays of beer.

As Thor was tormented by the mob, Aegir sat on his throne leering with satisfaction. This was the most delicious moment of glory and triumph that he had ever experienced. Like an eagle rising from its nest, his ambition took wing and soared into the flame streaked sky of possibilities. With Loki in a bottle, Thor in a cage, and Mjollnir above his head, what now could stop him from unseating Odin? Aegir felt sure that Odin alone, even with his fearsome spear Gungnir could not resist the power of Mjollnir. Tyr and the rest of the Aesir gods, once they learned of Thor and Loki's defeat, would switch allegiances to his side in a heartbeat. Aegir gave a low chuckle as he considered the fickle loyalty of his fellow gods. But then his mind returned to the main prize. He would claim Odin's hall, Valaskjalf, for himself and turn Odin out into the wastes of Jotunheim. In his mind he could feel the cool smooth touch of Odin's silver throne under his finger tips, see the haughty valkyries bow to him in reverence, and hear the throaty roar of his minions echo from Valaskjalf's rafters.

Suddenly the sound of steel against iron cut through Aegir's contemplations. A giant dressed in a fish-leather jerkin was hammering against Thor's cage with a huge mallet and making it toll like a bell. "Enough," shouted Aegir.

Like settling leaves, the crowd went silent, all eyes turned to where the sea god sat. Aegir adjusted his seal-skin tunic, cleared his throat, and held up his hand. He was going to make a grand pronouncement, to put this shining moment of victory into golden words. The mob waited breathlessly to hear what glorious path their triumphal king would now lead them down. Slowly and majestically Aegir stood up and opened his mouth to speak. Yet before he could utter a word, a high-pitched voice cut him off, crying out sharp and clear, "You're a coward and a cheat, Aegir!"

Startled and offended, Aegir looked for the source of the insult and his eyes rested on Samuel.

Samuel's face was white with fear and desperation, but his chin stuck out and his body shook with defiance. Next to Samuel stood Rag, glaring like a bird possessed. Thokk, standing a little apart, was gawking at his friends with mouth agape and goggle eyes.

Aegir's face darkened, his moment of glory now tarnished. With a dismissive flick of his hand, he said "Oh my, I forgot about you three. Well, I can always use a couple more net menders . . . Guards!"

Chapter 21

Ever since Samuel was magically transported away from the Geyser Inn so long ago, events had carried him along like a flood. As he was swept from one fantastic adventure to the next, his emotions had ricocheted from fear to wonder to terror. Now, at what seemed the darkest moment of all, he was gripped by near madness, a desperate need to rebel against the fate which seemed to be sweeping him up. In a voice on the brink of hysteria, Samuel spat at the Sea God sitting so smugly on his throne, "Are you afraid of me, Aegir?"

A chorus of cruel guffaws rang from one table to the next and someone threw a chicken bone at Samuel's face. The greasy joint glanced off his cheek and skittered along the floor. Two soldiers, alerted by Aegir, began edging their way through the crowd. One carried a length of coiled chain with an iron bracelet welded to it.

Suddenly Thokk squawked, "Wait! Just a minute. I pray your majesty to let me speak."

Aegir glowered at Thokk, but did not say a word, an expression of scorn frozen on his face.

Stuttering as he spoke, Thokk blurted, "Did your lordship know that nobody has ever beaten us at riddles?"

Both Samuel and Rag turned to stare at Thokk with looks of disbelief and incomprehension. The crowd hooted in disdain, and Aegir raised an eyebrow. Desperately, Thokk continued, "Why, Samuel, just the other day didn't we tell a real poser to Odin, and he swore that no one was better at telling riddles than the three of us?"

The guards had nearly reached Samuel and the ravens. All three could hear the rattle of the chains above the hum of the crowd. Suddenly, Aegir asked, his voice thick with disbelief, "Really, is this so?"

"Oh, yes, it's true; we can even outsmart Loki," sputtered Thokk. Then, just as a soldier was about to lay hands on him, he squeaked, "Just ask us a riddle and we'll prove it."

Aegir held up his hand and the two soldiers halted. "By my soul, I don't believe a word you're saying. The idea that a mere boy and two wormy birds might converse with the Aesir gods on equal terms is so unimaginable that it's laughable. But I find your audacity amusing. For whatever good it will do you, I'll give you a chance to prove your boasting. Here, I'll go first. Just let me think . . . "

After a pause, during which the hall fell quiet, Aegir cleared his throat and said in a deep, booming voice. "I'll give you an easy one."

Once there was a giantess great,
Whom in a fit the very firmament ate.
Swiftly she chewed across the opal gray sky
Causing in a wink the stars to die.
Next she swallowed the ashen moon
And cast the land in an inky gloom.
Then down on Midgard her mighty fury bore,
Her passage marked by a rolling roar.
In a raging, bellowing, sparking crash,
Trees, rocks, and homes were turned to mash.
But a rage like hers could not last,
Soon a curtain of tears came quick and fast.
In shame and regret she rushed away,
Leaving nothing in her passage but a sparkling
     clear day.
All this monster's violence was done
Without wings to fly, mouth to shout, or legs to run.
Speak this terrible giant's name.
To win the golden apple of our game.

Samuel's mouth gaped open and he looked at Aegir in bewilderment. This kind of riddle was far beyond the simple word twists he had solved before. Rag frowned, unable to help in any way. At first Thokk was also completely flummoxed. But then a distant look filled his eyes, and he seemed to stare at something far away. The bit about the giantess swallowing the stars was somehow familiar to him. Like a half-forgotten dream, he began to remember a night two summers ago when he was perched on the roof of the Geyser Inn. There had been a full moon that evening and everything was cast in a dream-like illumination. Suddenly the light had dimmed and Thokk had looked up to see a fast-moving cloud quickly devouring the moon and stars. This billow turned out to be the leading edge of a midnight thunderstorm, a roaring gale with hurricane winds and great sheets of lightning. A tree near the inn had been struck by a bolt and had exploded in a shower of sparks and flame. Yet in spite of its initial fury, the tempest had quickly died to a gentle downpour. Thokk turned and whispered to Samuel, who then looked straight at Aegir and said in a loud voice, "A thunderstorm, at night."

Aegir remained silent for a second, a blank look on his face, and then in calm voice said, "Very good. But one riddle does not give you the cunning of Loki. Now it is your turn to pose a question to me."

Samuel bowed his head and began to think, trying desperately to remember a riddle—any riddle. Time slipped away quickly. Aegir began to tap his fingers on the arm of his throne and to click his tongue against his teeth. All Samuel could think of was the tired old nursery rhyme:

> There is a creature very strange to meet,
> Who begins its life on all four feet.
> Then for something new,
> It goes along on two,
> Until it decides that three legs can't be beat.

Fortunately for Samuel, this riddle was not at all familiar to Aegir. In fact it was quite strange and difficult. Aegir paid scant attention to his many human thralls and so the details of their lives were alien to him. Aegir frowned and began to rub his forehead. Finally in exasperation he said to Samuel. "Since there are three of you, you must allow me also to have two assistants."

Samuel looked at Thokk and Rag and then back to Aegir and shrugged. The sea god quickly summoned Eldir and a shabby old troll dressed in a patchwork of cow hides. They conferred in a low whisper for a long time. Eldir seemed to do most of the talking while Aegir just listened and nodded his head. An air of expectancy hung in the Hall and a low buzz of conversation echoed off the walls. Finally Aegir turned to Samuel and said, "The answer to your riddle is humans because they start life by crawling on four legs, go to walking on two legs, and end up using a cane, three legs."

Samuel nodded and the crowd clapped and cheered. When the ruckus subsided, Thokk licked his lips and said, "Perhaps your majesty would like to make a little wager on the next set of riddles. I mean, if that's not too much to presume."

Aegir's eyebrows shot up in mock surprise, and his belly jiggled with a silent chuckle. "What kind of bet did you have in mind?"

"Well, you mentioned that we were trespassers, I believe. That sounds rather serious."

"It is. All who trespass on my sacred island become my slaves."

Thokk cleared his throat and then said, "I am sure all three of us would prefer to retain our freedom. Perhaps you might reconsider your sentence upon us if we were to win the next round. Not that we stand much of a chance against your cleverness."

Aegir sat back in his chair, considering what Thokk had suggested. With a shrug he said, "It is customary that the winner of a contest of riddles be granted a boon by the loser. Therefore, if you win, I will grant you a wish. You can use it to regain your freedom. But be warned, I will increase the time of your thralldom to me if you lose. Such is the price of audacity."

Samuel and the ravens reluctantly nodded assent. Aegir then bent over and conferred with his two assistants. After a few minutes he nodded his head, sat up straight, and said in a loud and cocksure voice:

I am from the very deep,
Wandering endlessly beyond the pale.
My teeth are like needles
My hide like a suit of iron ring mail.
My eyes bulge like a frog's,
My body puffs and swells like a toad.
I have a tiny husband,
Who never ever spares me the goad.
Amid the depths I roam
Lighting the dark in my own clever way.
I have a glowing charm

Which turns inky night to pallid day.
It lures the unwary close,
Like the fairy light of a sprite.
Then, like a trap, I snap,
And eat the fools in one vicious bite.
My, oh my,
Who am I?

Aegir sat back with a look of complete self-satisfaction. He glanced at the troll and gave him a smug smile. Eldir, who was standing nearby, nodded his head and crossed his arms. Someone in the back of the room gave a loud whistle and another clapped.

Now it was Thokk's turn to feel stumped, and he turned to Samuel with a grimace. What he saw was not confusion though, but a look of eager confidence in Samuel's eyes.

Aegir was counting on Samuel and the ravens being like any other Midgard creature, totally unfamiliar with the depths of the ocean and never having seen the weird animals that lurk there in total darkness. Unfortunately for him, Samuel was not what he seemed to be. All the countless hours Samuel had spent in the Geyser Inn reading lounge perusing its beat-up set of encyclopedias or skimming through countless scientific web pages on the Internet suddenly came into play. Samuel's fascination with odd and interested natural facts and figures was like a secret weapon which he could now unleash. The image of a bloated fish with bug eyes—not too dissimilar to Aegir—needle teeth, and a glowing bait suspended at the end of an antenna came quickly to Samuel's mind.

Breathlessly, Samuel shouted triumphantly, "An angler fish."

Aegir was stunned. He had been so sure of himself. A gasp of amazement erupted from the crowded hall. Even Thokk and Rag looked surprised. Aegir's astonishment gave way to embarrassment, his features darkened. "No man has ever seen that fish, it lives at the very bottom of the ocean. How did you know the answer to my riddle!"

Samuel shrugged and said, "I saw a picture of it in a book."

"There is no book like that in Midgard," snarled Aegir.

"The book is not in Midgard."

"Then how, by the gates of Gimli, did you see it?" scoffed Aegir.

"I'm not from Midgard either. I'm from Earth. The book is back there, at my home. I'm just a visitor here in your world," replied Samuel, with a shrug of his shoulders.

This caught Aegir off balance and a flicker of doubt and confusion flashed across his face. But after a moment's pause he growled, "Well, never mind, it's your turn."

Samuel bit his lips and began to think. Again the moments seemed to fly by. The harder Samuel thought, trying desperately to remember a real poser, the more elusive remembering any riddle became. Like trying to catch butterflies, they seemed to slip and flutter just out of reach of his mental grasp. Thokk and Rag only shook their heads when Samuel turned to them for help. A grumble began to rise in the crowd. "Come on, come on," someone yelled. Suddenly, like a flash Samuel blurted out, "Why does Odin wear a black belt with silver studs and red rubies?"

Aegir spat on the floor and growled in an offended tone, "That's not a riddle! How would I possible know the answer to that?"

The mob let out an ominous hiss. Thokk looked horrified, and even Rag seemed doubtful. Samuel just stuck out his chin and replied, "It's a riddle, and I am sure you know the answer."

Aegir looked at Eldir and then the troll. They both shrugged and shook their heads.

Then Aegir turned back to Samuel and said in a disgusted voice, "Determining such a petty matter as someone else's choice in fashion does not constitute a fair riddle. You must give me another question."

Samuel grit his teeth and said: "It's a riddle, and you don't have to read Odin's mind to solve it. Do you give up?"

Aegir half rose from his seat and hissed, "I warn you! If you are cheating me, I'll cast you into the sea for the lobsters to eat!"

"Do you give up?" repeated Samuel in a hoarse whisper.

Aegir glared at Samuel for a long time. But then, as his face twisted into an ugly sneer, he sullenly said in a voice with more than a hint of threat, "I give up. Why does Odin wear a black belt with silver studs and red rubies?"

"Why . . . to keep his pants up, of course," crowed Samuel.

Aegir went white, and the hall fell into a deathly silence. Suddenly the dovekie who had mocked Thor earlier, burst out laughing, his shrill twittering breaking the quiet. Aegir glared at the bird, swore an oath under his breath, and then slowly sat down, his face ashen with suppressed fury.

Thokk piped up, "Well, I guess we can go now, right?"

"No!" snarled Aegir, as a blaze of white-hot anger welled up inside of him. "That last riddle was not fair; it didn't even rhyme. I get another chance. One more riddle! You must answer one more riddle of mine. If you are correct, then I will grant you a wish, any wish! If you are wrong though, you are mine until your hair grows gray and all your teeth fall out!"

"Now wait . . . " began Samuel, but Rag reached out and tapped his hand with his beak, as if to say "It's all right, we have no choice." Reluctantly, Samuel nodded his head in acquiescence.

Aegir stared at Samuel and the ravens for a long time. Nervously, he chewed a strand of his beard. With a violent gesture he waved away Eldir and his troll advisor when they tried to speak to him. Slowly, like the dawning of an evil sun, a wicked glint filled his eyes. Finally he said in a quiet voice as he stared at Samuel, "You say that you are not from our world. Then perhaps what is obvious to any Midgard human will be strange to you. Just as what should have been unknown to a Midgardian seems to have been common knowledge for you." A few more seconds passed during which Aegir stroked his beard from its very base to its scraggy tip and a cruel smile creased his face. Then, in a strong voice which filled the hall like the pronouncement of a death sentence, he began. "Here is my final riddle, strange boy. Answer it if you can:

I will come at the end of three winters jointed,
Blood stained, fire burnt, frost coated,
Ravenously devouring the golden sun and pale moon,
Teeth gnashing, mouth ripping, belly bloated.

While Midgard in pain moans and wails,
Walls tumbling, tree wilting, realms sighing,
Down I'll cast the rainbow bridge,
Horn blowing, halls burning, gods dying.

A final battle I will stage,
Fear shot, terror full, horror filled,
For good and bad to slay each other,
Thunderer poisoned, wanderer swallowed, watcher
    killed.

Last I will cast open the gates of Hel,
Demons rise, wolves howl, giants rage,
So that fire and ice will sunder time and earth,
In a shield age, sword age, axe age.
    Speak my name if you dare.

As Aegir spat out the last verse he leaned forward on his throne, gripping the armrests until his knuckles went white. His eyes were on fire and his ugly face was screwed into a terrible leer. A heartless, gloating murmur rose from the crowd now standing in a sweaty crush around the contestants. Samuel glanced about and saw that he was hemmed in by a ring of cruel, pitiless faces, each cast in harsh relief by the flickering fire. A dark glint of meanness filled all their eyes. Even Thor, who was standing and gripping the iron straps of his cage, suddenly looked alien to Samuel's eyes.

Samuel became pale and his mouth went dry. He had no idea what the answer to the riddle might be, not even a glimmer of a clue crossed his mind. All at once his contest with Aegir seemed deadly serious. A life time of dreary, dangerous drudgery stretched before Samuel's eyes. He would now never get home, never see his parents or the Geyser Inn again.

Desperately, he asked Thokk for help. The raven just shook his head and looked sadly at the floor. A twitter of excitement went through the crowd, victory for Aegir hung in the air like thick smoke.

The moments ticked by. Someone in the crowd began stamping on the floor. Soon there was an uninterrupted rhythm of pounding feet, slowly swelling to a roaring crescendo. In his cage, Thor hung his head. One of Aegir's soldiers began to shake a chain above his head, and a hideous troll with four heads began to hoot in a great bellowing voice, "Time! Time! Time!"

Samuel looked at Thokk and saw only hopelessness. For once his friend was speechless. In panic, Samuel turned to Rag for whatever help the mute bird could offer. He was stunned by what he saw. Instead of despair or desperation, Samuel saw Rag transformed, the raven's eyes were radiant, even his dusty feathers seemed glossy and newly made. He was shivering violently and one wing twitched uncontrollably. Suddenly, he opened his beak and in a trilling croak, which cut through the cacophony of pounding feet and jeers like a crossbow arrow through a sawdust dummy, he cried, "Ragnarok! The answer to the riddle is Ragnarok!" And then in a whisper, heard only by Samuel and Thokk, he added, "It is also my name."

Dead silence fell in an instance. Aegir's eyes bulged in amazement and then in sheer rage he smashed a stone dish in front of him with his fist. He shook his head from side to side, and then, in a bitter tone, he turned to Samuel and said, "You have your wish. Freedom is yours."

"No!" cried Samuel. "You said that I might have a wish, *any wish*, and I do not wish for my freedom."

Thokk nearly fell over in a faint, and Rag gasped.

"Then for what do you wish?" snarled Aegir.

"I wish for Thor to have Mjollnir!" shouted Samuel.

Aegir's mouth fell open and his face went violet with rage. "You presume too much. No human can wish for such a thing!"

"But I do!" yelled Samuel

"Never!" shrieked Aegir.

Aegir sprang from his throne in wrath, intending to smite Samuel himself, but before he could take two steps, he stopped dead, his expression changing from fury to horror. Mjollnir, like a loose window pane in a storm, began trembling in its holder above his head. It quivered and rattled until the whole wall shook and the swords and shields which were hanging there came crashing down. All eyes were turned toward the source of the clatter. A gasp of amazement rose like steam from the mob and Aegir's face went gray. With an explosion of fragments, the holder flew apart and Mjollnir went whizzing across the room and straight into Thor's outstretched hand. As it touched the Thunder God's palm, it blazed to a cherry red and a sheet of white flame erupted about it like a halo. In one great sweeping blow and a shower of sparks, Thor shattered the iron cage like so many brittle sticks.

With Mjollnir in one hand, Thor advanced toward Aegir. The mob evaporated before him like water on a hot stove. Aegir shrank into his throne, wriggling one way and then the other. Thor stopped beside Samuel and in a voice thick with anger said to Aegir, "Now you evil son of a shark, release Balder from the spell you have cast on him or I'll pound you into a mass of bone and blood."

Aegir was so paralyzed with fear that at first he did not respond. Like a deer caught in a wolverine's gaze, he just sat blinking at Thor. But then, with a jerk, he turned and snapped his fingers at Balder. The god of kindness fell into a heap where he lay moaning and holding his head. Thor then pointed to the jar containing Loki and said, "Now him."

With shaking hands, Aegir motioned to several guards cowering nearby. They quickly uncorked the bottle containing the fire god and hastily retreated into the shadows. Dripping wet Loki emerged, looking as arrogant as ever and saying, "Well, well, Aegir; it looks like you're the one in a pickle now."

Thor then looked up at the rows of kettles hanging from the ceiling and pointed to a particular large one and said, "Fill that cauldron with gold and have it loaded onto our ship, along with enough food and water for us for a month."

Without so much as a whisper of protest, Aegir nodded in agreement.

Thor turned to Samuel and asked, "Is there anything of Aegir's that you would like?"

Without hesitation, Samuel pointed to Jetta, who was standing by her well. "I want her to come back with us."

Thor didn't even look at Aegir for approval; he just nodded and waved Jetta forward.

By now Balder had regained his feet. He was groaning and shading his eyes. "What happened?" he whispered.

"Betrayal and treachery. Much too long a story to tell right now," answered Thor. "But satisfy your curiosity with this: the least among us, the skraeling child from beyond our world, and his two ravens have put Mjollnir in my hand, freed us all, and saved Odin's throne."

Chapter 22

Aegir's thralls moved quickly to fulfill Thor's demands. A long pole with a hook was produced to retrieve the brewing kettle chosen to be filled with gold from its hook along the ceiling. Once the cauldron hit the floor, it was quickly taken away to the sea god's treasury. Meanwhile, a regiment of Aegir's servants rolled barrels of water and carried bags of food from a side room and stacked them next to the main entrance. In the hushed chamber their labors seemed loud and discordant. Orders were shouted and angry replies cast back.

Aegir's minions sat surly and downcast, for once their raucous party at an end. Trolls and dwarfs, gnomes and pirates sat in the fetid darkness snarling at each other or slowly drinking from tankards of ale. As a low growl pervaded the room, Thor stood over Aegir with his hammer raised and his face darkened to a menacing scowl.

In a very short while the giant kettle returned, brimming over with neck rings, arm bands, plates, cups, goblets, helmets and even a coat of mail. Jewels flashed and glittered amid the warm and brassy glow of gold.

The cauldron was carried under a stout pole hefted by ten men, tottering under the weight. A gasp of amazement accompanied the treasure trove as it passed through the chamber and toward the front of the hall. More than a few hands reached out in a vain hope of snatching away a stray coin or loose ring.

On tiptoe, Jetta made her way through the crowd and over to Samuel. She carried just a single ragged bundle under her arms. In a tense whisper she asked, "Are we really going? Can we really escape?"

"I hope so," Samuel replied in a nervous voice.

Suddenly from across the room, Eldir called to Thor. "All that you have requested is now set here in a pile. If you wish, my men will help you load it onto your boat."

Without a word, Thor turned his back on Aegir and headed straight for the hall's tall outer doors. The sea god was left slumped on his throne, muttering and chewing on his beard. Loki and Balder fell into step behind the thunder god, while Samuel, Jetta, and the two ravens ran along in their wake. They all marched, eyes forward, through the sullen crowd—now dead quiet and ominous. A thousand bitter eyes watched their passage. In the morose silence, only the hissing and popping of the fire could be heard.

Outside, the early evening sun shone in brilliant radiance, casting everything in a golden glow. Great woolen clouds, flashed with orange and scarlet, raced across the dark blue sky. Purple twilight was spreading across the eastern horizon. The bay rippled and sparkled like a field of gems. The sea-washed air was so clear that it seemed to Samuel that he could reach out and touch crags and rocks that were miles away. Waves lapped along the dock, the armada of boats creaked against their moorings and in the distance an occasional sea bird cried. The air was cool but not cold. A strong breeze, smelling of salt, ruffled Samuel's hair.

Samuel and his friends quickly walked down the steps in front of Aegir's palace. The entire company was anxious to leave the sea god and his hall far behind, before there was some sudden and unexpected change of fortune. They trotted onto the dock, heedless now of the beautiful drakars and longships. They were followed by Eldir's soldiers in a long line, gasping and grunting, each carrying a keg or sack or helping with the kettle of gold. Finally they reached their own little knarr.

Thor and Balder jumped into the midship hold and quickly began stowing supplies, heedless of order or neatness. Loki loitered on the pier, leaning on a piling and grinning as the other two gods labored. Samuel helped Thor and Balder as best he could, while Jetta and the two ravens found resting spots near the back of the boat. With many curses and groans, the kettle of gold was heaved on board. It was gingerly set on the keel block and tightly lashed to the mast. All was nearly ready for departure, when suddenly, with a flurry of squawking kittiwakes above his head, Aegir emerged from his hall. Balder let out an audible groan.

Slowly the sea god hobbled down the stone steps, one hand held above his head. His face twisted into a sheepish smile. "Wait, wait!" he croaked.

Aegir painfully limped along the pier. Samuel saw that his ankles were swollen from gout and that in the open sun he looked pallid and pockmarked, like an overripe mushroom. Finally he arrived beside the knarr, wheezing for breath.

"I hope that we are now all squared away and that no hard feelings remain between us," Aegir said hopefully, glancing at Thor, Balder, and Loki in turn.

Thor just grunted and glanced away while Loki sneered and shook his head. Only Balder looked Aegir straight in the face and said, "Time will tell."

Samuel could not help but look at Aegir, unable to pry his eyes away from the strange and compelling ugliness of his face, now highlighted in the broad daylight. Aegir noticed Samuel's stare and said, "Here now, my son, let me give you a gift to make up for our, um . . . disagreement."

Aegir rummaged under his beard, sending the crustaceans that lived there hopping madly about. Finally, with a yank, he produced a silvery disk the size of a large coin and handed it to Samuel. The disk was hard and iridescent like the inside of a clam and it shimmered in the sun light.

"What is this?" gasped Samuel.

"It's a Jormungand scale," said Aegir.

"What!" roared Thor who whirled around and looked ready to strike the sea god.

"Wait, wait!" squeaked Aegir. "Let me explain. It's really a most wonderful gift. As Thor obviously knows, but perhaps Samuel doesn't, the Jormungand serpent is a gigantic snake that lives at the bottom of the ocean. It is extremely venomous; one whiff of its breath can kill a whale. As the Sea God, I am able to collect Jormungand scales when they break off and sink to the bottom. The shard in Samuel's hand has the power to not only counteract Jormungand venom, but to draw out any other poison that might enter a man's body or soul. To make it work, its owner need only hold it up and gaze upon its surface."

Samuel turned the scale over in his fingers and then put it in his pocket. He smiled briefly at Aegir who winked at him, a strange discombobulated action given his wandering eye.

With a sigh, Aegir look hopefully back at the other three gods. None of them would return his glance and so with a shrug, he turn and shuffled back toward his palace. As he limped away, followed closely by his guards, Thor scoffed and Loki made a snide remark.

As Aegir disappeared through his door, Thor nodded to Balder. The god of kindness then retrieved the last rope holding the knarr to the pier with a flick of his wrist and a strong pull. As the boat gently floated free and out into the bay, Thor ordered Loki to the tiller and, with Balder at his side, took his place amidship at the oars. Quickly they began to row. With a majestic pirouette, the knarr came around until it was heading due west. The rocky cliffs ahead were sunk in purple shadow, but the sky above was aflame with great curtains of sunset orange and flame yellow. The knarr's figurehead caught the rays of the sinking sun

and leapt to fiery life. The knarr and its crew were headed home.

Across the bay the knarr slid toward the narrow
canyon that led to the open sea. One last time before
the rocky cliffs blocked his view, Samuel turned and
caught a final glimpse of the entrance to Aegir's Hall.
Its smooth black face was brilliant in the luminous
light. A flock of birds, like flakes of snow, whirling in
the crisp air, called softly to Samuel.

By nightfall they were out in the open ocean. The
sail was unfurled and a following wind drove them
steadily to the east. As Hlesey grew faint and then disappeared in the darkness, a jubilant mood fell on the company. As they talked and laughed, Balder produced from
his pack a set of clothes. They had been meant as spares
for Samuel, but now Balder gave them to Jetta. Behind
the mast she quickly discarded the sooty and frayed rags
that Aegir had given her and stepped back out transformed. She was now dressed in a long tunic of pale
reindeer hide that reached to her ankles. Around her
waist was a narrow leather belt tied in a knot. Over her
shoulders was a pale blue cloak clasped at her neck with
an intricate bronze ring pin. Jetta no longer resembled a
dismal urchin, but instead shone like a golden-haired
princess. Her eyes danced with joy. The only strange
thing about her was the black tail that peeked out below
the fringe of the tunic.

Suddenly Thor's face reddened and he gasped, "Say!
You're a Hudler, aren't you? I've never seen one before

but you certainly fit the description. You have the looks of a fairy princess, but the tail of a cow."

Balder and Loki joined Thor in staring at Jetta, their faces clouded with uncertainty. Jetta's face, which had been so happy, went pale and she took a step back.

Quickly Samuel stuttered, "It's all right. She's my friend. She's not going to turn us into dirt or anything. She was kidnapped by Vikings, just after we left the crossroads."

"You mean she's the very same Hudler that almost entrapped you?" Balder said incredulously.

Samuel blushed and nodded. A moment of stunned silence followed until, with a great bellow, Thor began to laugh. Soon Balder and Loki were chuckling also and the happy mood of the evening was restored. Through tears of mirth, Thor said, "What a royal court we three gods have: a skraeling from beyond the world, a little lost Hudler, and two shabby old ravens."

On through the night they ate and drank, glad of their freedom and buoyed by their success. At first they joked and told stories, but as the hour grew late, they all became quiet, each contemplating the day's events. Finally, Balder asked Rag the two questions that were on everyone's mind. "How did you know the answer to Aegir's final riddle and why did your voice suddenly return?"

In a halting voice, Rag replied, "I'll answer your second question first. My voice returned because I remembered my name, which is indeed Ragnarok. That is the way with ravens. If we lose our voice and memory, we can regain them by simply remembering and then saying out loud our name. I think that Thokk once explained this curious fact to Samuel a long time ago back in the attic of the Geyser Inn."

"Surely it can't be as simple as that?" Balder remarked with a frown.

Rag stopped to think for a moment and then said, "No, you're right. But to explain further, I have to tell you how I lost my voice in the first place. It's a long and sad story and it starts with my birth. I was born in late fall—not at the usual time, which is in early spring. I grew and demanded food during a time of year—winter—when everything is very scarce. I was also an enormous chick, far larger than any normal raven. I soon became a great, gawking monster, ugly and unkempt. I was a freak and my mother knew it. She saw me as a dark omen and gave me an old raven name that means forbidding and ominous—*Ragnarock*. After a while she would have nothing to do with me. It was my relatives who ultimately took care of and fed me. They shortened my name to Rag and my real name was soon forgotten."

"In spite of my mother, I had a wonderful family—aunts and uncles, sisters and brothers, and numerous cousins. We all lived along a beautiful stream in a grove of trees, deep in the wilderness. I can still see in my mind the aspen leaves whirr and flicker in the wind above my nest and hear the tumbling brook below. Then my second winter came, a terrible season of bitter cold. Snow was deeper than usual and all that we might eat was buried. Famine stalked my family. In desperation, one of my uncles went on a raiding party to a human town. He returned ill and soon all my family was sick and weak. Only I escaped the disease that ravaged them. And then to compound catastrophe with disaster, we were attacked and driven from our home by a rival clan of ravens, desperate themselves. We were forced to live on a barren hillside, devoid of cover and blasted by the wind. Without shelter or food, my family began to perish. It was like the end of the world. One by one they all died and I was left alone. My mother's premonition about me had come true. I was a horrible omen, a bringer of famine, disease, and war. Overcome by guilt, I spoke no more. As I fluttered about my family's frozen corpses, half buried in the snow, even my memory slipped into gray oblivion. I then became an exile, without family or friends, living only in the moment."

Here Rag paused. The company had fallen quiet and all that could be heard was the gentle rustle of the sail and the hissing of water under the keel. With a check in his voice, he began again, "When we were in Aegir's hall and the sea god was confronting Samuel and Thokk with his riddles, I felt utterly helpless. I was unable to assist in any way or fight against the evil fate which seemed to be swallowing us up. I was filled with an overwhelming feeling of helplessness and despair. When Aegir posed his final riddle, a tale of an endless winter full of famine and disease and war cumulating in the death of all that was good, it touched something deep in my soul. The story sounded bitterly familiar and in a rush, all the dark memories of that evil winter, so long ago, when my family had died, came back, like a sunken wreck brought to the surface. With them up bobbed the name Ragnarok. Involuntarily, I cried it out and with its sound my past and tongue completely returned."

For a long time the company sat and considered Rag's story. Finally Loki said, "However it happened, Rag's recovery was certainly a wonderful turn of luck for us."

"I don't know if it was luck," answered Balder. "Ravens are a sensitive and intelligent race. The gods have, after all, always revered them as prophets and allies. Rag has already proven on many occasions to be a most unusual bird. There is a mystery about him."

"What do you mean?" asked Thor.

"I'm not sure. Rag is more than any other ordinary raven. He is brave beyond measure and endowed with amazing foresight. It's as if the blood of Odin's royal ravens flows in his veins. The three Norns must have woven a silken thread of poetry into the cord of his life."

"Norns? Who are they?" asked Samuel.

"The Norns are three goddesses who sit at the roots of Yggdrasill and spin the destinies of all who live, including the gods. For thralls they spin rough twines of coarse wool, which they often cut very short. For free farmers the threads are of linen, and for kings, long strands of steel. The gods are allotted a nearly endless skein of gold or silver. The Norns are named Fate, Being, and Necessity," Balder answered with a faint smile.

For a long while everyone sat in peace and looked up at the stars. The Milky Way's vast arch stretched directly over their heads like a spray of snow against black water. Finally Samuel asked, "What exactly is Ragnarok?"

"Ragnarok is the end of our world," answered Balder with a sigh. "It will be just as Aegir's riddle describes, a tremendous cataclysm. It will begin with a winter that lasts three years. Famine and pestilence will stalk every land. Clan will war with clan, family will fight family, brother will murder brother. It will indeed be a sword age, and an axe age. When Midgard lies in ruins, a final battle between the Aesir gods and the frost giants and all their evil allies will be fought. The rainbow bridge will be broken and Asgard burned. Surt, a great fire demon, will rise from his lair beneath the ground and set everything, even the sky above, afire. Ultimately both sides will destroy each other and Asgard and Midgard and all the other realms of the world will sink into the void. The sun and the moon will be caught and eaten by the wolves of darkness. Only Yggdrasill, the great ash tree at the center of the universe, will survive, and from her a new world will sprout."

"It all sounds horrible and sad," Samuel said with a shudder.

"It will be," answered Balder with a slow shake of his head, "It will be."

Chapter 23

The voyage back to Njord's hall was much quicker and easier for Samuel and his friends than the outward-bound journey to Hlesey had been. A strong westerly wind continuously blew, pushing the knarr quickly on. Because of the favorable breeze, the knarr no longer needed to be tacked or rowed. All that was required of the crew was to man the tiller, bail out the hold, and a few other minor chores.

The knarr was a serious cause for concern though. Everywhere little trickles of water oozed through the seams. Even some of the iron rivets holding the strakes together had popped out. Each day more and more water had to be scooped out from between the ribs and from around the keel. In the back of everyone's mind was the fear that the knarr might suddenly sink before they reached home.

Now that Loki was along to man the tiller, Samuel had little to do. He spent most of his time fighting off boredom amid the cramped confines of the stern deck. For long hours he would just sit and watch the sail as it billowed in the wind. Sometimes, when it was caught by a gust, it would madly flap and snap about like a hooked fish. Mostly though, it just gently puffed and rippled like an ocean swell or pulled taunt against its restraining ropes.

Samuel also spent a great deal of time playing "Tables" with Jetta. This game consisted of moving pawns made of reindeer antler around a wooden peg board. One side had a king, which the other side would try to capture. There were starting positions and a castle spot and a number of complicated rules. Although Samuel soon caught the gist of it, Jetta won most of their games. Thokk, much to Samuel's irritation, would help Jetta. The raven's devious cunning was a distinct advantage, and Thokk seemed to take tremendous pleasure in Samuel's frustration. After each victory, Jetta, suppressing a smirk, would quickly set up another round.

After a few vexing games, Samuel would usually give up and take to wandering about the boat, often ending up at the bow. There he could watch the prow cleave through the sea and feel the spray on his face. So it was no surprise that Samuel found himself four days out of Hlesey sitting on a bucket at the front of the boat, arms resting on the gunwale, staring out at the sea.

As he sat, Samuel looked out on a vast landscape of gray-green waves cut here and there by a whitecap. Mist and scudding banks of clouds obscured the horizon so that it was hard to tell where sky began and sea ended. Eventually, his eyes wandered to the rushing bow wave, a gushing, pulsating fountain of white foam and glittering spray. The quiet hiss and rhythmic frothing of the water nearly lulled him to sleep. Through heavy lids, he watched passively as bits of flotsam and jetsam, a jelly fish and bit of seaweed, were pulled into the maelstrom and under the keel. In front of the knarr, the surface of the ocean seemed without depth or substance, a green opaque film veined occasionally with creamy foam. Samuel's mind drifted and his senses seemed cocooned in batts of heavy cotton. He blinked. When his lids slowly opened there was an eye staring back at him from the deep. It was a monstrous eye, the size of the knarr itself, with a yellow pupil, shot with orange and black. Samuel felt stunned and paralyzed as if grabbed by an electrical shock. The fierce orb appeared to be just below the surface, touchable if Samuel were to reach out his arm. It was an animal eye, a fish eye, devoid of spirit or soul. Suddenly from behind, Samuel faintly heard Thor yell, "Samuel! Samuel! Watch out or you'll fall in."

Samuel shuddered and shook his head, trying desperately to raise himself from the torpor that had seized his body and was pulling him over the side. As if in slow motion, he caught himself and rocked drunkenly back on his heels. When he looked at the sea again, the eye was gone but in its place was a subterranean rush of golden scales, an endless train of iridescent armor. Yet for all this motion, no undercurrent buffeted the boat, the knarr kept placidly gliding along undisturbed. Finally, Samuel's muscles and nerves broke the paralysis that gripped them and he sprang up in horror. He stumbled back away from the edge of the boat and then giddily turned to face his companions. They were all staring blankly at him.

Samuel's mouth gaped open, as if to shout a warning or to scream in panic. But then he glanced back at the sea and where the monster had been and there was nothing, not even a ripple. He refaced his friends flabbergasted and embarrassed, struck dumb by confusion.

Finally Loki spoke. "I wouldn't go dozing at the edge of the boat if I were you. You're liable to fall in and then Jormungand will have you for lunch. Especially after he finds out that you have one of his scales."

"Wh . . . What do you mean?" stuttered Samuel.

"You wouldn't know, would you," chuckled Loki. "Here in our world people and creatures are very particular about the odd bits of skin that fall off their bodies. If you have a lock of someone's hair or a flake of their skin, you can use it to concoct an evil spell against them. I myself take a great interest in old toe and finger nails. That is why Jormungand would be very upset to find you in possession of one of his scales. He would suspect you were up to something very nasty."

Samuel was suddenly consumed with an overwhelming urge to toss Aegir's gift overboard. Loki—as if reading Samuel's mind—said, "Now I wouldn't do anything rash like throw away that scale Aegir gave you. If the world serpent was going to gobble us up, he would have done it already. He's probably afraid of Thor, who gave him a sound thrashing the last time they met.

Keep the scale—it is indeed as valuable as Aegir made it sound—or better yet, give it to me."

Samuel just shook his head and touched the scale in his pocket. He also never went near the bow of the boat again.

Fortunately, the rest of the voyage to Njord's harbor was uneventful and without any further visits from Jorgumand. The wind continued to be strong and at their backs. Finally, one day, an unbroken landscape of green and white hills rose out of the waves. Soon, with great weariness and relief, they spotted through the haze the dark brown buildings of Njord's home and the mounded dunes that marked the entrance to the inlet where the kindly old god kept his small fleet.

They were welcomed politely and graciously by Njord. He had regained much of his good humor and seemed to have forgiven Thor and Balder their previous rudeness. He even ignored the pitiful shape of the knarr, which was by now little more than a battered wreck.

The travelers spent several days in Njord's hall recuperating from their long voyage and gathering supplies for the final leg of their journey back to Asgard. The god of warm winds and gentle seas held a tremendous banquet for them on the second night after their arrival. A whole walrus stuffed with oatmeal and horseradish roots was roasted over the central fire. Accompanying this main dish was an oyster stew flavored with cumin and a bread laced with pine nuts. There were also platters of sausages, which Njord called cauldron snakes, and bits of grilled seagull wrapped in seaweed.

Even though Njord's home was heaven after the cramped and ever-moving confines of the knarr, Samuel began to feel an uneasy restlessness as the days passed. He had an increasing desire to be through with this adventure. He spent his time wandering listlessly around the hall or sitting by the beach throwing stones into the ocean. Jetta made friends with several girls in Njord's household and consequently was not much of a companion. So, it was to Samuel's great relief that after he woke one morning he was told by Balder that he should pack his few possessions and be ready to leave in an hour.

At the appointed time, Samuel stepped from Njord's hall and mounted the back of Thor's sled. He was soon joined by Jetta, Thokk, and Rag. Toothgnasher and Toothgrinder were harnessed to their halters, snorting and shaking with impatience. As he waited, Samuel noticed that lashed to the inside of the sled was the kettle of Aegir's gold, now covered by a leather tarp. Finally, Balder and Loki stepped aboard and Thor, after one final bear hug with Njord, followed and took his place at the reins. With the crack of a whip, they lurched forward and were on their way.

The sled soon left the beach and the roar of the ocean behind and reentered the forest. Once again the company was surrounded by deep snow and ice. There had been several new storms since their outward journey and strong winds had laid enormous drifts across the road. They were forced to carefully thread their way around these barriers, avoiding trees and wells of soft snow into which they might become permanently stuck.

The weather was clear, and Samuel noticed that the air was ever so slightly warmer and softer than a month ago. The snow seemed heavier on the branches and the drifts more dense. Winter had lost the vigor of youth and gained the lumpishness of middle age.

Thor, Balder, and Loki were in a jovial mood and spent much of their time singing, joking, or telling stories. Thokk acted like a hero, bantering and chatting with the gods without the slightest note of diffidence. Loki even seemed to ingratiate himself to Thokk, as if hoping to claim the raven's success as his own. Rag spoke rarely and even then with great difficulty. When he did speak, it was either to Samuel or Balder.

Late on the second day out from Njord's hall, the company arrived back at the crossroads where Samuel had first met Jetta. They decided to camp once again in the ring of spruce trees. It was here that they were forced to confront a sticky problem, which until now had been left unsaid—what to do with Jetta.

Of course, Jetta wished to return to her parents. Unfortunately, both Thor and Loki felt that she should be taken to Asgard and made a servant. "If we let her return to her parents, she'll just end up luring some unlucky soul underground," argued Thor. "Better to take her back with us and keep everyone safe. After all, a life in Asgard is not such a bad fate."

Balder, on the other hand, thought that she should be released to her parents. With the passion that he always showed when arguing for mercy, he stated, "I have always thought that Hudlers were an evil and treacherous race. Now that I have met Jetta, I find that I was wrong. I believe that Jetta is incapable of doing anything so wicked as imprisoning another person against their will. I say, let her go home."

In the end a compromise was reached. Jetta would be allowed to visit her parents now, and then, perhaps, in time, be allowed to return home.

Unfortunately Jetta's parents seemed to have disappeared. They never answered her calls as she walked through the forest with Thor and Balder in tow. All the secret entrances to her underground home were caved in or otherwise blocked. Dejected, she returned to the ring of spruce trees, tears streaking her cheeks. Even Thokk seemed moved by Jetta's sadness.

"What do you think happened to your parents?" asked Samuel.

"I was their last child and when I disappeared, it must have been a terrible blow. Perhaps they just gave up and died or moved to some other cavern far away," Jetta answered, her voice hoarse with despair.

The next morning dawned overcast and gray and the company was quickly back on the road. All, except Jetta, were eager to be away from the unlucky crossroads. The day passed uneventfully until late evening when they reached the upended boulder marking the edge of Midgard. Odin's stone eye still glared out over the frozen landscape like a menacing talisman.

As they traveled on the next day, the snow turned hardpacked and glassy. They flew along like a skater on ice and the trees rushed by in a blur. The air became colder and it bit at Samuel's nose and cheeks. Swiftly they pushed on, riding far into the evening. Finally, when they could see no longer, they stopped for the night and set up camp in a small clearing.

As Balder and Loki built a fire and Thor fed his goats, Samuel began to look about. In the middle of the clearing was a large mound of snow. With a shock, Samuel suddenly realized that this indistinguishable lump was the remains of Loki's snowman. This was the very clearing in which he and the two ravens had appeared, with a flash of light, so long ago. Samuel would have gone in search of Loki's old campsite if Balder had not called him to dinner.

After eating, everyone was much too tired to do anything but go to bed. As always they slept on a pile of pine boughs and in between great fur pelts and wool blankets. Curiously, Samuel was unable to sleep. As he lay there in the frosty air, listening to the others snore, he gazed up at the night sky. Above him spread a vast glittering dome, clearer than a still pond, a thousand cold sparks in a jet black void. As his eyes wandered, they caught a movement, a ghostly glow swimming across the northern horizon. A phantom curtain of iridescent green and pink, eerie in its silence, rippled and undulated like seaweed in an ocean current. Streamers of red shot out like tossed spears, arching across the vault of the sky and vanishing like puffs of steam.

Samuel turned his head and saw that Balder was also awake and watching the luminous spectacle.

Balder smiled and said, "They are the Northern Lights. Although many think that they are bad luck, the fiery breath of Surt seeping up from his underground lair, I like to see them."

The next day the sun rose in a cloudless sky. A vast glorious canopy of blue spread out above the clearing. The company quickly packed up and was on its way. Nearly everyone was joyous. In just a few more hours they would be home. Only Jetta was quiet as the sled bucketed along. Concerned, Samuel leaned over and shouted through the rushing wind, "What's the matter, Jetta, why are you so sad?"

Jetta nodded and in a cracked voice answered, "With my parents vanished and my home gone, I don't know what will happen to me. What does it mean to be a servant in Asgard? Will I be again hauling water out of a well? I miss my mother and father more than ever now."

Samuel shrugged his shoulders and replied, "I am sure everything will work out once we reach Asgard. I know that Balder will take good care of you."

In spite of his confident answer, Jetta's worries reminded Samuel that his own fate was far from settled. For the first time in a long time he began to think about the Geyser Inn. It seemed like a lifetime since he had last seen his own mother and father. How would he ever get back to them? With the magic of the ring pin apparently gone, his way home seemed irrevocably blocked. He had to fight back a tear.

Just before noon the sled rounded a corner and the forest gave way. Before them, across a few barren slopes, was the great rumpled glacier that was the doorstep to Asgard. Samuel craned his neck upward and saw, ever so tiny and fenced in by ranks of rocky crags, the city of the gods itself. Across and up the glacier they sped, hurtling past sinkholes and icy ravines. Soon they found themselves once more on the glorious rainbow bridge. As the sled clattered over the span's many-hued stones, a flock of jays flew up and disappeared behind the walls. A lone trumpet, beautiful and resonate, sounded in the afternoon air.

Thor's sled thundered past Heimdall and then along the breathless catwalk, the great chasm of ice and stone yawning just below their eyes. At full speed they rushed through Asgard's outer gates, down the dark tunnel under the walls, and finally into the great courtyard beyond.

Like the opening of a weir, a flood of gods and their servants poured out into the courtyard and came running along the log street to meet the sled. Thor reined in his goats and, with an ever-growing crowd following, proceeded slowly up the walkway toward Odin's palace. Jetta's eyes were wide with wonder, as she took in the glory of Asgard's halls and palaces—their tremendous sizes, beautiful shapes, and rich embellishments. Finally they came to a stop at the doorstep of Odin's home.

Like a swallow darting from its nest, Nanna emerged from Balder's hall and came running up the road, followed closely by Kvasir. She elbowed her way through the press and when she reached her husband embraced and kissed him. She then began to scold him loudly for being away so long. The crowd laughed and clapped, then cheered as Thor and a group of his servants unloaded the kettle of gold. As the boisterous and happy throng swirled about the sled, Loki stayed on board, leaning over the side, a smug and secretive smile pasted on his face like a mask.

Amid the celebration, the tall silver doors to Odin's palace creaked open and a giant bird strutted out. It was one of the two ravens Samuel had seen perched on the arms of Odin's chair. In a deep croak, which silenced the hubbub, it said, "Odin commands that Thor, Balder, Loki, and their companions present themselves at the foot of his throne."

Loki rolled his eyes, Thor grew serious, and Nanna began to grumble. Everyone reluctantly followed the raven into Odin's home. Even the uninvited gods and their servants came along, too curious to stay away. After the cheerful din of the courtyard, the cavernous hall seemed ominously quiet.

Odin was seated on his throne, with a blank expression on his face. Surrounding him was a single line of berserkers, their demeanor as fierce as ever. After everyone had crowded around, he spoke, "I see that Mjollnir again swings from Thor's belt. I am very glad that the great thunderer has found that which he so carelessly lost."

Thor's face colored, and he said, "I didn't really lose it."

"No, of course not," replied Odin. "Loki did that for you." Odin then turned to Loki and said, "You're beginning to be more trouble than you're worth, blood brother. And by the way, I thought that I had banished you from Asgard for the winter."

Loki stared back at Odin, but said nothing—his face a blank slate. A stiff silence filled the hall.

Balder coughed, and said, "Odin, have you seen the tribute we extracted from Aegir? A cauldron, as big as Ymir's cup, full of gold."

"I would have preferred Aegir's head instead," Odin said, without humor.

"Come, come, Odin. All has ended well. We should be rejoicing," Balder said with a smile.

Odin glared at Balder and then replied, "Don't humor me Balder, it doesn't befit you."

Balder pursed his lips, and then said, "And jealousy doesn't suit you, either."

Odin's eyebrows shot up and an angry spark flickered across his face. A murmur ran through the line of berserks and a moment of frozen silence followed. But finally and grudgingly, Odin said, "I suppose this is a victory of sorts and therefore deserves a celebration. Tonight, my hall is open to any who wish to feast in my presence."

Chapter 24

As suddenly as it began, the audience before Odin's throne ended. The gods and their servants passed through the outer doors of Odin's hall, like grain through a funnel, and quickly dispersed. Everyone was anxious to start preparing for the evening's celebration. Samuel, Jetta, Balder, Nanna, Kvasir, and the two ravens left as a group and headed straight to Balder's home. As they walked along, other gods or their servants called out congratulations, their voices floating softly in the chill winter air.

The barren oak trees surrounding Asgard's courtyard cast long blue shadows on the snow as the late afternoon sun hung low in the sky. The everlasting leaves of Yggdrasill flickered in a slight breeze, each leaf touched with pale yellow. The air had turned colder and the crunching of everyone's feet in the snow sounded loud and sharp.

Balder's hall was almost directly across the courtyard from Odin's palace. Consequently, Samuel and his friends had a long way to march. As they trudged along, the great square emptied and went quiet. The sun passed behind a cloud and the light became somber. With the initial excitement caused by their arrival over, a melancholy mood fell over Samuel. He suddenly felt very tired and let down. Ahead, Nanna was laughing and walking hand in hand with Balder, and Thokk, Rag, and Jetta were all talking at once to Kvasir. Samuel fell further behind and deeper into thought. Jetta's worries of the day before came back to him. How long had he really been gone from the Geyser Inn? Had a day passed back on earth, or had an hour, or had a year? Were his parents still searching the inn and the countryside for him, or had they given up in despair? Would he ever see the Geyser Inn again? As he pondered these questions, his mind filled with visions of his home and parents. He imagined his father, with his big black beard, plaid shirt, and scuffed shoes, and then his mother, dressed in a flowered blouse and laughing at some small joke. Next he saw his small room at the inn. There on his bed was his frayed comforter, and scattered about the floor and shelves were his model ships, dog-eared books, and school pictures of old friends.

Samuel felt very low. His shoulders drooped and a mist seemed to fog his vision. As he crossed the threshold of Balder's home, Nanna, who had waited behind to latch the door, saw his distress and stopped to comfort him. She knelt, lightly grasped his shoulders and in a gentle voice asked what was wrong.

At first Samuel only shook his head and looked away. But then, with a rush, he poured out his homesickness. When he finally paused, Nanna asked, "Please explain to me why you can't go home?"

"Because the ring pin that brought me here has lost its magic."

"Are you talking about the brooch that Rag and Thokk found back in your world, the silver one with Odin's inscription on it?"

Samuel nodded.

"Balder told me a little about it before you left for Aegir's hall. But I don't understand what you mean when you say that it has lost its magic," said Nanna.

"It just doesn't work any more. It won't send us back. I've tried it a thousand times. I've held it in every possible way and said 'Odin' so many times that I say it in my sleep."

Nanna frowned and then asked, "May I see the ring pin?"

Gently, Samuel lifted the ring pin from around his neck and handed it to Nanna who studied it carefully for several minutes. Slowly she said, "Samuel, I want you to remember exactly what you were doing and saying just before the ring pin sent you to our world."

Samuel paused, gathered his breathe, and then said, "Thokk, Rag, and I were in the attic of the Geyser Inn and we were arguing. Thokk was very angry. He was mad that I had forgotten to bring him lunch. He was yelling and, as sort of a joke, he blurted out 'Odin' three times. There was a flash and all three of us were standing in the clearing, the one where Loki found us. That's all I can remember."

Nanna studied the ring pin for a long moment, and then, with a gleam in her eyes, she smiled and handed the brooch back to Samuel. She asked, "Are you Odin's servant?"

With a puzzled look, Samuel said, "No, I don't think so."

"Then that's your problem. The brooch says: *'Servant, say my name, Odin, thrice.'* In other words, only a servant of Odin can activate the magic of the brooch. If I remember right, you said Thokk was the one who uttered 'Odin' three times in the attic."

Samuel nodded his head, but then asked, in a puzzled tone, "But Thokk isn't Odin's servant either, is he?"

"Oh yes, he is," Nanna said with a laugh. "All ravens are Odin's servants. Before any other animal or plant—even before man—Odin created ravens. It is through them that Odin keeps track of creation. They are his sentinels and watchers, sages and scholars, spies and emissaries, his most loyal subjects sent to every corner of every realm from Midgard to Alfheim. When Odin wants to know what is happening in a far land he sends a raven to investigate. If he wants to remember what happened a thousand years ago, he asks a raven. That is why the brooch worked for Thokk and not for you."

"Then all I have to do is get Thokk or Rag to say 'Odin' three times and the brooch will work again?" Samuel said, his face lit with new found hope.

"That's right. You are now free to go home at any time," Nanna said with a smile. "Although, I would suggest that you wait until after the celebration in

Odin's hall tonight. It will be a pleasant experience and a nice way to end your stay in Asgard."

Just then, Kvasir appeared and laid out Samuel's old clothes on a nearby bench. Nanna patted Samuel shoulders and said, "Even good old Kvasir thinks that it is time for you to go home."

Nanna left to attend to other matters, leaving Samuel to put on his old clothes. Reluctantly, he took off the tunic and pants he'd been wearing and began pulling on his faded cotton shirt, jeans, white socks, and blue nylon coat. They seemed garish and cheap in comparison to what he had been wearing, plain and utilitarian without a hint of mystery or intrigue. Kvasir noticed Samuel's disappointment, held up a feather and waddled off. In a moment he returned, carrying a bundle of dense blue-black cloth, and said, "Please take this cape. It will help you to remember us when you are back home."

Samuel took the garment and let it cascade to the floor. It was patterned with a thousand tiny silver stars, piped along the edges with a scarlet thread and embroidered with Balder's symbol, a yellow glacier lily. Samuel's face shone with delight as he draped it over his back. It was huge, reaching nearly to the floor and swallowing him up like a big blue jellyfish. Samuel laughed as he spun it around his body. With a flash of inspiration, he took the magic ring pin from around his neck and used it to clasp the cloak together. The ring pin shone silver bright amid the sea of dark blue wool.

While Samuel was changing into his old clothes, in another room Nanna had been helping Jetta assemble a new outfit. With a laugh, Jetta suddenly danced into the main hall and over to where Samuel was standing. She was wearing a long, two layered, pale-blue dress. About her shoulders was a white woolen shawl dotted with hundreds of tiny blue embroidered flowers and drawn together at her neck by a fine gold chain. On her feet were low leather boots with pointed toes, tanned to a creamy white. She looked even prettier than when Samuel had first seen her that night in the forest by the crossroads. In response to Samuel's dazzled stare, a broad smile crossed her lips.

In a happy breathless voice, Jetta said, "Guess what, Samuel? Balder and Nanna are going to let me live here with them. I'm to be one of Nanna's servants, in charge of her threads and needles. You were right, everything did work out." Before Samuel could answer, she twirled around and with a laugh ran back out of the room.

As the last glow of twilight filtered into Balder's hall, a lone horn sounded in the distance. "It's time to go," said Balder, and together with Nanna, he ushered Samuel, Jetta, and the two ravens out the door and toward Odin's palace. Once outside, Samuel could see small parties of gods and their servants moving in the dim light. Some were carrying bright yellow torches, which winked off and on as their bearers passed behind trees. Samuel felt as though he had joined a giant, joyous midnight parade. Gradually all the scattered groups congregated into one sparkling mass on the front step of Odin's hall. Gods and servants stamped their feet to keep warm and talked and laughed in hushed voices. Everyone's cheeks were rosy and their eyes glittered in the flickering light. A warm orange cloud of exhaled breath hung over the crowd like a fog bank.

Like the leaves of some giant book, the silver doors of Odin's hall creaked open, their surface burnished gold in the torch light. Two enormous ravens stepped out to greet the crowd. One by one the gods, their servants, and guests trooped inside. The hall had been transformed. The dusty floor was now covered with a carpet of hay. Row upon row of tables and benches had been set up in orderly lines. The livid tapestries of gory battles had been taken down or covered with curtains of amber red. Torches were set in brackets and their dancing light suffused the air with a mellow glow. In one corner a musical quartet of drums and pipes sat ready to play. Servants dressed in white and brown tunics crowded the room and ushered guests to their seats.

At the far end of the chamber, under the spreading branches of the oak tree, a raised platform had been constructed. On it was a long table covered by a white cloth decorated with blue and red ribbon beasts. Along the table, several chairs were positioned so that their occupants could look out over the room. In the very middle was a throne, covered by carvings and inlaid with chunks of amber and quartz. The table itself had been set with gold plates, platters, knives, and spoons. Everything twinkled in the fire light like morning dew on sunlit grass.

It was to this grand table that Odin's wife Frigga, Thor and his wife Sif, Balder and Nanna, and Loki and his wife were directed. Samuel, Jetta, Thokk, and Rag were lead to a smaller table nearby. Their spoons and knifes were of silver and their plates, cups, and bowls were of wood and soapstone. Samuel had noticed on his way in that the tables farthest away from the head table had been set with only a thick slab of bread, leather cup, and a single knife. He was secretly glad that he was not eating off a slice of stale bread.

When all the gods and their retainers were seated, a big drum was struck and the hall went silent. Odin appeared from an antechamber and strode across the room. As he stepped up onto the platform, all present in the hall rose in one great rasping of benches and rustling of clothes. Odin looked out over the crowd, a haughty smile on his face, and said, "Welcome to Valaskjalf, the shining heart of Asgard. Tonight let us celebrate that Mjollnir has been retrieved and that our enemy Aegir has been humbled and humiliated." He picked up a drinking horn, turned to the gods present at his table and then raised the cup in a toast. "I salute you, Thor, for your strength; Balder, for your wisdom; your wives for their industry and beauty; and you, Loki, for no good reason at all." A ripple of laughter swept across the room and Loki managed a sickly smile. Odin took a drink and then sat down. A storm of conversation immediately broke forth as everyone took their seats and the musicians began to play.

This celebration feast was a magical experience which Samuel never forgot. Everyone was in a festive mood; even Odin looked and acted less severe than usual. All the gods wore tunics or dresses of brightly colored silk and cloaks that had been embroidered with threads of precious metals. No one wore mail or any other kind of armor. Numerous courses were served. Of some, like salmon and apples roasted together in honey, Samuel could not get enough. Others, such as a gelatinous codfish steak that had been cured in lye and boiled in onions, he wasn't even going to taste.

As Samuel ate, he watched the musicians ply their instruments. One, a squat man dressed in striped trousers, held to his lips a plain block of wood through which five holes had been drilled lengthwise. The man played on it like a pan flute while stamping his right foot to keep time. Next to him a great auk, its black feathers shiny in the dim light, beat a drum with its stumpy limbs. Nearby a dwarf strummed an oaken harp with his knobby but agile fingers. Finally, in back of everyone else, a large man with a braided moustache played a simple bagpipe. Samuel grinned and tapped his finger in time with the rhythm.

After a while Samuel leaned over and tried to talk with Jetta above the din. He asked her about her old home underground. Jetta was more than happy to reminisce. She described, in great detail, helping her mother make bread and cheese, and the comic disasters that happen when you are responsible for farm animals.

Samuel was especially fascinated when she spoke of the other magical denizens of her cavernous home. In a hushed and secretive voice she described the tiny tooth-ache troll who preyed upon people who slept with their mouths open, and the gnome that lived in the barn and fed all the cats, and finally the mischievous house elves who blew out candles when your back was turned.

As the evening wore on, dishes of sweet fruit and cakes were offered, along with fire-warmed wine. The lights dimmed and voices were lowered. A sleepy, dream-like quality fell over the crowded hall.

Finally Odin called out for Samuel to approach his table. When he reached the table, Samuel found that he had to stand on a chair in order to see over the edge. Odin looked at Samuel for a long moment and then said. "I see that you have something of mine."

Samuel, taken aback, stammered, "I do?"

"Yes, you do; the brooch pinned to your cloak. Give it to me now." Here Odin held out his hand.

Blushing, Samuel, unclipped the ring pin from his cape and, while standing on his tiptoes, placed it in Odin's outstretched hand—a hand that Samuel noticed was smooth and manicured, without callous or scar, so unlike Thor's hands which looked and felt like a plowed field. A faint smile creased Odin's mouth as he turned the ring pin over in his fingers and said, "It's been a very long time since I have gazed upon this chunk of silver."

"Is it as special as its inscription makes it sound?" asked Balder.

"Oh yes," answered Odin. "It is a treasure of great value. I made it, or rather I had the dwarfs of Nidavellir make it. They formed it from a single nodule of silver, beating and shaping the metal until it rang like a bell. Then they carved my eye into its face, using a chisel made from the tooth of a frost giant, and attached the stick pin. Finally they fired it till it glowed white and then with tiny bands of silver solder welded the magic runes to its surface. When all was finished, they plunged it into a stone trough filled with water from the Well of Mimir, the fountain of knowledge. I had to pay the dwarves dearly for their labors, a lump of gold as big as a skiff."

"Why did you make such a thing?"

"To allow either myself or a small group of my servants to journey quickly from Asgard to any other world and then back again. This includes Samuel's world. Only Gimli is inaccessible. I also made it so that any tongue is understandable to the wearer of the brooch. I anticipated that my spies would need to understand languages other than their own."

"So you know about Samuel's world then—this place called Earth?" exclaimed Balder in surprise.

"A little. The universe has many quirks and corners, and Samuel's world is one of them, a shadow image of Midgard, devoid of magic and enslaved to the dictates of nature. A world frozen away from the gods, where humans play out their puny lives bereft of glory and divine purpose. Thousands of years ago, I sent numerous emissaries to this world to inspire its inhabitants. After years and years of patient work, a civilization developed that revered me and honored my name. These people were called Norsemen, and I tried to help them the best that I could. Unfortunately, in the end, they betrayed me, trading glory for humility, and pride for subservience." Here Odin grimaced but then continued.

"Often the servants I sent to Samuel's world would be ravens. Always they would return, bringing news and carrying the brooch back with them. That is until I sent a raven named Hobrok. He was my last hope for Samuel's world, a final emissary to advise the few humans still loyal to me. One day he enthusiastically reported to me that a new home had been found for those still faithful to me. It was a land far away from the corrupting influences which had driven me from the hearts of so many other men. A country called Vinland. Unfortunately, after Hobrok rejoined these adventurers he met some unknown fate. He never returned to Asgard and the ring pin disappearing with him."

Odin sighed and stared at his plate as if lost in a day dream. He then abruptly looked up and, in a stern voice, asked Samuel, "How and where did you find my brooch?"

"I didn't find it. Rag did," answered Samuel.

Odin turned to Rag, and the raven said, "I found it at the bottom of a hole being dug by a group of humans. How it got there, I have no idea."

Odin turned a questioning look back to Samuel. Unfortunately all Samuel could do was shrug his shoulders. Odin then frowned and said, "I wish I knew what happened to Hobrok and the few humans who still confessed loyalty to the Aesir. Their fate has always puzzled my dreams and slept at the edge of my thoughts. But alas, unless you are hiding something from me, this appears to be the end of the story."

For a long time Odin gazed at the brooch, turning it over slowly in his fingers. A bittersweet smile crossed his lips as if it were bringing back fond but distant memories. Finally, and without looking up he said, "You have a problem Samuel. This is my brooch and I will not lose it again, but without it you cannot return to your world."

Samuel went pale. Suddenly all his hopes, which had seemed so sure, now appeared dashed. The thought of never seeing his parents or the homely old Geyser Inn again made his throat constrict and his ears burn. He suddenly felt sick to his stomach.

Balder spoke, "Surely, something can be worked out?"

Odin remained silent, his features set in stone and his eyes never leaving the brooch. Nanna coughed and said, "Odin, didn't you create the brooch so that you could obtain information about other worlds such as Samuel's? It has been a very long time since anyone from Asgard has visited earth. From Samuel's description a lot has changed there since Hobrok's time. Why not send Samuel back as a special emissary? He could return to you in a set amount of time."

"No," said Odin. "I don't think Samuel would return. Why should he? This is not his home. Earth is. I know that I would never return, if I were Samuel."

Nanna's features darkened ominously, but before she could speak, Odin held up his hand and said, "Before you say something that you will regret Nanna, let me continue. I have a solution. I will send Huginn." Here one of the two giant ravens perching on the back of Odin's throne looked up, "And Samuel can go along as his companion. Perhaps Huginn can discover something concerning Hobrok's fate. How soon can you be ready to go, Huginn?"

"Whenever you wish, master," croaked the great raven.

"And you, Samuel?"

"Right now," answered Samuel, his hopes completely restored.

"Then say your goodbyes."

Samuel turned to Balder and Nanna, who both rose from their seats and came around the table and stood next to him. Balder knelt down and grasped Samuel by both shoulders in his giant hands. "You are a brave and clever young man. Keep hopeful and cheerful and all will work out for you in life."

Then Nanna spoke, "Samuel, I have made a gift for you. Actually it's a gift for your mother. Give it to her as soon as you return." Nanna held out her hand and in it were a pair of simple earrings, plain chips of white quartz wrapped in bits of copper wire. "They are magic, so take care of them." Nanna added with a smile.

As Samuel put the earrings in his coat pocket, he faced Jetta and in an awkward voice said goodbye. For a moment Jetta hesitated, but then she leaned over and quickly gave Samuel a kiss on the cheek. Samuel blushed a deep crimson and mumbled something under his breath. A touch of red colored Jetta's pale cheeks and she glanced at the floor. A second passed, and then Samuel and Jetta looked each other in the eyes, smiled, and laughed out loud. Finally and reluctantly, Samuel turned to Rag and Thokk and asked, "Are you two ready to go?"

Thokk and Rag looked at each other and then back to Samuel. In a quiet voice Rag said, "I'm sorry Samuel, but we're not going back."

Samuel's mouth dropped open and he stammered, "What do you mean? Don't you want to go home?"

"Come on, Samuel!" scoffed Thokk. "A raven's life is the pits back at the Geyser Inn. It's cold, windy, and dinner's usually stale garbage. Here we're royalty. We even get a place at the table. Balder has asked Rag to be one of his servants, and I am to become Loki's messenger. We'd have to be crazy to go back to the inn. Frankly, I hope the place burns down."

Samuel nodded his head, but as he did so, he was overwhelmed by a stabbing sadness. As Samuel bit his lip, Rag leaned over and whispered, "We are friends, and friends are never forever separated. Have faith and look for the unexpected."

Suddenly, Thokk boomed. "Come, come, Rag's right. You'll see us again. No need to feel bad. You're going home. Be happy. We are."

Finally, Samuel hugged Thokk and Rag one last time and then looked up at Odin. The All Father pointed to Huginn, who was standing at the far end of the table, impatient to leave. Samuel drew his cape around his shoulders and walked up to the giant raven. Odin's magic brooch now hung from a slender silver chain around Huginn's neck. With a raspy croak the raven said, "Are you ready?" Samuel nodded.

Suddenly there was a commotion from the far end of Odin's table. Thor had staggered to his feet, groggy from innumerable cups of mead. In the process, he had knocked over several plates and goblets. Ignoring the distress that this caused, Thor raised a horn cup high above his head, looked out over the entire hall, and in a booming voice shouted, "Come on, all you blue-toothed charcoal chewers, let's have three cheers for Samuel!" The hall erupted in a thunderous roar of hurrahs—once, twice, and on the third, Samuel and Huginn disappeared like snow in hot water.

Chapter 25

Sound was the first sensation that Samuel experienced as he and Huginn appeared in the attic of the Geyser Inn. A terrific gale was blowing outside. Shingles were rattling, timbers were creaking, and wind was whistling through every little crack and chink in the Geyser Inn. Samuel could hear trees moan and hiss beyond the walls and what sounded like sleet pattering on the roof. A faint breath of cool air touched his skin. Samuel guessed that it must be night or nearly so, because the attic was almost pitch black.

Samuel glanced around and saw Huginn, nearly invisible amid all the darkness. The big bird was prancing in a circle, croaking with irritation, "Where am I? How do I get out of this dismal cave?"

"It's okay. It's okay," Samuel said. " You're in the attic of the Geyser Inn. All you need to do is fly through that hole up there and you'll be free." Samuel pointed to the broken roof vent, through which a few stars could be seen.

"Well then, I'll be gone. Goodbye!" And without even a thank you, Huginn fluttered up to the opening and disappeared into the twilight.

Samuel was left all alone in the cheerless attic. With a shock, he suddenly realized that the air was much warmer than when he, Thokk and Rag had left so long ago. Surely it could not still be the dead of winter anymore. It must be spring. Samuel's mouth went dry and a flood of questions cascaded through his mind. How long had he been gone? Had time passed at the Geyser Inn at the same rate as it had passed in Odin's world? Samuel quickly estimated that he had been in Asgard and Midgard for around a month and a half. Was it now a month and half later here at the Geyser Inn? Or had just a few hours passed? Maybe he had been gone for weeks, or months, or perhaps years. Were his parents even still at the inn or had they moved away, never to be seen again?

A sudden overwhelming desire to see his mother and father overtook Samuel. He rushed across the floor boards, heedless of the dark. Like a blind man, he blundered into the storage boxes that surrounded the attic hatch. With a crash, he knocked several over and went sprawling across the floor. Slowly he gathered himself together and, on hands and knees, groped about till he found the trap door. It was still propped open. Down the ladder he ran and through the closet door and into the maintenance room beyond. Unfortunately, the light bulb in the maintenance room had burned out and the space was entombed in total darkness. With mincing steps and outstretched arms, Samuel carefully felt his way across the room. Finally he found the exit door, burst out into the hall, and ran to a nearby window.

Samuel half expected to see green grass and bushes with leaves outside. Instead little had changed, snow still covered the ground in one great blanket and the wind was blowing as fierce as ever. Yet things were different. The sky was clear of whirling snow and glowering clouds, a blizzard no longer raged about the inn. The western horizon was dyed a somber yellow, touched with pink, while the rest of the sky was darkening toward night. Low scudding clouds hurried by like tattered rags caught in a fast-moving stream. Rivulets of melt water cascaded off the roof and spattered against the window.

Prying himself away, Samuel hurried to the stairs. Down he flew, two steps at a time, level to level, till he was on the first floor. He raced across the great central lobby, gloomy and empty as ever, and toward the kitchen where he knew, or hoped, his parents would be. With a flood of relief he could hear them talking beyond the kitchen door. Unfortunately they were arguing. His father's voice, thick with sarcasm, snapped out like a whip. Samuel pulled up short in front of the door, suddenly afraid to confront his parents, especially his father when he was in such an angry mood. But then, with a knotted stomach, Samuel opened the door and entered the room.

A stunned silence fell when Samuel appeared. All three stared at each other for a long moment. But then, in a voice edged with acrid anger, Samuel's father said, "Where have you been!? You missed dinner and *what* have you got on?"

Samuel had forgotten about his cape. He quickly removed it, folding it nervously between his arms. He
stammered that he had found it while exploring.

"Make sure you put it back where you found it. *Understand?*" Jim growled.

Samuel looked fearfully at his father. The big man's
eyes were narrowed to slits and the skin on his forehead
was pulled unnaturally taunt. His lower jaw and beard
were thrust out into the air. He sat on the edge of his
chair tense and furious, arms crossed and back straight
like a piece of iron rod. Carol, in contrast, was standing
meekly behind a counter, her face slightly flushed, eyes
disorientated, and tear tracks streaking down her cheeks.
Out of nowhere, Samuel suddenly blurted, "I have a
gift for Mom."

A look of extreme irritation passed over Jim's face.
"Make it quick! Your mother and I have important things
to discuss."

From his pocket Samuel pulled out the earrings
which Nanna had made and handed them to his mother. Carol took them and mumbled thanks, turning
them over in her hands. She looked completely bewildered by them.

"That's enough, Samuel. Go to your room. We can
talk about your missing dinner later," Jim spat.

Samuel turned to go, but then, on impulse, he reached
into his pants pocket and dug out the Jormungand
scale that Aegir had given him and said, "Here, Dad,
you can have this."

"What?" Jim snarled. "What? What are you talking about?" And then, when he saw the scale he hissed, "Look, Samuel. I don't collect junk."

In the face of his father's bile, Samuel almost retracted his hand and put the scale back in his pocket. But something made him keep his arm outstretched. After the horror of Nidhogg and the snide viciousness of Aegir and all the other adventures he had just experienced, his father's surliness seemed suddenly petty and small. A new flintiness armored Samuel's soul. He continued to look calmly at his father and again offered him the scale.

Finally, with a snort of disgust, Jim said, "Well, let me have it. Then leave us alone."

Jim took the scale with a jerk, barely glanced at it, and reached to put in his shirt pocket. But then something happened. As if drawn by a magnet, his eyes returned to the scale.

He began to slowly turn it over in his fingers. Its iridescent surface caught the kitchen's fluorescent light and it shimmered to life casting faint rainbows on the room's white walls. As it flickered and sparkled, Jim stared at it transfixed. As he did so, the lines of frustration eased from his forehead, his eyes softened, and his scowl disappeared. Years of bitterness seemed to drain out of him. All the hoarded anger he had kept stashed away in his heart, like ice buried beneath sawdust, melted away into nothingness.

Suddenly, as if snapped from a dream, he closed his fist around the scale and in a quiet, even voice said to Carol, "Why don't you try on your new earrings?"

Carol's mouth dropped open and she stared at her husband. Then, with a nervous shake in her hands, she put on Samuel's gift.

Nothing changed. Neither Carol's face, nor body, nor clothes transformed in any way. There was no flash of light or sparkling rain of stardust. Yet to both Jim and Samuel, Carol suddenly became more beautiful than she had ever been before. All that was attractive about her shone forth.

Now it was Jim's turn to be amazed and all he could do was stammer, "They're beautiful on you!" Carol's face beamed and Jim smiled in return.

The rest of the winter at the Geyser Inn was a wonderful experience for Samuel. His father forgot all about the furnace in the basement and it did fine without him. Jim began helping Samuel with his homework. He became genuinely interested in the things that Samuel was studying, discovering in himself a long-lost academic streak. Jim and Samuel learned how to play cards and they, along with Carol, spent many evenings playing pinochle and other games.

This made Samuel's mother very happy and considerably lightened her sense of isolation. She quit smoking, burning up her entire stock of cigarettes in one enormous bonfire in the central room fireplace. Jim and Samuel took up ice fishing and Carol was overjoyed to practice her culinary skills on fresh trout.

One afternoon Jim discovered an old yellow snowmobile moldering away in a small storage shed attached to the inn. He applied all his tinkering know-how and soon had it roaring to life. After that the family spent numerous afternoons sightseeing. The park's geysers and mudpots took on an altogether different and magical aspect when surrounded by ice and snow.

Curiously Samuel had no desire to tell his parents about Rag and Thokk, or Odin's world. His travels seemed almost a dream, with only the cloak and his mother's earrings to remind him of its reality. Even though he had been in Asgard for about a month and a half, only a few hours had passed at the Geyser Inn. Consequently, he had not been missed and therefore had no real explaining to do. His parents had forgotten about the cloak and after admiring it for a few days, Samuel had stored it away in a secret box with other precious mementos.

There was one thing that continued to puzzle Samuel about his adventure. It was the extreme change of temperature that had occurred during the mere five hours—earth time—he had been in Asgard. When he and the ravens had been transported away, the Geyser Inn had been locked in sub-zero cold. Yet, when he reappeared in the attic, snow was actually melting and running off the inn's roof. Cautiously, he asked his father how the weather could change so drastically in such a short time. Jim laughed, replying, "It was a chinook—a warm windstorm that can descend on this country in a matter of hours and last several days. Sometimes temperatures can rise forty to fifty degrees in one hour—from ten below zero to forty above in minutes."

Unfortunately, as Samuel soon found out, a chinook is but a temporary reprieve from winter. The very next day a new cold front buffeted the park. A tremendous snowstorm piled yet another deep layer of snow upon an already smothered landscape. Howling winds lashed the inn, ripping off lose shingles and forcing everyone inside. After the initial gale, a stretch of bone-chilling cold invaded the park, seeping into the building and turning it once more into an icy prison. But soon, winter truly began to loosen its grip.

The sun shone brighter and stayed in the sky longer each evening. The air turned warm and soft. Great rivers of melt water cascaded off the roof of the inn. Snowstorms still came rolling over the trees, but they were not followed by days of numbing cold. Slowly the piles of snow blown up against the building began to lose more than they gained.

One day, when all that was left of winter were dirty snowdrifts in sheltered areas, the first of the Geyser Inn's summer staff began to arrive: restaurant and reservation managers, maintenance supervisors, and park rangers. With them came an excited team of archeologists, the same ones that Thokk had so enchanted the summer before. They immediately returned to their excavation site, the one where Rag had found the ring pin. The hole had been covered with a blue tarp that now sagged in the middle from accumulated melt water. Because of its distance from the inn, Samuel had not noticed the survey pit last fall before the first major snow storm had covered it up. He now curiously hovered around the hole as the scientists noisily unloaded tents and gear. One of the archeologists, a blond-haired young woman in a blue parka, noticed Samuel and said, "Hello." Samuel waved, and then asked what was going on.

She explained, brushing strands of wind-blown hair out of her eyes, that they were digging up artifacts at what had once been an important Native American campsite. Samuel asked if they had found anything interesting and the woman replied, "We've found amazing things. Sea shells from British Columbia that the Indians used as money, pottery shards from the southwest, and, believe it or not, a Viking amulet, a small reproduction of Thor's hammer."

Samuel's mouth fell open and he gasped, "How could something like that get here?"

The woman answered, "The native people traded among themselves. Their culture and commerce were much more complicated and sophisticated than we often give them credit for. The Vikings had some contact with Native Americans; that's a proven fact. As strange as it may sound, it's quite possible for something acquired by an Indian on the East Coast, from say a Viking who was living in Greenland, to have found its way, through trade, gift giving, and warfare, to the West Coast or even here. Numerous Viking artifacts, from a Norse penny to a wooden tool, have been found scattered around North America." The scientist smiled at Samuel's astonishment and then turned back to her work.

Later that afternoon Samuel went for a walk along the shore of Yellowstone Lake. He was happy because his father had just accepted a continuing position at the Geyser Inn. In spite of its brooding presence, the inn had become more of a home than anywhere else had ever been. He had also noticed that, among the incoming summer staff, there were a few families with young people his own age. Finally, he might have some friends.

As Samuel strolled along the lakeshore, waves lapped quietly at his feet and a cool spring breeze rumpled his windbreaker. The sun was bright and the air was warm. He stopped at the tip of a little promontory jutting out into the lake and looked back at the inn. It sat, dark and immovable, amid the bursting green of spring. He then turned his gaze back to the lake. The water spread out before him like an indigo plain, rippling gently in the wind. Beyond the lake a forest of pine and spruce stretched into the distance, turning slowly from olive green to slate blue. Finally, pale, rugged, and still snow-capped, a marching line of mountains stretched along the horizon like a giant's fence. Above it all hung a sapphire sky, graduating from pale blue as it rose from behind the mountains to nearly black at its summit. Samuel smiled at all this beauty and then turned toward home, only to freeze in place. From across the water and echoing in the trees, he heard, clear and sharp, the deep, harsh call of a raven.

The End

Glossary

Aegir: Viking god of the sea. Lives apart from the other gods and is sometimes in competition with them. His hall is traditionally set under water, where he resides with his wife Ran.

Aesir: The chief tribe of Norse gods. Led by Odin.

Angrboda: Loki's giantess lover, and mother to the monsters Hel, Fenrir, and Jormungand.

Asgard: Fortress of the Aesir gods and the land that surrounds it.

Balder: God of goodness, beauty, and light. Husband of Nanna and father to Forseti, the god of justice.

Berserks: Viking warriors who, before going into battle, worked themselves into a crazed fury. Reputed to have eaten hallucinogenic toadstools and to have fought in the nude or wearing only the skins of bears—hence their name "bear shirts."

Bragi: God of poetry.

Brisings' Necklace: A fabulous necklace made by dwarfs and owned by Freyja.

Drakar: Literally, a dragon ship. A huge longship used to transport kings or a large number of warriors into battle. The biggest, found in Denmark, was approximately a hundred feet long.

Eldir: Aegir's loyal servant.

Fenrir: A giant wolf and son of Loki. Fenrir is bound with a magic ribbon which will not come undone until Ragnarok. It will attack and swallow Odin during Ragnarok, only to be killed in turn by Odin's son Vidar.

Frigga: Odin's wife, and first among the goddesses.

Frey: A Vanir god who came to live with the Aesir as part of a peace treaty between the two races. He is most famous for giving away his sword in order to win the hand of a beautiful giantess named Gerd. Will fight Surt the fire demon during Ragnarok with only a pair of antlers.

Freyja: Frey's sister and Norse goddess of love and lust. Owns a chariot drawn by cats.

Giants: Primary villains of the Norse universe, always plotting to overthrow the Aesir and conquer Asgard. They represent chaos as a counterpoint to the gods' embodiment of cosmic order. Most dangerous are the frost giants.

Gimli: Home of the gods who survive or come back to life after Ragnarock.

Gungnir: Odin's dwarf-made spear which, once thrown, never misses its mark.

Heimdall: The watchman of the gods, ever vigilant for invading frost giants. He owns the horn Gjall, which will sound when Ragnarok commences. Has an especially keen dislike of Loki. Credited with creating the three races of man: thralls, freemen, and kings

Hel: Where all who die from illness or old age go; a bleak and terrible place.

Hel: A woman half alive and beautiful, and half dead and decaying. The ruler of Hel and offspring of Loki and Angrboda.

Hlesey: An island in the great western ocean near which is located Aegir's home.

Huginn: One of Odin's two raven servants. The name means "Thought." Odin's other raven is named Muginn (Memory).

Idun: A goddess who tends a magical tree that produces golden apples. This fruit keeps the Norse gods forever young.

Jormungand: A venomous serpent who encircles the earth. Another evil spawn of Loki. Is destined to kill and be killed by Thor during Ragnarok.

Jotunheim: A forbidding wilderness of ice and stone inhabited by trolls and frost giants.

Knarr: The work-a-day ship of the Norse world. With a deep hull and strong construction, it can carry a large cargo, including livestock, while remaining remarkably seaworthy. Knarrs were the ships that Norse explorers used to colonize Iceland and Greenland and ultimately travel to North America.

Kvasir: A wise man (or god) murdered by evil dwarfs. A drink was brewed from his blood that, when sipped, inspires poetry.

Loki: The trickster god of Norse mythology. In the beginning of time, Odin and Loki swear allegiance to each other and become blood brothers. With Loki's aid, the Aesir, and especially Thor—outfight and outwit many enemies. Unfortunately, Loki becomes progressively more evil and ultimately instigates the murder of Balder and fights on the side of the giants during Ragnarok. Loki is also the Norse god of fire.

Midgard: "Middle World." The realm of man.

Mjollnir: The magic hammer that is Thor's chief weapon. It always returns to Thor's hand after he hurtles it at an enemy. It was made as a gift for the gods by the dwarfs Brokk and Eitri. Loki's interference during its construction resulted in a disproportionately short handle.

Nanna: Balder's wife and goddess of homemaking.

Nastrond: Nidhogg's lair and nightmarish home for the souls of wicked Vikings.

Nidhogg: A dragon who eats the bodies of the dead and chews at the roots of the world tree. His name literally means "Corpse Tearer." Every day a squirrel named Ratatosk carries insults between Nidhogg and an eagle, who lives in the uppermost branches of Yggdrasill.

Niflheim: One of the nine Norse worlds; land of the dead. Hel is contained within.

Njord: Another Vanir god and father of Frey and Frey-ja. Associated with wind and the sea, and reputed to be good-natured.

Norns: Three goddesses who determine the length and quality of every man's and god's life. They are named Fate, Being, and Necessity.

Norse: The people and culture of medieval Scandinavia. Norse influence stretched through Russia to Constantinople and across the Atlantic to North America.

Odin: King of the Aesir gods and creator of the world. Values honor, wisdom, and order above all else. Also known as "All Father," "Vegtam, the Wanderer," and "Father of Battle," among other names. He gave up an eye in order to have a drink from the well of wisdom. In doing so he exchanged physical sight for insight. He provokes war among men so that he can raise an army of "gloriously slain" warriors. These fighters he brings to a heavenly hall named Valhalla where they await the coming of Ragnarok. He is always accompanied by two ravens and two silver-gray wolves.

Ragnarok: A series of disasters and wars that culminates with the death of the gods and the destruction of the world. The finality and completeness of this cosmic termination is unique to Norse mythology.

Rainbow Bridge (bifrost): A bridge that links the world of the gods with the world of man.

Sif: Thor's wife. One night, as a trick, Loki shaves off her hair. When confronted by Thor, Loki replaces the hair with locks of spun gold.

Skraeling: Norse derogatory name for Native Americans; means Ugly or Screecher. The Native Americans ultimately ejected the Norse from North America and were able to adapt to climatic change when it occurred in Greenland, whereas the Norse were not.

Skadi: A goddess associated with hunting and skiing. The estranged wife of Njord.

Surt: At the end of Ragnarok, the fire demon Surt will appear and set what remains of the world on fire.

Thokk: An old hag who prevents the return to life of Balder after that god's murder. Most likely Loki in disguise.

Thor: Thunder god and hero of every freeman in the Norse world. With his magic hammer, iron gauntlets and belt that doubles his strength, he protects Asgard from monsters such as frost giants. He is noted for his quick anger, simple straightforward manner, and huge capacity for food and drink. Rides about in a cart drawn by two goats.

Thrall: Essentially the slaves of the Norse world. Often captured during Viking raids from places like Ireland. Sometimes they were freed by their masters and even became prominent citizens.

Tyr: The Norse god of war. He lost his right hand when the monstrous wolf Fenrir bit it off.

Vanir: A secondary tribe of Norse gods who live in Vanaheim. At one time the Vanir and the Aesir were at war with each other. In order to guarantee peace, the two sides exchanged hostages. Njord, Frey, and Freyja went to live with the Aesir and the gods Honir and Mimir went to live with the Vanir.

Valaskjalf: Odin's hall in Asgard.

Valkyries: Odin's shield maidens who select and carry away, from the midst of battle, brave warriors.

Vikings: Seafaring Scandinavians who explored the North Atlantic and terrorized medieval Europe between approximately A.D. 800 and A.D. 1100. They raided and conquered places such as England, Ireland, and northern France, and even ventured as far as Spain and North Africa.

Yggdrasill: The world tree, an ash, and a living spine upon which the Norse universe is centered. In its bark a man and woman will hide and survive Ragnarok to repopulate the world. In the Norse world sacrifices were often hung upon holy trees.

Ymir: A huge giant who preexisted every other living being in the Norse universe. In the beginning there was only a great void, called Ginnungagap, bordered in the north by ice and to the south by fire. When ice from the north met the heat of the south, the ice began to melt. From the resulting drips, Ymir was born. Odin and his two brothers, Vili and Ve, kill Ymir and create the world from his body.

Major Sources

The Norse Myths. Introduced and retold by Kevin Crossley-Holland. Pantheon Books, New York, 1980.

Nordic Gods and Heroes. Padraic Colum. Dover Publications, Inc., New York, 1996.

Norse Mythology, The Myths and Legends of the Nordic Gods. Arthur Cotterell. Lorenz Books, New York, 1997.

The Vinland Sagas, translated by Magnus Magnusson and Hermann Palsson. Penguin Books, New York, 1965.

The Oxford Illustrated History of the Vikings. Edited by Peter Sawyer. Oxford University Press, New York, 1997.

Vikings: The North Atlantic Saga. Edited by William W. Fitzhugh and Elisabeth I. Ward. Smithsonian Institution Press, Washington, 2000.

To Write to the Author

If you wish to contact the author or would like more information about this book, please write to the author in care of Llewellyn Worldwide and we will forward your request. Both the author and publisher appreciate hearing from you. Llewellyn Worldwide cannot guarantee that every letter written to the author can be answered, but all will be forwarded. Please write to:

John Anacker
℅ Llewellyn Worldwide Ltd.
P.O. Box 64383, Dept. 0-7387-0433-4
St. Paul, MN 55164-0383, U.S.A.

Please enclose a self-addressed stamped envelope for reply, or $1.00 to cover costs. If outside U.S.A., enclose international postal reply coupon.
Many of Llewellyn's authors have websites with additional information and resources. For more information, please visit our website at http://www.llewellyn.com.

For a free set of rune dice, write to
megana@llewellyn.com
and tell me what your favorite part of this book was.
Feel free to write any other suggestions you might
have for books you want to see in the future.
We welcome your input!